Faerie Fool

by

Silver James

This is a work of fiction. Names, characters, places, and incidents are either the product of the author's imagination or are used fictitiously, and any resemblance to actual persons living or dead, business establishments, events, or locales, is entirely coincidental.

Faerie Fool

Contact Information: info@thewildrosepress.com

Cover Art by *Rae Monet, Inc. Design*

The Wild Rose Press, Inc.
PO Box 708
Adams Basin, NY 14410-0708
Visit us at www.thewildrosepress.com

Publishing History
First Faery Rose Edition, 2012
Print ISBN 978-1-61217-559-1
Digital ISBN 978-1-61217-560-7

Published in the United States of America

Rory stared at the woman, knowing her somehow. Her face wavered, like a badly tuned television, two faces not quite lining up—the ghost of a ghost. She stared back.

"Out of time." The words were out of his mouth before he could define their meaning.

She nodded, bending to begin mouth-to-mouth resuscitation on Delaney.

Rory continued chest compressions, almost on autopilot as his brain chewed over events. Out of time. Those afraid of Becca had whispered that. A woman out of time. A woman sent back by the fae to marry their beloved clann chief. Ciaran. His cousin. As close as any brother.

"One, two, three, four, five." He counted the beats. He'd seen Manannán mac Lir take Becca away on that fateful *Lughnasadh* night, seen Finvarra and Onagh of the fae court arrive and gift Ciaran with the MacDermot Knot. And he'd watched his cousin fade away, willing himself to die in order to join Becca in Tir Nan Óg. He'd sworn never to love a woman that much, even as he celebrated Becca's return on *Samhain*.

And then the O'Neill raided the small O'Beirne keep. And he'd rescued a little girl. Delaney. He'd waited for her to grow up, despaired as she loved Conor, and knew in his heart that he was never meant to be the man of her heart.

"One, two, three, four, five."

"Riordan. Cease, man. She's gone." Ciaran's hand rested heavily on his shoulder, fingers digging in to pull him away from the lifeless girl.

"No."

Praise for Silver James and…

***FAERIE FOOL*:**

"Unrequited lovers finally unite!—with a twist. Silver James does a wonderful job of blending old world and new, enchantment and reality. Age-old wounds that lead to new heartbreak keep this story rocking and rolling until the very last page! I highly recommend Faerie Fool!"

~Karin Tabke, aka Harlow, best-selling author

~*~

***FAERIE FATE*:**

"This is a wonderful mix of adventure and humor, with an unforgettable heroine who follows the voices in her head and travels back to a time of handfasting, dreamy Irish men and clan wars. Although Ciaran and his Irish ways are not new to romance novels, Becca is extremely humorous and fun, and makes the reader laugh out loud as she waltzes into yesteryear."

~Romantic Times Magazine (4 Stars)

"Captivating, Timeless and Passionate! *FAERIE FATE* crosses the boundaries of time and faerie law to reunite two souls in the sacred binding of love. Silver James is a writer to watch!"

~Jennifer Lyon, award-winning author

~*~

***FAERIE FIRE*:**

"From the prologue to the epilogue, I was hooked. …I keep replaying Moira and Duncan's story over in my mind and I just adore it! Reading this book was wonderful. *FAERIE FIRE* is worth every penny and minute the reader spends on it!"

~Night Owl Reviews (4.5 Stars, Top Pick)

Dedication

As always, my love and thanks go out to my first line of defense—my family, Greg, Clary, and Jeremy, my critique partner, Heidi, for making me stretch, and Justin because he cares. I couldn't hide out in my imagination without your support.

This book is dedicated to them; and to Liza, who never gave up hope for Rory's story; to Chrystal, who won the chance to create Delaney's BFF, Bronwyn; to the Penumbra Street Team (y'all know who you are!); to my most patient of editors, Frances Sevilla; and to all the wonderful folks at the Wild Rose Press, including Rae Monet, who designs the most amazing covers.

And finally, many thanks to Deputy Jason Ruegge for his inspirational and technical advice.

Prologue

The wolfhound awakened Delaney before the raiders arrived, whining and urgent as he tugged her nightclothes, pulling her downstairs and out the door. She stumbled on a rock, barefoot as she was, and cried out, but the dog yanked her forward. Shivering in the cold night air, she followed. No moonlight lit the inner courtyard of her father's keep. The huge dog let go of her gown and raised his head to sniff the faint breeze blowing in from the north. He growled low in his chest, his white canines visible even by nothing but starlight, and chased her into the low wooden structure her father used as stables.

The sweet scent of new-mown hay tickled her nose, and she fought the urge to sneeze. A horse stamped his foot and whickered, a question in the sound. The wolfhound gave her no time to stop to pet the horse's nose as she would have under normal circumstances. The dog bullied her to the back of the stable where a stack of straw rose higher than her eight-year-old head.

A short time later, Delaney cowered under the hay. Her fist stuffed in her mouth to muffle the screams crouched in her chest just in case they clawed their way out. Swords clanged. Men shouted. Women screamed. Pandemonium ruled her world. As long as she remained silent and hidden, she might survive the slaughter. The screams of others echoed in her ears, and chaos reigned all around her. A whimper escaped around her hand. She didn't breathe for a long moment as a scream echoed, a rising keen to rival the banshee. Her skin prickled as she forced her muscles to remain still. Every ounce of her being urged her to jump up and run away. The dog had burrowed into the hay with her. Even now he curled up in front of her, head down but ears perked, the grin splitting his muzzle full of malice should anyone discover them. His warm presence helped keep her calm despite the periodic shudders that racked her whole body.

A familiar voice yelled out in the courtyard. Her father. He shouted orders to rally the clann. She heard her mother scream her name then the names of her brother and sister, and finally, a weak wail followed. More shouts drowned out her father's cry until his voice was silenced as well. She squeezed her eyes shut as tears threatened. Biting down on her fist, she kept her anguish silent.

Where was her brother? Her sister? Had they escaped the slaughter? For slaughter it surely must be. Her father wasn't a warrior. He was a farmer, a breeder of horses, cows, and sheep. An occasional moan wafted on the wind then a wail, followed by a sound resembling a cleaver splitting a piece of meat. Death stalked through the keep. Eventually, complete silence descended, the effect more ominous than even the screams had been before.

Shhh, cailín, a voice as sweet as spun sugar whispered in her ear. "Stay very still and yee'll be safe." The voice crooned a lullaby so soft Delaney was positive no one but she could hear it. Not even the wolfhound stirred. She curled up at the dog's back, huddling against him for warmth.

Voices echoed in the stables—two gruff, boastful men chortling over their conquest. She recognized neither. She felt the growl rumbling in the dog's chest even though she couldn't hear it. His muscles tensed. She prayed they remained undiscovered, knowing the dog would die trying to save her. His sacrifice would be in vain for she would likely die, too—or worse. She might be only eight but the raiders came every year to take what they could, leaving death and destruction behind them. The voices edged closer, muted now. Delaney pictured the men creeping along, checking in each stall before snagging the horse and trotting it out as spoils of war. The horses in her father's stables were known far and wide, prized by friend and foe alike.

She was doomed to discovery. Fear permeated her very bones, making her feel like they could snap in two from the tension of waiting. A little part of her brain nudged, urging her to jump up and surrender, to throw herself on the mercy of the raiders.

Then a shouted name penetrated the fog of her fear. *O'Neill.*

She curled into a tighter ball, her head butting against the hound's back. She'd heard terrible tales of the O'Neill raiders, of what they did to their victims. No quick death for her should she be discovered. The big dog she huddled against was her only weapon. He'd given her no time to grab the small scian she kept beneath her pillow. The little dirk wouldn't be much defense but perhaps by putting up a fight, she'd annoy the O'Neills enough to kill her outright.

Time held its breath. The raiders took their own

sweet time investigating the stables. At last they reached the haystack, their voices loud and raucous in her ears. The dog tensed, ready to spring despite the hand she laid across his shoulders to keep him still.

One of the O'Neills kicked at the hay. She strained to listen, her brain desperate to identify the sounds. His trews rustled as he bent over. His mantle unraveled from his shoulders and the end whispered across the hay. Each breath he took rattled like the wind in the rowan trees.

Just as she was sure they'd be discovered and the dog would leap from beneath their cloak of straw, someone yelled in the courtyard. The two men pounded out of the stables, their rapid exit kicking up puffs of dust that threatened to choke her. Her nose burned and a fierce tickle tormented her, teasing her unmercifully until she was positive she would sneeze and give away her hiding place.

"Shh, small one."

She opened her eyes, straining to find the source of that voice.

He comes for you and all will be well.

Who? Her mouth formed the word, but she was still too terrified of discovery to ask the question out loud and too stunned to wonder where the voice originated.

No reply came but she swore she could feel the answer as real and warm as two arms wrapping around her in a hug. The sweet crooning sang in her ear, and in moments, she drifted into a peaceful daze.

****

The growls alerted him. Riordan tiptoed toward the pile of hay in the back of the stables. "Peace," he murmured to whichever dog crouched beneath the straw. He heard rustling and pinpointed where the animal hid.

With great care, he dug through the hay. He didn't fancy a dog bite. A furred head, massive with glinting teeth, reared up from the pile. Riordan recognized the beast. "Easy now, Bród."

The big dog whined low in his throat. He held out his hand for the dog to sniff. With a grace belying his size, the brute pushed up to his full height and shook. Hay flew off his brindled coat like sleet driven before the north wind.

Riordan's breath caught in his chest when he recognized the small figure curled up in the hay. The youngest of the O'Beirne children stirred and shivered in the cold left in the wake of the wolfhound's abandonment. Riordan pulled off his mantle and wrapped the little girl in it. With great care, he lifted her into his arms.

"Ah, child, 'tis safe you are now. I have you." Her head lolled against his shoulder as she snuggled into his warmth. His arms tightened instinctively even as his heart clutched. So far, she was the only survivor of the slaughter left in the wake of the raiders.

Outside the barn, Riordan's cousin and clann chief, Ciaran MacDermot sat his horse like a legendary Finian warrior. In the courtyard, bodies lay in disarray, broken and bloody, as if thrown by a giant's hand. Ciaran's expression remained impassive, but his eyes mirrored the pain and disgust felt by every man riding with him. Riordan hugged his treasure closer, nodding in answer to Ciaran's suddenly hopeful look.

Niall McDonagh, Ciaran's captain, walked up,

leading a horse by its reins. Refusing to surrender the girl, Riordan stepped up into the saddle with only minimal assistance from the other man. He urged his horse closer to Ciaran's.

"Any sign of the others?" He murmured the words so as not to wake the sleeping child.

Ciaran shook his head. "None. Taidhg is tracking the raiders. They took all their wounded and dead with them so they will be slowed down."

Niall stood between the two horses and nodded to his clann chief. "Taidhg will follow until he catches them, and then he'll send word. There's no better tracker in Roscommon." He glanced at the child. "Is she all right, then?"

Riordan nodded. "She is. I found her buried in the hay pile at the back of the stable, guarded by Bród. Poor little cailín."

As if he knew the men spoke of him, the big dog woofed and lunged up to put his front paws on Riordan's knee. He nosed the girl and whined. The wolfhound stared up at Riordan, his liquid brown eyes showing his worry.

With the little girl resting across his thighs, Riordan risked letting go with one hand in order to pet the wolfhound. "You did well, Bród. You're aptly named, boy, for you served the little cailín with pride." He ruffled the dog's ears and patted him on the shoulder. Seeming satisfied, the big dog dropped to all fours and waited patiently beside Riordan's horse.

He looked down and realized the little girl stared up at him. Her eyes shimmered with tears but she didn't speak, only watched him like a bright little bird, both curious and skittish. In the light of the torch Niall held,

Riordan could tell her eyes were dark brown, framed by impossibly long lashes. He smiled at her, though his normally easy grin was stretched a bit to hide his angry reaction to the night's events.

"Hello, cailín. So you're awake after all. Do you remember me?"

She nodded, her pinched little face solemn. Arching her neck, she shifted so she could peek out of his mantle. Her eyes widened when she recognized Ciaran, and then they resembled the waters of Galway Bay as they filled with tears. One lone drop quivered at the corner of her eye, poised on a long lash before diving onto the soft cream of her cheek and rolling away, a silvery trail the only sign of its passage.

"Are they all gone?" Her voice whispered and, quaking with the certainty of his answer, sounded resigned. She shivered and closed her eyes awaiting his reply.

"We're still looking for your brother and sister." He could only hope he sounded more optimistic than he felt. The raiders had left no one alive. Other than the child in his arms. Her survival was a miracle.

A delicate hand appeared from beneath his mantle, and she cupped Riordan's cheek. "You found me," she whispered.

He had to swallow around the lump in his throat before he could speak. "I did, yes."

"Thank you." Those dark lashes drifted over her soft brown eyes, shuttering them, and she drifted back to sleep.

Riordans' heart stuttered in his chest, filled with an emotion he had no name for. It couldn't be love. An overwhelming wave of coldness strangled his heart at the thought of losing the tiny cailín sleeping in his arms.

He looked up to find Ciaran studying him.

"We'll see her safely to Becca," Ciaran promised.

Riordan's stomach clenched and bile rose in his throat. He didn't want anyone else looking after the child.

Mine! His brain roared the claim.

Yours, a voice as sweet as spun sugar affirmed.

Chapter 1

Rory MacDermot did not cool his heels well at all. He paced up and down the hallway, resisting the urge to put his fist through the wall at the far end of his path. Instead, he executed a precise about-face and stalked back to the other end. For a man whose business depended on patience, he had absolutely none at the moment. The little blonde receptionist stuck her head out of the doorway and waited until he drew even with her.

"Are you sure you won't come in and sit down? Can I get you something to drink?" Her hesitant voice rose at the end of each sentence, making a question of everything. "Dr. Burns won't be too much longer? She just called to say she was on her way?"

He shook his head. The last thing he needed was more caffeine. As it was, adrenaline zinged through his body, snapping across muscles and nerve endings as it passed. "I can't wait much longer. I have stuff I need to do."

The blonde looked apprehensive. "You have to stay until the doctor gets back." She tried to sound insistent, but it came out as a plea.

Normally, he would have felt some pity for the girl, but today? Nope. Wasn't happening. This was the last place he wanted to be. In fact, it pissed him off royally. He didn't need further debriefing. Not now. Not ever.

He watched the little receptionist cower away from him. Catching a glimpse of his face in the glass window in the door, he understood why. His scowl made him look like a mad man. Angry, he amended. He wasn't mad. Or crazy. Rory scrubbed a hand across his face. He had to admit he did look haggard. But considering his lack of sleep, his appearance was understandable.

"Look, this is a really bad idea. I need to be somewhere else, doing something else. Tell the doctor I'll call to reschedule." He turned on his heel, stalked down the hallway, and made it as far as the elevator before his pager went off. "Damn." The curse came out like a sigh, muttered under his breath. A call out. His team had been activated. The little blonde still stood at the entry to the doctor's office, watching. "See? I just got paged out to an incident." He didn't wait for the elevator, turning instead to the door marked "STAIRS." He bumped it with his shoulder, pushed through, and took the stairs two at a time.

The adrenaline surge he'd been fighting since arriving at the doctor's office ramped up another notch. Action. That's what he needed. Not sitting penned up in some therapist's office, puking his guts out to her about an incident that couldn't be changed, couldn't be fixed, and shouldn't be erased.

Reaching the first floor, Rory bounced the bar on the stairwell door. It slammed open and he stood, hesitating for just a moment. Noon. The place teemed with office drones. One part of his brain registered the fact they looked like ants after their hill was disturbed. He, however, had to cross the lobby of the office building. He stepped into the crush of bodies. With the ease of a running back dodging tacklers, he executed a broken-field run through the crowd and made it out into the humid air of the hot August day. He snagged his cell phone, punching the autodial even as he jogged for the corner.

His partner picked up on the second ring. "Scotty, I'm at Airline and Montgomery. Grab my gear. I'll meet the truck at the scene." He listened for a moment, his trot slowing to a walk before he halted completely. "That's bullshit, man. Tell the captain I'm coming anyway. New Boy isn't ready." His hand clenched the phone, his grip so tight the electronic device almost cracked. "Just bring my gear, Scott. I'll deal with Captain Davis." Flipping the phone closed, he jammed it in his hip pocket.

"Great. Just fucking great," he snarled, unaware he spoke aloud until a little old lady thumped him with her handbag.

"Watch your language, young man," she chastised him primly.

"Yes, ma'am. Sorry, ma'am." He didn't stop to see if the grandmotherly woman accepted his insincere apology. He'd parked his truck around the corner, lucky to find a space on the street. Turning the corner, he kicked his jog up a couple of gears and sprinted to his pride and joy. The big four-wheel drive pickup was rigged to run and looked completely out of place on this urban street.

Rory dug his keys out and hit the fob, deactivating the door locks with a loud beep. The meter maid taking down his license plate number jumped. She marched around the back of his truck, glaring at him.

"You did that on purpose!"

Under normal circumstances, her accusatory tone

would have him teasing and bantering with her. Today, though, he was a man on a mission. "Sergeant Rory MacDermot," he announced. In a smooth and practiced gesture, he pulled his wallet from his hip pocket and flipped it open. "SWAT. I'm headed to a call out."

"Oh no you aren't, big boy." The meter maid fisted her hands on her hips and scowled up at him. The drab brown uniform did little to hide her curvaceous figure, and her dark eyes snapped as she blinked rapidly. "You are twenty minutes out of time on this meter, and I'm in the process of writing you up. You are not going any place until I finish writing this ticket and you sign it. You think I was born yesterday?" She shook her head and muttered under her breath. "That badge don't mean nothing to me. Flashing it like a get out of jail card. Humph."

Rory shoved his badge wallet back in his pocket and pulled out a couple of ten-dollar bills from the front pocket. As he approached, she opened her ticket book and returned to filling out the form. He never broke stride as he tucked the money in the book and closed it. "To pay the ticket. And remind me to send you chocolate." He paused, reading the name placket on her uniform. Pasting his most devastating smile on his face, he added, "Officer Ramirez."

Before she could recover, he was in his truck and pulling out into traffic. Glancing in his rear view mirror, he realized she hadn't moved—that she stood in the same spot staring after him. He gunned the accelerator to pull around a slower car. He was less than a mile from the incident. Hopefully, he would arrive at the same time as the SWAT truck with his gear. His heart raced for a moment and then settled down to the steady thump-thump-thump of its normal rhythm. He lived for this. Always had. First in the Marines and now with the police department.

Uniformed patrol officers had the street blocked off. He pulled up behind one of the squad cars and left the truck parked in the middle of the lane. He climbed out, and his badge appeared in his hand. As it turned out, he didn't need his ID. The first street cop he met flashed a grin of recognition and lifted the flapping crime scene tape stretched across the road.

"Howdy, Rory. You must have been close."

He ducked under the tape and nodded. "About a mile away."

Both of them turned at the sound of a growling diesel engine. The SWAT truck rumbled up, men spilling from the back before it even rolled to a jerky stop. Rory ducked back under the tape, intent on retrieving his gear. Captain Davis stepped down from the front passenger seat, effectively blocking his way.

"Just where do you think you're going, MacDermot?" The captain barked the question, and Rory was reminded once again how much the man, with his jowly cheeks and narrowed eyes, resembled a bulldog. "If I'm not mistaken, you are still on mandatory administrative leave. Until you have the paperwork from the consult, you aren't cleared for duty."

Rory lifted one shoulder in a nonchalant shrug. "I went. The doc didn't show up. Then I got the page." He stepped closer, invading the older man's space. Lowering his voice, he added, "Look, captain, we both know I'm fine. New Boy isn't ready. He's never been tested, and this isn't the time to find out if he has the cojones for this job." He recognized the flicker of doubt in the captain's eyes and pressed home his advantage. "My gear's in the truck. Let me suit up, cap'n. I'll take New Boy with me. Watch him and evaluate. But if push comes to shove, the shot is mine." He schooled his expression. It wouldn't do to let Captain Davis see how important this was, how desperate he was to get back to his job.

Davis stepped back so he didn't have to crane his neck so much to look up at Rory. "Every instinct I have is screamin' at me, boy. I should kick your ass out of here and send you back to wait on that doctor."

Despite the huge smile blooming inside, Rory maintained his poker-faced expression. "But you won't. You know I'm right about New Boy."

Davis actually sighed. "Yeah. I know. Get your gear while I find out what the hell is going on here."

Rory dashed to the back of the SWAT vehicle and climbed inside. All alone, he let the smile appear. He stripped down and pulled on his jumpsuit, bullet proof vest, boots, and grabbed his sniper rifle. He pretended his hands weren't shaking as he loaded the weapon. Gulping in a deep breath, he squared his shoulders and emerged from the truck. His team clustered nearby, but he simply nodded to them and headed off to find Captain Davis. He didn't miss the scowl New Boy flashed in his direction. Sooner or later, he would have a come-to-Jesus meeting with the kid. But not today. Today he had a different mission. He found Davis talking to the patrol division supervisor, a lieutenant, who'd been in charge before Metro SWAT arrived. The lieutenant was just finishing his briefing.

"The first unit on the scene was only two blocks

away when the silent alarm went out. As he pulled up, a teen-age boy ran out the door. Shots were fired so the officer grabbed the kid and ducked. As near as we can tell, there are two perps and five hostages, one of them a baby or toddler. The victim who escaped mentioned two clerks, and two women with a child in a stroller." The LT snorted. "Talk about being in the wrong place at the wrong time. The kid walked in on the robbery. He took one look and high-tailed it out of there."

Rory winced at the mention of the hostages but steeled his emotions and his expression before either man saw him. As Davis turned his direction, he was already scanning nearby rooftops looking for the best firing position. "Is there any way they can get out the back of the store?"

The lieutenant shook his head. "Only way in or out is through the front door. Back door is blocked by the Dumpster. Go figure." He shrugged and continued. "They attempted to close the blinds on the window but something happened." He turned and pointed to a shop in the middle of the small strip center. Metal blinds hung askew, one end jacked higher than the other.

He could feel Captain Davis's gaze on him as he studied the layout. He pulled a pair of small binoculars from his flak vest and searched the area carefully. When he focused on the window, he could discern vague movement beyond the glass. Lowering the binoculars, he glanced up at the sun. In another hour, the sun's reflection on the window would make seeing inside the shop all but impossible.

Davis squinted up at the sun, too. "Maybe there's common crawl space. We could set up inside."

Rory growled under his breath. "We couldn't get

that lucky."

The captain's growl echoed his. "Take Carter and set up your firing position. I'll establish communications. Maybe we can negotiate."

A bark of laughter erupted before Rory could stop it. "Yeah, and maybe the Cubs will win the World Series." He turned on his heel and returned to the SWAT team. He filled them in and gave them their assignments. "Dutch, report to the captain for communications liaison. Andy and Luke, take the rear just in case. LT swears the front is the only egress. Let's not get caught with our pants down if he's wrong." He nodded to the single female on the team and the big man standing next to her. "Jessie, Hoss, take the front. Scotty, across the street for low cover." Rory glanced at Dean Carter, the newest member of the team. The kid bounced on his toes while his fingers alternately clutched and caressed his sniper rifle. "New Boy, with me."

Within minutes, Rory selected his vantage point on the roof across the street from the shop. He motioned for New Boy to set up about ten feet away so they'd have two angles. With an ease of motion born of countless hours of practice, Rory set up his sniper rifle and settled in to wait. This is what he did best, this waiting patiently for a target to appear in his scope. Stretched out on the black-tar roof, eye to his scope, cheek resting against the butt of his rifle, Rory let his breath out. Slow. Inhale just as slow, lungs expanding to capacity, diaphragm stretched and almost aching before the release of air, just as deliberate. *Breathe.* His heart rate spiked briefly before calming to a steady beat. Had he realized he was smiling, he would have been surprised.

"Target team Alpha set." His calm voice whispered through the microphone attached to his radio earpiece. Cutting his eyes to the left, he glanced over at New Boy. Sweat dotted the kid's forehead, soaking through the band of his cap. Rory's upper lip curled in contempt. He switched off the voice activation on his radio. Without moving his head, he said a bit louder, "Relax. We're going to be here awhile."

"I know." Carter sounded defensive.

"Then why are you sweating?" Rory wasn't in the mood to be nice.

"It's hot out here."

There it was, he thought, the New Boy whine. He should trademark the description. "And it'll get hotter yet." Rory had done his time as a field training officer. He didn't relish repeating the experience, especially since this pup wanted his job. "Once the sun goes down, it'll get cold. And you'll get thirsty. Or hungry. You'll need to piss, too, so you'd better learn to hold it." He heard movement, the faint brush of whipcord material against tar paper. He cut his eyes as New Boy swiveled to face him and then immediately returned his focus to the scope and the scene playing out across the street.

"I can outlast you, dickhead."

Rory snorted. "Yeah, you and your little dog, too, Dorothy."

The radio whispered in his ear. "Any movement?"

"Negative," Rory replied after switching the radio back to voice activation.

"Negotiator will be here shortly."

"Roger that."

He heard more rustling as Carter settled back into position. Sooner or later, the kid would push one too many of his buttons. Even though he knew his team would stand behind him and help put Carter in his place, deep down, he hoped it wouldn't come to that. Internal discipline on the team was crucial. A loose cannon only complicated matters, but if push came to shove, he was ready.

"Bravo Team in position." Luke's voice whispered in his ear. Rory could picture Luke and Andy taking up their positions on the back side of the strip. "Nothing but Dumpsters back here. LT's right. Rear door is blocked." Luke paused for a few seconds and Rory knew he was taking in the scenery. His earpiece clicked. "Looks like firewalls between each shop. No way to go inside high."

Damn. He didn't utter the curse out loud, but it echoed in his head. They'd be losing visuals soon.

"Charlie Team in position." Jessie's voice fluttered in his earpiece, interrupting his thought pattern. He grinned. She might look and sound all soft and cuddly, but she could take down any guy on the team, including Hoss. Hard on the heels of her acknowledgement came Scotty's as he announced he'd taken up a spot just below the sniper team, but slightly off to one side, using a pickup for cover.

Now all they needed was the man who did the talking. With luck, the negotiator could keep the perps engaged until the sun moved far enough toward the horizon so he'd have a clear view. Ultimately, Rory hoped the negotiator could do his job and talk them out. He shivered despite the heat and then tamped down on his emotions again.

His right index finger caressed the trigger like a lover.

Breathe. He was ready.

Dammit, he was always ready.

Chapter 2

Dr. Delaney Burns walked through the outer door into her office. Her nose twitched as the scent of newly-mown hay wafted into her nostrils. The familiar tickle and burn of an impending sneeze made her curl her lip, squint, and sniffle. After a tense moment, the sensation subsided and she exhaled slowly. She sniffed the air again but could only identify Mandy's perfume, the slightly noxious smell of the ammonia-based cleanser the overnight cleaning crew used to wipe down every surface, and stale air puffing through the over-worked air conditioning unit. There was no underlying odor that would have triggered her allergic reaction.

"I'm so sorry I'm late," she told her receptionist. She paused, looking around the empty office. "Is Sergeant MacDermot waiting in my office?"

Mandy shook her head, her bottom lip quivering as her eyes filled with tears. "N-n-no." The girl all but wailed.

Delaney sighed. There were times she wished she wasn't quite such a pushover. As dean of a local business college, her sister constantly saddled her with the students no one with any sense would hire. Luckily, none of them ever stayed long. "Get a grip, Mandy. It's not the end of the world. Did he reschedule?"

Again the girl sniveled. "N-n-no."

"Deep breaths, Mandy. And put your head between

your knees if you feel faint. When you can talk without crying, perhaps you will tell me what happened?"

The little receptionist leaned back in her secretarial chair, performed a series of deep breathing exercises—eyes closed, fingertips pressing into her abdomen just below her diaphragm. After a few moments, she opened her eyes and flashed a tentative smile. "He left."

Fighting the urge to roll her eyes, Delaney nodded. "I can see that, since he isn't here. Where did he go?"

Mandy shrugged. "I don't know. We don't have a television so I couldn't turn on the news."

Delaney opened her mouth but no words came out. Her brain was too busy processing Mandy's statement to actually form coherent speech.

Before she could make sense of her receptionist's response, her cell phone rang. The ringtone played the theme song from *COPS* and pegged the caller immediately. She answered with a brusque, "Doctor Burns." She listened intently, cutting her eyes periodically in Mandy's direction. "Of course. I'll be right there."

She hit the button to end the conversation and glanced at the girl. "That was police dispatch. I'm guessing you were about to tell me that Sergeant MacDermot left because he was paged out to an incident?"

Mandy nodded so energetically that Delaney wondered how she avoided whiplash.

"I've been called to the same incident. Just take messages if anyone calls. There is no need to tell them where I am. Right?" She caught herself leaning forward to emphasize and encourage an affirmative answer.

Mandy nodded again, a bobble-headed doll on the

dashboard of life. "Oh, of course, Dr. Burns. I won't ever make that mistake again!"

The involuntary shiver chilled her skin before Delaney could stop it. "You know how to lock the office in case I'm not back by five?" She got the bobble-head again. "Okay, Mandy. I'll see you tomorrow morning if not before." She felt like she was talking to a five-year-old.

Out in the hallway, she caught that scent so reminiscent of freshly cut hay again. This time, though, her heart thudded in her chest and sneezing seemed the furthest thing from her mind. For the first time since she'd accepted the contract to work with the city, she was nervous. Hired to consult on psychological issues during and after critical incidents involving the police and fire departments, she'd hoped this meeting with the sergeant was scheduled to further clarify her role. She thought she'd be, well, *consulting*—but by phone—if they needed her expertise. But the dispatcher insisted she come to the scene. ASAP.

The bell on the elevator dinged and the doors slithered open. Delaney hesitated a moment, peeking inside. The car was empty so she stepped in. The doors closed behind her and she stifled a gasp. Turning, she punched the button for the lobby. As if it were an express, the elevator dropped, leaving her stomach feeling like it was lodged on the ceiling of the car. Much relieved when the thing shuddered to stop, the bell dinged, and the doors opened, she jumped out, startling the group of people waiting to board.

"Excuse me. Sorry. Pardon me." She apologized right and left as she pushed through the returning lunch crowd. A man paused to hold the exit door for her and she darted out with a hurried, "Thanks!" tossed over her shoulder. At the curb, she managed to catch a cab and after getting in, she gave the driver the address.

She used the few minutes the ride took to compose herself. She was new to this hostage negotiation advisor gig. A trained police officer talked to the perpetrators, but she was expected to stand next to him and give psychological insight. She'd only participated in one other incident and that one had ended almost before it began.

Delaney stepped from the calm of the taxi cab's backseat into a tense sea of controlled chaos. As the cab drove away, she turned a slow circle, stopping at the cardinal points to survey the entire scene. Yellow crime scene tape stretched across the street and fluttered in the gentle breeze. When a stray strand of her hair tickled her cheek like unseen fingers, she ignored the sensation.

A uniformed police officer stood in the center of the intersection directing sporadic traffic. Beyond the ethereal yellow barrier, a crowd gathered. Too far away for her to hear clearly, she nonetheless recognized the speculation running rampant through the group. The expressions on their faces, their gestures—strangers talking avidly amongst themselves, acquaintances now due to shared experience and curiosity. Police cars and the SWAT van blocked the east and south side streets of the intersection, leaving the other half of the intersecting streets open. The officer made eastbound traffic turn left and southbound turn right. She caught a view of the expressions on various drivers' faces. No one was thrilled by the situation, though some rubbernecked more than others as human curiosity reared its head.

A black four-wheel-drive pickup looked oddly out of place among the police cars. For a moment, she wondered about the driver. To abandon such a vehicle in the middle of an active police incident was a bold gesture. She stared at the truck for a long moment. While it looked, at first, like it had been abandoned haphazardly, she now realized the big vehicle was precisely parked. Curious, she took a few steps to get a closer look.

Two things happened almost simultaneously. Delaney recognized the small badge tag attached to the truck's license plate and a very large and very belligerent cop bore down on her.

"Get the hell outta here, lady! Are you nuts or something? Or blind? Can't you see the emergency lights? Get back behind the yellow tape. Jeez! People are stupid. C'mon. Let's go. Right now. If you don't get moving, I'm going to arrest you!"

When he paused to take a breath, Delaney carefully raised her hand and pointed toward the knot of officers huddled around the trunk of a squad car close to the center of the action. "Captain Davis is expecting me. I'm Dr. Delaney Burns."

Honking horns and screeching brakes distracted the cop for an instant. He glanced over his shoulder and winced at the chaos in the intersection. "Don't move," he growled as he stomped off waving his hands and yelling at the drivers of the two cars sitting nose to nose in the intersection.

Delaney took the opportunity to continue her perusal of the area. The sharp sounds of honking horns and heated, exclamation-filled yelling faded into the background as she focused on the scene in the street to the east. The sun angled in from over her shoulder to bounce off car and building windows. The glint of sunlight flashing from a place where no glass should have reflected it caught her eye. *Sniper team,* her brain registered. Despite the heat of the afternoon sun, goosebumps prickled her arms and the hair on the back of her neck bristled.

That's why she was here. She knew with certainty that she needed to prevent whoever was peering through that sniper scope from ever pulling the trigger. She rubbed her palms up and down her arms in hopes of squelching the shiver doing the quickstep along her spine. What would it be like, she wondered, to stare at a person's face, to be so far away yet be able to read every expression, knowing that at any moment the order could come to terminate? How cold and unfeeling would someone have to be to hold steady, wait, and then pull the trigger? How could a man keep his eye glued to the scope, watching the face he'd become so intimate with simply explode in a rain of blood and torn tissue?

Her stomach clenched and bile rose in her throat. She swallowed it down and had to cough. Her face contorted for a moment with the effort to breathe. Her hands shook as the big cop approached again. He'd dealt with the miscreant drivers and sent them on their way. Another officer appeared to direct traffic in his place. His glare hadn't diminished nor had his mood improved.

"Now, what's this about Captain Davis?" His voice sounded gruff and growly as he focused narrowed eyes on her.

She swallowed again to school her voice and

clenched her hands into fists so he couldn't see her distress. "As I said before, I'm Dr. Burns. The captain is expecting me. I'm part of the negotiating team."

The cop snorted, his disbelief obvious but he pulled out his radio and made the call. "Command Post, I have a female civilian here, says Cap'n Davis is expectin' her?"

Delaney watched his demeanor change as a voice spit out of the radio. "How long has she been here? We need her at the CP now!"

The cop stammered a 10-4 and waved her through. If the situation hadn't been so serious, she might have smiled at the man's discomfort. As things stood, though, she couldn't summon up enough lightheartedness to put one on her face.

She approached the knot of men with some trepidation. She had two strikes against her, three if she'd admit to it. She was a civilian, a psychologist, and a female. Breaching this last bastion of male dominance still felt like walking into the lion's den.

"Glad you're finally here, doctor. Sorry for the trouble back there." Captain Davis tossed his head in the direction of the intersection. "I've put in the paperwork to get your official police department identification badge. You won't have that problem next time."

She swallowed hard again. Next time? How often did these incidents happen? When she'd signed the contract with the city, she thought she'd simply be doing psych evaluations and counseling, albeit mainly with police officers and firefighters. That was before Captain Davis learned about her graduate school paper dealing with Post Traumatic Stress Disorder, EMDR—

the somewhat controversial Eye Movement Desensitization and Reprocessing system to deal with PTSD—and her work with victims and perpetrators of violent crimes. He'd talked her into becoming a civilian consultant. It never occurred to her that she'd be expected to respond on-scene. Too late now to change her mind.

"Do we know anything about the hostages or the perpetrator?" Proud her voice didn't quiver, she pulled a notebook from her shoulder bag to take notes.

"Five hostages. Two female clerks, a mother and small child, and an older woman. Two male perps, at least one armed with a handgun." Captain Davis nodded toward a very scared looking teenager. "He walked in on it. Came out just as our first unit arrived on the scene. Shots were fired as he cleared the door. The kid's scared shitless." Davis coughed. "Sorry. I mean he's scared out of his mind."

Delaney studied the boy, ignoring the crude language the police officer used. Maybe eighteen or nineteen, the pimples on the youngster's pale face stood out like bright red stop signs. Shaggy hair fell over his forehead, the bangs flipping every time he blinked. He kept rubbing his palms up and down his legs, the light blue of the denim slowly darkening as it became sweat stained. The boy's Adam's apple bobbed every time he swallowed.

"May I talk to him?"

Davis looked surprised that she'd even ask for permission and nodded. "Go for it. On-scene, just do what you think needs doin', Doc. Unless you get in the line of fire, no need to ask permission."

She approached the boy with a serious look on her

face but also with a smile and introduced herself. "What's your name?"

"Josh."

"Do you feel all right? Would you like some water or something?" She wasn't sure where she'd get any, but she'd figure it out if Josh wanted something to drink.

Luckily, he shook his head in the negative even as he replied in the affirmative. "Yeah. I'll be okay. Just...dude! He was shooting *real* bullets at me!" His hands kept up their rhythmic rubbing.

"Did you get a good look at them?"

He shrugged, his expression looking unsure. "Sort of. Two guys. One's about my age. One maybe mid-twenties? The older guy had a gun for sure. And tats. Lots of tats." He blinked and paled even more. "Oh, hell. Do you think they're like…gangbangers?" He shifted from one foot to the other, almost hopping. "God, I hope not. That means their homeys will come looking for me."

Delaney sucked in a long breath but almost spit it out. Heat waves danced off the pavement and her lungs felt like they'd been seared. She licked dry lips and desperately wished for a drink of water. Almost as if someone had read her mind, an EMT walked by and handed her and the boy ice-cold bottles. Resisting the urge to press her bottle against her forehead, she gazed at the kid. "What about the other guy? Did he have a gun?"

The teen shrugged. "I'm not sure. It looked like he was hiding something down his leg. And he was…nervous. Like he was jonesing, ya know?"

She did know. She offered him a smile. "Thank

you. You've been a big help."

A uniformed cop appeared and moved the kid away, tucking him into the backseat of a squad car. AC churned cold air into the vehicle, and she longed for the wash of coolness across her clammy skin. Squaring her shoulders, she stepped over to the knot of men. Captain Davis held out a cordless headset. She stared at it but didn't take it from him.

"What's that?"

Davis blinked at her but he'd obviously played a lot of poker in his time. His expression gave nothing away. "Hands-free headset. So you can talk to the hostage takers once we establish contact."

She didn't intend to but she stepped backward anyway. "Me? Talk to them?" Her voice squeaked and she swallowed around the frog in her throat. "I thought I was here simply to advise the negotiator."

The captain shook his head. "No. You *are* our hostage negotiator."

She managed not to shudder under the cold scrutiny of his gaze. A brief smile touched the corner of his mouth, and she let out the breath she'd been holding. The situation was what caused his expression, not her reaction. He touched her arm, gestured for her to follow him a few steps away from the group.

In a quiet voice, he added, "Don't doubt yourself, Doc. You can do this. I've watched you. Listened to you. You have the touch. As long as the perp is talking, he isn't shooting. As long as the perp is talking, *we* aren't shooting." He paused, took a short but deep breath and huffed it out as he looked around the scene. Heat waves danced off the pavement and the hoods of cars. Windows glittered in the fierce sunlight. His gaze returned to her face, watching as he waited for her reply.

Moisture beaded on her forehead and upper lip, and then a thin trickle of perspiration rolled down her back. Even so, she shivered again. How could she feel chilled when the heat index was over a hundred and she was sweating like a race horse?

Meeting the captain's gaze, she swallowed again and finally nodded. "Yes." She almost choked on the word. Licking dry lips, she spoke again, her voice stronger this time. "Yes. I mean, no. No shooting is a good thing." She held out her hand for the device. "Let's get started." She sounded far more confident than she felt. Straightening her shoulders, she accepted the earpiece from Captain Davis and settled it in her ear.

The gruff cop nodded at her and turned on his heel. "Dutch? Have they answered yet?"

The cop with a laptop open on the hood of a squad car shook his head. "Still ringing, boss."

Davis reached into the front seat of the car and snagged a bullhorn. Delaney winced and covered her ears, knowing what was coming. He put it to his mouth, and his voice boomed down the street.

"You there, inside the store. I'm Captain Davis with the police department. We're attempting to contact you. Please answer the phone." He nodded to Dutch, who dialed again. The electronic ring echoed from the computer speaker even as the guy who looked more like Robocop than human held the cell phone to his ear.

Delaney was both amazed and dismayed by the array of electronic gadgets spread across the hood of the squad car. The command post vehicle hadn't been dispatched yet. If the incident dragged on very long, Captain Davis would request the modified RV. They'd be nice and comfortable with an air conditioner and other amenities all available. That glint of sun on glass drew her eyes again. If she was withering in the heat down here on the street, what was the sniper feeling up there on the rooftop. Was he anxious? Would he want to take the shot before she had a chance to talk the men into releasing their hostages and surrendering? Fear turned her knees to jelly for a minute before she locked down on the emotions. She could not—would not let that happen. Her doubt banished, she gestured for the bull horn and told Dutch not to hang up.

"The ringing will irritate them, wear them down," she explained. Hefting the bullhorn she watched as Captain Davis showed her how to activate it. "Hello?" Her voice echoed in her ears and she grimaced. "My name is Dr. Delaney Burns. Please pick up the phone so I can speak with you."

Chapter 3

What the hell? Rory gritted his teeth as the woman's voice ricocheted off the brick and glass canyon of the street. That voice didn't belong to Jessie, the only female member of the SWAT team. "Alpha team leader to command."

"Go." Dutch didn't sound upset.

"Who's on bullhorn?" He schooled his voice.

"Negotiator."

Oh, hell no! The words he didn't say out loud bounced around inside his head like her voice over the bullhorn. He swallowed his irritation even though his gut twisted when he heard her voice again.

"Please, I'd really like to speak with you."

Something clicked in his earpiece. An unfamiliar voice growled, "Yeah, bitch. What the hell do you want?"

Dutch had activated the link so Rory could hear the exchange between this Dr. Burns chick and the perps. He glanced over to New Boy. The kid hadn't moved. Interesting that Dutch kept the exchange semi-private. Rory settled in to listen.

"My name is Dr. Burns, not 'bitch.' Please show me the same respect I am showing you. What name shall I call you by?"

"They call me Music Man." Boasting. Rory envisioned Dutch running the name through the gang unit's database.

"Interesting nickname. Are you a singer? A musician?" Rory's gut clenched again. She sounded so naïve, and that fact was rammed home as the gangster's laughter echoed in his earpiece.

"I make the girls sing, bitch. Just like I'm gonna make you sing if I ever get my hands on you."

The hackles on the back of Rory's neck actually bristled, and he bit back a growl.

"Dr. Burns if you please, Music Man. And I doubt I'm your type. I'm plain old white bread, and I suspect you are used to far more exotic flavors."

Rory grinned in spite of himself. The doc might be all soft voice and politeness, but maybe she wasn't as naïve as he'd thought. He heard the banger stammer and swallowed his laughter as the guy's response whispered in his ear.

"D'uh...huh?"

The blinds twitched and a face peered between the slats.

"Target acquired." Rory's voice whispered through the microphone. He heard Dr. Burns gasp, followed by Captain Davis's quiet affirmation.

"Music Man, you need to listen to me." The doctor sounded flustered and a bit desperate. Not a good sign. "This thing is going to escalate out of control. I want to make sure everyone gets out of this in one piece. Okay?"

"Ha, bitch. Shows what you know. You think the cops'll let me 'n'Big Tee walk out of here?"

"If you don't hurt anyone, things will be easier."

"That's bullshit."

"No, it's not. Right now, you and Big Tee are

looking at minor charges. If you hurt one of the hostages, then—"

Wailing echoed in Rory's earpiece right before Music Man yelled, "SHUT UP!" The static of dead air hummed in his earpiece. The perp had hung up and the face disappeared from the window.

"Lost target."

"The baby is crying." Jessie's voice sounded a little tense. "We can hear it from here."

His chest tightened and Rory forced slow, measured breaths to loosen the strain. Babies cried, often for no reason. There'd been no sound of gunfire from the shop. What had been incessant phone rings, as the doctor attempted to reestablish contact, faded to silence. Dutch likely cut the link to keep from annoying the team.

"Music Man? Please answer the phone." Dr. Burns' voice boomed through the bullhorn. Long moments later, she tried again. "Music Man, why don't you let the baby and its mother go? Things will be calmer and that's a good-faith show for the police."

The gangster picked up the phone, and his voice snarled through Rory's earpiece as he answered. "Fuck you, bitch. I'm gonna kill the kid if it don't shut up."

"Music Man, please think this through. Babies cry. They can't help it. Let the baby go, okay?"

The front door opened abruptly. Unseen hands shoved the stroller out. Before anyone could react, the door closed, and Scotty darted from his hiding place. Like a pro-football running back, he swooped in, grabbed the bawling toddler, and sprinted for the safety of the command post.

Rory kept his eye glued to the scope, desperate to

cover his best friend. He didn't loosen his finger on the trigger until Scott and the child were safely under cover. Only then did he glance over at New Boy. The man was tense, his finger curled tight on the trigger.

"Stand down." The other sniper ignored him. "Carter, look at me." He kept his voice low but compelling, the whip of command inherent in the tone. The other man didn't move except to tighten his finger on the trigger. "Carter! I said stand down. Release the trigger."

"Carter?" Captain Davis tried to contact New Boy, too. When he got no reply, he called Rory. "Alpha team leader, status?"

"Tango two froze." Stuck between a rock and hard spot, Rory swore under his breath. He couldn't get up and knock some sense into Carter. He had to stay focused on his primary mission. Dammit, if Carter screwed up this incident, Rory would personally take the guy apart. He lifted his head slightly, to look around for something to throw then realized that could be a bad idea. If he startled Carter, the man might pull the trigger out of reflex.

"Carter." He ground out the two syllables. "CAR-TER." Rory heard the other cop take a breath. He exhaled his own. "Stand down, Carter. Disengage."

"No."

"That's an order, Carter." The captain's voice cut in. "Secure your weapon and return to the command post."

Rory listened, with furtive glances to confirm the sounds. Carter ejected the bullet in the breach and removed the clip from his rifle. He disassembled the tripod, grabbed his pack, and shimmied backward from the edge of the building. At least he did that part right. Once he was far enough from the building parapet so he couldn't be seen from across the street, he stood and marched to the stairwell door. He darted into the shadows of the doorway without a word.

"Good riddance."

"Say again, Tango One?" Dutch's voice whispered in his ear.

Had he really said that out loud?

"Tango Two is headed to the command post."

"Roger that."

The sun shifted farther toward the western horizon, its light glinting off the windows of the shop below.

"Alpha two, do you have a visual?" Rory could only hope that Scott had a better view.

"Negative, Alpha One."

Damn. Dr. Burns tried periodically to reestablish contact with the perps but there'd been none since the toddler was shoved out. She was quiet at the moment and Rory was glad. When her voice murmured in his ear, his body did funny things. His brain shifted from the job to thinking about more pleasurable pursuits. He didn't even know what she looked like but his libido didn't care. His shaft swelled with every breath she took, the microphone picking up every blessed erotic sound she made, and his imagination supplied the pictures of her breasts rising and falling.

A drop of sweat escaped from the band of his cap and trickled between his eyes. He squiggled his nose until the sweat dropped off the end of it. Shadows crept across the roof deck. In a few minutes, he'd be in shade and would have a view through the shop windows below.

"Yo, Doctor Bitch."

Rory's finger jerked where it lay next to the trigger guard, and he breathed through the reflex. He wanted to shoot the sonavabitch simply for calling Dr. Burns names. What the hell was going on in his head?

"You know my name, Music Man. There is no need to be rude." Her soft voice went straight to his groin, and he could almost feel her words caress his erection. He shifted slightly, trying to find a position that wasn't painful.

"Whatever. We're hungry."

"I'm sure you are. How are the hostages?"

"Hungry, too, only I'm gonna start carvin' 'em up for food if I don't get a pizza or somethin'."

"Really? Raw human flesh is full of bacteria and not at all like eating a rare steak."

Rory choked, and recognized the sounds of his other team members doing the same through his earpiece. The doc had some serious balls. Music Man didn't respond for a moment and no wonder. How did a guy from the hood answer that?

"What the hell, bitch? Talk English. Get us something to eat or I'm gonna mess up this little momma and then throw her bleeding body out and shoot her."

"You don't want to do that, Music Man. The only thing standing between you and the death penalty is the health and well-being of those people."

The blinds twitched, drawing Rory's eye to the movement. A big man, with a cordless phone pressed to his ear peered out between the slats. Sunlight no longer blocked his view of that section.

"I have target."

"Maintain target. You do not, I repeat, you do not have a go." The captain's voice left no room for argument.

Rory couldn't decide if he was pissed or relieved. As he stared through the scope, all he saw was the face of a thug who went through life intimidating and hurting people. He didn't see green eyes wide with fear despite the laugh lines at their corners. He didn't see the plump, middle-aged cheeks and wide forehead fringed with dark hair. He shoved that memory away. That ghost had no place here. Not now. Now he had a job. Four lives depended on his rock steady nerve. He inhaled slowly. Four innocent lives. Truth be told, six lives depended on him, and on Doc Burns with the hypnotizing voice.

She gave the thug time to reflect, and when he didn't smart off to her, she continued. "My goal here, Music Man, is to make sure everyone walks out alive and healthy. You and Big Tee haven't hurt anyone, right?"

"Yeah." At least the banger sounded thoughtful.

"There's still a chance to get out of this. Right now, the only charges are attempted robbery and unlawful detention. You can do the time standing on your head, right? But if you hurt anyone, if they die, what happens? You'll be facing murder charges."

"If I'm lookin' at kidnapping, those sumbitches better just shoot me now. I ain't doin' that kinda time. An' I damn sure ain't goin' down for murder!"

"Then think about it, Music Man. Think long and hard. You don't have to hurt those people. You don't have to go out in a blaze of gunfire. It's an ugly, painful way to die. What would your mother say? Do you want her crying over your casket?"

"You leave my momma outta this."

"I can't, Music Man. What you do here…what you do now affects not only you but the people in that shop. Your family. Their families. Friends. It's like tossing a pebble into a pond. Those ripples just keep spreading."

"Talk normal, bitch. You sound like one o'them shows on PBS or somethin'."

"Your actions, Music Man, aren't all about you. But it's up to you. You control what happens. You can stop it now. Or you can take the consequences."

The man said nothing for long minutes but he didn't hang up. Maybe everyone would walk away in one piece today. Voices hummed in the background, both deep but one highly excited. Music Man and Big Tee talking over their options.

"What do we get if we let these bitches go?"

"I can't make deals, Music Man. That's up to the DA. But, no one leaves in a body bag if you let them walk out. And if you put your guns down and follow them."

The male voices hissed and popped in his earpiece. He caught the words "get away," "car," "hell." Through the entire exchange, the shadow of the big body didn't move from the window, though his face disappeared when he wasn't talking directly to the doc. The face reappeared.

"Here's how it's gonna be. We send out the whiny old bitch and one other. But me n'Tee are keepin' the other two. We want a car. We're gonna drive outta here. Nobody follows us. When we're free, we'll turn the other two loose."

"No."

Rory's jaw dropped. The doc had been all honey until that one word. That "no" stopped the world.

"You are going to free all four people, and then you and Big Tee will surrender your weapons and be placed under arrest."

"You don't call the shots, bitch."

"That's Dr. Burns to you. And I do call the shots. We play it my way, Music Man. You don't want to die today. If I let you leave, do you really believe the police won't end things here and now? That means a bullet to your head. I don't want you to die. I don't want Big Tee to die. But I will sacrifice you both to keep all four hostages safe. Do you understand?" She waited a few heartbeats before continuing. "Tell Big Tee what I just said if I'm not on speakerphone. Tell Big Tee he doesn't call the shots. You're the big man, the one in charge. You decide, Music Man."

Rory breathed and didn't try to hide his grin. Holy shit could she play that guy. She knew all the buttons. Maybe she was a good fit after all. The male voices in his ear rose in a yelling match. The doc had Music Man in the palm of her hand and he was shouting down his partner in crime.

"Alpha One." Scott's voice called him.

"Go, Alpha Two."

"When they come out, I'll take the first suspect."

"Roger that." He agreed with Scott. If trouble erupted, it would come from Big Tee, not Music Man. They both anticipated that he'd be the last one through the door.

"Bravo One and Two in position in the shop to the west."

"Charlie One and Two still in the rear."

Rory counted the time by his heartbeats. The blinds twitched several times, and then the voices stopped. Music Man had hung up.

The front door opened and a frightened female voice screamed, “Don’t shoot!” The woman slid through the door and hesitated looking far too much like a deer in headlights.

The doc’s calm voice reverberated through the bullhorn. “Walk to your right. Down the sidewalk. Keep walking no matter what.”

Luckily, the woman did as directed. As she neared the door of the next shop, Jessie appeared, covered her, and rushed her down the street. A few moments later, Jess affirmed, “Hostage one secure.”

The door opened again and a second hostage appeared. This was the older woman. She instinctively turned right and scuttled down the sidewalk. She looked shocked when Hoss appeared but didn’t scream when he all but picked her up and rushed her to the command post.

“Hostage two secured.”

Jessie and Hoss both crept back up the street, hugging the front of the buildings. Two down, four to go. He didn’t dare hope this incident would go off like clockwork. The door opened a third time and he caught shadowy movement in his scope. A third woman appeared, bolting through the door and running pell-mell down the sidewalk. She never even looked at the two SWAT cops, flying past them like she was running for a gold medal. Dutch’s voice acknowledged that the third hostage was safe. The door hadn’t closed and Rory’s attention never wavered.

A hand holding a pistol appeared in the fading

sunlight. "Don't shoot." Music Man stepped outside, his hands high above his head, the gun dangling from his little finger.

"You fuckin' asshole." Big Tee screamed, but Music Man ignored him.

He'd seen Jessie and Hoss, their message clear as they pointed their assault rifles at him. He walked very carefully and extended his hand with the gun still hanging. Hoss snatched the weapon, passed it to Jessie and snapped handcuffs on the guy before hustling him away. Two patrol cops met Hoss halfway and secured the prisoner.

And that left two. The situation was going to hell. The sun was almost down but that did little to cool off the temperature or abate the humidity. Rory blinked sweat from his eyes and grabbed a chance to wipe his face across his sleeve. His respirations sped up and he made a conscious effort to slow them. *Breathe.* He couldn't relax until the fourth hostage was safe.

The door opened again and the last hostage appeared. Big Tee's arm circled her waist in a death hug. The woman's mouth gaped open in a silent scream, her eyes so wide the whites showed all the way around her irises as Rory watched through his scope. Big Tee pressed an automatic pistol against her temple. Rory blinked rapidly as his eyesight swam—a different face overlaying the hostage's.

Inhale. Exhale. *Breathe.* He schooled his vision as Big Tee's face moved into the scope's crosshairs. *Breathe.* Inhale. Exhale. "Target acquired."

"Roger that, Alpha One." Captain Davis turned control over to him with those four words. The decision to shoot/don't shoot rested entirely in his trigger finger.

Rory watched Big Tee's finger tighten on the trigger.

Breathe. Inhale. Exhale. His own finger tightened on the rifle's trigger. The woman sagged against her captor's arm and Big Tee stumbled.

NO! Not again. This wasn't happening again. He reacquired his target. Tee's fingers loosened on the pistol grip, and the gun slid from his hand. The woman collapsed to the ground as Tee raised both hands to the sky. In moments, Hoss and Scotty swarmed over him while Jessie led the sobbing woman away.

"Fourth hostage secured."

"Subject in custody."

"Scene is secure. Alpha One, stand down."

The reports tumbled over each other. *Breathe.* Exhale. Inhale. Rory flexed his fingers to ease the tension. Everyone had survived. He had survived. *Breathe.* Inhale. Exhale. Just another day at the office, right?

Chapter 4

"I know you don't want to be here. None of you ever do."

"I don't need a shrink. But the captain gave me no choice."

"Calling me a shrink is derogatory, Sergeant MacDermot. I don't shrink minds. Technically, I am a licensed psychoanalyst and therapist. I have a PhD in clinical psychology."

Rory shrugged. "Fine. I don't need whatever the hell you are. I'm not one of your test subjects. You want me to spill my guts. Get in touch with my feelings. I am in touch with them. I've been debriefed. We're done. Sign the release and I'm outta here."

This was the first time he'd seen Dr. Delaney Burns since the incident at the strip mall. She wanted information about the other situation. The one he didn't want to talk about. All of her questions circled back to it. He'd been debriefed on that one, too. The whole team had. Together. Like they should be.

The doc leaned back in her chair, her head tilted slightly to the left like a curious bird. She watched him without replying. The mass of gold, silver, and copper bracelets on her wrist slithered together with a metallic whisper as she reached for the pad on her desk. The sound reminded him of a bullet sliding home in his sniper rifle. He managed to stifle the shudder the sound created.

“You don’t sleep.”

As it wasn’t a question, he remained silent.

“Nightmares?”

He shook his head at her question. “No.” He maintained a noncommittal tone in his voice.

“I know you think about it.”

He blinked at her. “Well, d’uh. What was your first clue, Sherlock?” Sarcasm wrapped around his voice like a winter muffler. “I was the sniper for Team Alpha. I had the target acquisition. I didn’t hesitate when I got the go order.”

“What went wrong?”

“The hostage moved.”

“That wasn’t your fault.”

“Doesn’t matter whose fault it was. The hostage is still a vegetable. She didn’t go home to her family. She didn’t get to finish her lunch. She didn’t get shit but an existence hooked up to tubes and machines.”

His voice rang bitter in his own ears. He glanced at the doctor. She stared back at him, meeting his gaze squarely. And she did him the favor of not smiling in triumph.

“Yes. The hostage is all but dead. The bad guy *is* dead. Do you even regret taking his life?”

He jerked like she’d landed a left hook on his jaw. Royally pissed now, he pushed out of his chair and headed for the door.

“We aren’t done yet, sergeant.”

“Oh yeah we are.” He twisted the door handle viciously.

“You need my signature on this release. I haven’t signed it, and I’m not going to until you answer my questions."

Rory froze. He pivoted in place and pinned her to her chair with his gaze. "Is that a threat, Dr. Burns?" The words cut like ground glass as he spit them out.

"I don't make threats, Rory."

One part of his brain registered the fact that she was a gutsy broad. According to everyone who knew him, he was a scary-ass dude when he was pissed off. And he was. At that moment in time, he could put his hand through the door or… He continued to stare at her. His mouth curled into a cocky grin though he knew the expression in his eyes never changed. He didn't have to glimpse his reflection in a mirror to know he had the eyes of a killer. In three strides he was back to her desk. He leaned over it, wrapped one hand in her shirt—silky and cool beneath his hot skin—and pulled her forward. Nose-to-nose, he watched her, unblinking, barely breathing. If he inhaled, her scent would fill his lungs and he'd have a whole different set of reactions.

"We're done. At least for now." He let the implication hang between them for a couple of heartbeats before he leaned closer—just close enough his lips could brush across hers. With infinite regret, he loosened his grip and straightened. Oh yeah. He'd made a lasting impression. Her eyelids drooped and a surprised smile touched the corners of her mouth. Her breathing quickened and the thrum of her pulse beat a tattoo under the soft skin where her throat met her jaw.

He reached the door, had it open and was about to make his escape when her voice cut him off.

"I'll see you tomorrow at one, Sergeant MacDermot."

****

Delaney watched Rory stiffen and his free hand fisted at his side, but he didn't turn around, didn't argue with her. He simply walked through the door, leaving it open in his wake. Thirty seconds later, Bronwyn Allen, her best friend breezed in.

"Oh, honey, who the heck was that? Please tell me he's single. And then tell me he's not nuts." Bronwyn plopped in the chair Rory had so recently vacated.

She smoothed her blouse and glared, hiding her reaction to Rory's behavior behind the expression she directed at Bronwyn. "*Nuts* is not a medical term."

"Is he a patient?"

Delaney stared pointedly.

"Okay, okay. Confidentiality. I get it. But dang, girl. He is sexy." Bronwyn drew out the last word, adding several syllables as she emphasized her point.

Still amused, she arched one brow. "Oh? Really? I hadn't noticed."

"Yeah, right. And snowflakes dance the Nutcracker in hell. I'm hungry. Let's do lunch and you can tell me all the non-patiently things about that guy. Like his phone number and whether I'll have to kill his girlfriend or wife so I can go out with him."

Delaney laughed and grabbed her purse from her bottom drawer. Bronnie was the perfect antidote for Rory's dark, brooding presence. "Like that's going to happen."

Several minutes later, they settled in a booth at a nearby café—a place more sports bar than restaurant and notorious for attracting local athletes. Incorrigible and much too concerned about Delaney's love life, Bronwyn often dragged her off on mad escapades to such places. Today's lunch would be no different evidently. At the moment, her friend was waving madly at someone who just walked through the door.

"Connor! Over here, Connor!"

The man, backlit from the multitude of big screen televisions, remained a dark shadow as he maneuvered toward their booth. Delaney got the impression of height and broad shoulders and figured he was one of Bronwyn's sports cronies. As he reached them, she could do nothing but gape. Black hair and blue eyes so brilliant she could tell their color even in the bad lighting, and he was dressed in an impeccable three-piece suit and tie. His appearance was completely unexpected—so much so that Bronwyn kicked her under the table reminding her to close her gaping mouth.

"Hi, Connor." Bronwyn didn't quite simper but she did bat her eyelashes. "Are you meeting anyone for lunch?"

His easy grin revealed a dimple and Delaney remembered to breathe after he agreed to join them.

"This is my best friend, Delaney. She's a voodoo doctor."

She rolled her eyes. That was a sterling endorsement—not. She offered her hand, hoping some semblance of professionalism would cover up her nerves. "Delaney Burns. I'm actually a clinical psychologist. The PhD type doctor."

His strong fingers wrapped around her palm, and she couldn't suppress the shiver dancing through her.

"Connor MacDermot. I'm actually an attorney." His eyes twinkled merrily as he almost winked at her. He continued to hold her hand longer than necessary and seemed almost reluctant to release her.

With a pointed look at the space beside her, he waited for her to scoot over. Which she did with a stunned look. He wanted to sit next to her? She glanced over at Bronwyn, relieved to see her friend grinning madly. She'd been set up. Again. But this time? Just maybe Bronwyn had gotten it right.

Lunch flashed by in a blur. She didn't remember what she ordered and couldn't remember actually eating the food the waitress placed in front of her. Every last one of her senses was filled with Connor. Her leg tingled from the heat radiating from his thigh so tantalizingly close. He was a feast for the eyes—his thick, wavy hair almost glinting blue it was so dark. And his eyes! Gazing into his eyes she all but swooned. Dark blue, they flickered like a sapphire ring in bright sunlight. His scent washed over her with each breath, completely blocking the odor of greasy food and beer. When she closed her eyes and inhaled she sensed a big, blue sky stretched in a canopy over open water—fresh, not sea—the wind in her face teasing her with a hint of spice to warm the crystal-cool sensations.

Standing on the hot sidewalk outside the café, she didn't want to say goodbye. Connor seemed averse to leaving as well.

"Are you doing anything this weekend?" He sounded almost shy as he asked.

Delaney shook her head. "No, I don't think so. Why?"

Connor looked relieved as a grin teased the corners of his mouth—his very luscious, kissable mouth. "I'd like to take you to dinner Friday night. At Gatsby's?"

Gatsby's was a five star restaurant and she'd been dying to try it, but it was such a date place she didn't want to go alone. “I’d love to.” She snapped her mouth closed before she started gushing.

“Excellent.” He fished in his breast pocket and pulled out a pen. “Address and phone number?”

Delaney dug through her purse until she found one of her business cards. Taking the pen, she scribbled her home address and cell phone number on the back. “What time?”

“I’ll pick you up Friday at six?”

She smiled and nodded. “I’ll see you then.” Holding out her card, she remembered to breathe as his hand caressed hers for just a moment before he took the card from her.

“Right. See you then.” He glanced at Bronwyn and grinned. “I owe you one, darlin’.” He winked, turned, and strode off.

Delaney punched Bronwyn on the arm. “He owes you one? This was a set up, wasn’t it?”

Bronnie did her best to look innocent—for about ten seconds. “Of course it was. Connor is one of the attorneys in the law firm. He’s new in town, and the moment I saw him, I was positive the two of you would be perfect together.”

“Sometimes, it’s a good thing you’re a paralegal, Bronwyn. And no, I will not call you Friday night and dish all the details of my date.” She giggled as the other woman assumed a comically crestfallen expression.

Back in her office, Delaney flipped open Rory’s file. MacDermot. Rory MacDermot. And Connor MacDermot? What were the odds? Were they related? She knit her brow in consternation. Both were tall and well-built though Rory was in much better shape. They were about the same age—late twenties or early thirties.

But that's where the resemblance ended. Dark-haired and blue-eyed, Connor could be a model. Rory reminded her of ginger spice—close-cropped auburn hair, casual, outdoorsy. He'd more likely appear in a sporting good store's ad than in a fashion magazine. While MacDermot wasn't that common a name, she doubted they could be related. They just seemed too…different.

After dictating her notes on Rory's session, Delaney took a few minutes to indulge herself. She had a date. With Connor. To Gatsby's. Which meant shopping for a new outfit. Panicked, she grabbed the phone and speed-dialed Bronwyn.

Chapter 5

Abhean plucked a few notes on his harp, still smarting from Manannán mac Lir's visit. He'd argued with the king. Again. Putting away his instrument, he stood with the inherent grace of his kind. Above his craggy ledge, the standing stones beckoned and he answered their siren song. King Manannán had not forbidden him access to their lives, but the order to let the mortal fools spend their precious chances irked him deeply.

He climbed the narrow path on nimble feet and entered the circle of stones. In the very center, the altar summoned him, colored fog already swirling above its cold surface.

He stood, feet spread, hands outstretched, and watched the mist. Hazy figures danced within its core. Abhean set his harp upon the rough stone and tugged a wooden flute from the folds of his mantle. As he put his lips to the chanter, a simple tune floated through the air. The mist formed, drifted apart then transformed, all in time to the notes. Spectral walls solidified and ghostly figures acquired shape and substance within the confines of Caisel Ailfinn—the home of Ciaran MacDermot, chief of Clann MacDermot. The frost in Abhean's eyes was not warmed by the smile frozen on his face. Reuniting Ciaran and Becca had created the first of many rifts between harper and king.

People scurried through the foggy scene in front of him, carrying pots and trays laden with food and bread. By defying mac Lir, Abhean had thrown a boulder into the river of time and even now the ripples continued to affect the lives of many. A slip of a girl appeared and he fixed his gaze upon her.

****

Delaney watched from the arched doorway leading from the kitchens. The group of warriors strode in looking like Fenian warriors to her girlish eyes. Her foster father stood tall and straight, a full head taller than even the tallest among them. His eyes, the color of the midnight sky, searched the great hall for her foster mother. A delighted cry echoed from above her head.

"Ciaran!" Becca, her foster mother, skipped down the stairs, her booted feet barely touching the worn stones.

Delaney's heart clutched at the love radiating from the two of them. She could only dream of finding so abiding a love. Ciaran met Becca at the bottom of the stairs, caught her in his arms, and kissed her. Delaney shrank back as the scene continued to unfold in front of her like some mummer's play at *Samhain*. Ciara, her foster sister, followed her mother down the stairs. She tracked the other girl's gaze, suspecting she only had eyes for Keegan, Delaney's older brother. His expression lit up at the sight of Ciara descending a bit more sedately than her mother's reckless plunge. The older girl paused long enough to hug her father, and then slid around her parents to join Keegan in the center of the hall. The two stared at each other but made no move to touch or greet the other beyond covetous glances. Keegan cleared his throat several times while digging the toe of his boot in the straw littering the floor. Ciara simply blushed, dropping her eyes for a moment, only to raise them to gaze at the slightly taller boy.

Delaney rolled her eyes. Silly fools. Those two needed to sneak off behind the stable and do some serious kissing and petting to get it out of their systems. Of course, whenever Ciaran returned from an extended absence, the whole place seemed enchanted. Love and some feeling she couldn't quite define wafted through the very air, infecting everyone. The back of her neck prickled and she gazed around the room looking for the source of her unease. Her gaze collided with Riordan's. Not as old as her foster father, he was still Ciaran's cousin and much older than her. She always felt odd in his presence. He'd rescued her the night her family was slaughtered. Delaney felt the heat creep up her throat and across her cheeks, certain they were now stained red.

The light streaming through the door blurred again and her heart raced as she recognized the young man striding in. Conor. Foster brother he might be, but she harbored such feelings for him as surely Ciaran and Becca shared. She stepped forward, her hand rising in unconscious greeting and longing but stopped when her sister, Neasa, screamed in glee. The older girl brushed past her, almost knocking her down. Conor looked over, distracted by the commotion. Moments later, his arms were full of screaming girl, his face peppered by her kisses.

Delaney shrank behind the arch, her face flaming. How could she ever think Conor would notice her? Neasa was light to her dark, full of fun and frivolity.

She dashed the back of her hand across her eyes, banishing the tears welling up, as her friend, Bronwen, skipped up beside her.

"Aren't they fine for sure, Laney?" The girl issued an exaggerated sigh. "That Riordan is so handsome, as 'tis your brother and Conor. But any fool can see Keegan an' Conor are both matched already."

Delaney squared her shoulders and peeked around the corner. Keegan and Ciara and Conor and Neasa certainly seemed oblivious to anyone but each other. Sadness settled around her like a tattered mantle. Would she ever find someone to love like that?

****

Riordan's heart lightened when he saw the little cailín hiding behind the arched entry. Her presence never failed to make him smile. He watched her face light up as she saw him, and he smiled in return. Then he realized Delaney glowed because young Conor walked in right behind him. He felt oddly deflated until a saucy cailín approached, her eyes glinting with mischievous lights, and her smile so broad both dimples were engaged.

"Here to welcome me home, sweet Alys?"

The little maid threw her arms around his neck, and he lifted her up so he could buss her mouth. Even as he did, his eyes sought Delaney, found her hiding in shadows, her face sad as she watched her sister and Conor. His heart twisted.

Alys whispered in his ear. "'Tis not the time, Riordan. Not yet. But it'll come an' that's a promise."

He didn't understand the meaning of her words but her kisses silenced his questions and drove any thoughts from his mind other than slipping away with her. Even so, he glanced back for one last glimpse of Delaney. Riordan smiled when he caught her watching him, and her gaze felt like sunshine spilling into his heart.

****

Abhean waved his hands, dispelling the misty scene. Dark, angry reds and blacks swirled in the depths of his eyes. The silly cailín longed for love in all the wrong places. And Riordan? The arrogant fool swore never to fall in love all those years ago without a moment's thought for the soul of his other half.

"No."

He jerked like he'd been slapped. With effort, he schooled his emotions and the mad whirlpool churning in his eyes stilled. "No what, mac Lir?"

"I know your thoughts, harper. I know your heart. Riordan MacDermot made his choice."

"But what of her? Do you condemn her to life ever after, suffering because she loves a man who will never be hers?" Sadness flickered across Manannán's expression, and Abhean pressed home his suit. "Is she destined to suffer an empty heart then?"

The king growled and stomped away, his back to the fae harper. "You try my patience, Abhean."

"That goes both ways."

"Why do you do that?" Manannán's voice rang with a sadness so profound the birds stopped singing and the playful breeze died in a faint rustle of leaves. He turned and grief painted his beautiful face with sorrow.

For a moment, however brief, Abhean felt guilt. He remembered how many mortal lives the other fae juggled, and how the weight of caring bore down on his broad shoulders. "What is the duty of the harper,

Manannán? The keeper of tales and legends, surely, but am I not also the voice of your conscience?"

He watched the king pace from the altar to the edge of the stones to stare out over the valley to the misty-blue mountains framing the horizon. Beyond those crags stretched the white-foamed sea that separated Tir nan Óg from the realm of human existence. Abhean had studied his antagonist for a millennium but still had little insight as to his current thoughts. That Manannán had a soft spot for the humans was a tightly held secret. And the harper knew the king doted on certain mortals—much to the chagrin of many in Faerie. Abhean would exact his revenge eventually. After all, what was the passage of time to an immortal?

Manannán spoke without turning his head. "What plot are you concocting now, Abhean? I can almost hear the thoughts boiling in the cauldron of your vengeance."

"Vengeance, my king? You speak of such to me?" Bitterness coated his tongue as he spat the words. "Vengeance is an emotion best left to the mortals. In our existence, vengeance is a cold dish but the humans serve it hot and bloody as it's meant to be."

"Do you now regret my decision, Abhean? You who begged me on your knees for absolution?"

Abhean clutched his hand in a fist so tight he snapped the wooden flute. The sound cracked through the still air, startling a flock of birds. They shot into the aquamarine sky, their wings sounding like polite applause. "How dare you speak to me of absolution, mac Lir! 'Tis my forgiveness you should seek, not the other way round."

The king did turn, finally, his face a mask etched in stone for all the emotion he displayed. "Do you wish to return to the mortal realm, Abhean? I can make it so."

In a flash of light, Abhean disappeared. Manannán closed his eyes and breathed deeply, reaching for self-control. "If you persist in testing me, Abhean, prepare yourself to face the consequences! Do not play the fool, or the cost may be more than you are willing to pay."

Chapter 6

The SWAT team gathered around the command post for a briefing from Captain Davis. Rory leaned against the side of the truck, his weapon held loosely in one hand and pointed at the pavement. There as backup to serving a warrant, he felt relaxed but ready. This was a smash and grab operation, nothing like lying on a roof top watching a suspect through the crosshairs. At the sound of a car door shutting, he glanced over at the late arrival and his gut twisted. Doc Burns. What was she doing here? This wasn't a hostage negotiation.

Captain Davis waved her over and included her in the briefing. "I've asked Dr. Burns to observe tonight. We already know she's a great negotiator—" Murmurs of agreement from the team interrupted him. "But she needs a crash course in what SWAT is all about. Jessie, I asked you to bring your extra vest. Will you help the doctor suit up? She'll be part of Team Two, and I don't want to take any chances."

Rory bit his tongue. She could watch the action from the command post just fine. She did not need to be anywhere close to the action. This might be a routine warrant service and search, but things could still go wrong.

Scott jabbed him in the side with his elbow. He cut his eyes and caught the almost imperceptible shake of his best friend's head. Scotty's message came through loud and clear, but he still didn't have to like it—and he didn't want to take the time to analyze his feelings. He'd gotten along just fine being out of touch with them, thank you very much. He hated the meetings with Dr. Burns. But, if he were absolutely honest, he looked forward to them because they meant he could see her, be in the same space with her. Her voice and perfume washed over him like… He chambered a round in his weapon to jerk his thoughts back from that uncomfortable path. The damn woman burrowed under his skin like some sort of parasite. And despite his protestations, her safety—and her happiness—remained paramount to him. He was one screwed up sonavabitch.

"Team One, head to the target location. Team Two, standby."

Rory hoisted his weapon to the ready position and moved out. Scott and New Boy followed. Hoss, carrying the battering ram, brought up the rear. Sticking to the shadows, they drifted down the street to the house where their suspect remained holed up, according to the snitch. Scott peeled off and jogged between the house and its neighbor to cover the back entrance. Most of the windows remained dark. One window on the first floor flickered with the light cast by a TV screen.

Hoss moved to the front as they climbed the front steps. Rory banged on the door and yelled. "Police. We have a warrant. Open the door." The lights switched off as Rory counted a hurried ten in his head. "GO!"

With one swing of the ram, the front door shattered. Rory was the first one through, New Boy hard on his heels, as Hoss tossed the battering ram aside and pulled his weapon to follow. They cleared the front room and headed toward the kitchen when Scott's shout kicked them into a higher gear.

"Stop right there!" Scott commanded from the other room. "Face down on the floor."

In the play of flashlights, Scott handcuffed and patted down the man on the floor.

"Suspect in custody," New Boy claimed as he keyed up his radio. "Team Two can enter for the search."

Rory whirled on him. "What the hell? This scene is not secure, and we don't know this is *the* suspect."

New Boy glared at him, chin jutting defiantly. "Nobody else is here."

Before Rory could countermand the transmission, Team Two entered the front door. "Dammit." He muttered the curse before raising his voice. "Jessie, we haven't cleared the house yet. One suspect in custody."

"Roger that."

"Scott, you good?"

The other man nodded.

"We need to secure the rest of the house." He turned on his heel and backtracked—and bumped into Delaney Burns as she stepped into the hallway in front of him. Rory grabbed her to keep her on her feet. The vest did nothing to hide her curves, and he was thankful for the darkness. He knew his face was flushed, but the majority of his blood had rushed south as soon as their bodies made contact.

"Oh." The sound whispered from her mouth and tickled the skin on his throat.

His breath hitched. He had to concentrate to loosen his grip and step back from her. Every part of him wanted to crush her to his chest. "Sorry." He growled the apology.

"My fault." She still sounded breathless. Was it from fear or from his touch? "I should have watched where I was going."

Fear, then, or at least from being startled. "It's dark, Doc. Just hang back a little until we get the place secured."

"Okay."

He moved away but reluctance made him drag his steps. Rory focused on the job. The only way to still the mad beating of his heart was to secure the house and ensure Delaney's safety. As they cleared a room, they left a light burning. Rory and Jessie approached the last bedroom. Someone—or something—whimpered from the far side of the bed. Jessie pinned the spot with her flashlight as he brought his weapon to bear.

"Hands where we can see them," Jessie ordered.

Two little hands appeared, followed by the top of a head and two terrified eyes. A child. Before he could react further, Delaney pushed past him and scurried across the room to the little boy. Rory recognized the click of a bullet jacking into the breach a millisecond before he launched across the room. The bright flash blinded him for a moment and the sharp retort of the shot left his ears ringing. He landed on top of Delaney and took her to the floor.

"He had a gun! He had a gun!" New Boy yelled over and over.

Someone wailed, a terrified scream that undulated like a siren. Delaney lay still beneath him. "Doc?" Rory whispered her name, afraid to breathe, afraid to let his heart beat.

"What happened?"

Adrenaline surged through him. That's why he

shook. Just adrenaline. “Are you okay? You aren’t hurt?”

She squirmed beneath him and his groin liked it. A lot. Embarrassed, he rolled off her and sat up. Delaney followed suit and stared around the room, the whites visible all the way around her warm brown eyes. Someone flipped on the overhead light while people argued out in the hall. The moaning continued, much closer to hand. He followed that sound to find the little kid balled up behind the bed. Delaney started to crawl toward the child but Rory stopped her.

“Even kids have guns in this neighborhood, Doc. Let me.”

He shoved the mattress toward the middle of the room, opening up space between the bed and the wall. The kid, maybe nine or ten, stared at him, his face shiny with tears but quiet now.

“Nobody’s going to hurt you, son. Let me see your hands.” The kid stuck his hands out, and they trembled violently. “Are you hurt?” The boy shook his head. Rory stood and helped the kid to his feet. He patted him down before he allowed Delaney to reach for the boy. The child buried his face against Delaney as she hugged him. Rory took the time to check between the mattresses and under the bed. No weapon.

“I’m telling you, I saw a gun in the kid’s hands. I was just following protocol.” New Boy’s voice climbed into the range of whining.

Rory turned around. The asshole stood just inside the room. Hoss had taken away New Boy’s weapon. In two steps, he reached the knot of people and without stopping to think, he pulled back his fist and nailed New Boy on the jaw with a vicious right jab.

"Protocol? You haven't been on this team long enough to know what the hell our protocol is, you jackass. And if I have my way, you won't get the chance." Rory was so angry the words came out flash frozen, heat replaced by dry ice.

"You…you *hit* me!" New Boy sounded incredulous, but he'd stopped whining at least.

"I did and if you don't get your ass out of here right now, I'm liable to hit you again."

Scott and Jessie slid between them. Jessie placed her palms on Rory's chest and backed him up. Scott grabbed New Boy and marched him away.

"Ease up, Rory." Jessie kept her voice low and soothing. "Don't make it worse."

He nodded once, a quick, curt dip of his chin. She dropped her hands and turned her attention to Delaney and the boy.

Rory didn't move. He had to force air into his lungs while he willed the shakes to go away. He didn't want to check, but he needed to find out just how close that bullet had come to hitting Delaney.

Pivoting, he marched to the wall, looking for the bullet hole. There wasn't one. He glanced at the tousled covers on the bed. There. In his mind's eye, he revisited the scene—where the bed was situated before he kicked it aside, where Doc stood before he took her down, where the child huddled, hiding from the scary people wearing black clothes and helmets, and with drawn guns.

Rory glanced over his shoulder at Delaney's gasp. "What?" She pointed at his back and he tried to see what she pointed at.

"Shit." Jessie never cussed. He stared at her as she

stepped closer and bent over. “You gotta see this, boss.” She grabbed his arm and pulled him over to a dingy mirror hanging above a dresser. She turned him so he could see the ripped cloth along his side.

Ice filled his veins as he stared at his reflection. If he hadn’t reacted— No. He couldn’t go there. He couldn’t think about Delaney taking a bullet, about her laying on the floor bleeding. One part of his brain remembered she wore a vest, but that didn’t matter. That bullet had come too damn close. He wanted to punch New Boy all over again. In fact, he wanted to beat him senseless.

Breathe. He had to breathe through the rage. He forced his fists to relax. He forced air deep into his lungs. *Breathe.* He swallowed and stopped clenching his teeth. *Breathe.* He turned to watch Delaney as she comforted the frightened boy. *Breathe.*

“Child Services has been notified. They’re sending a case worker.”

Rory nodded, only vaguely aware of Jessie’s report. His eyes remained fixed on Delaney. Half a second. A centimeter. *Breathe.* He didn’t want to think about his reaction, about his deep-seated fear for the doc’s safety. None of it made sense. But this woman was as important to him as breathing, as important as his life. He knew it with a certainty he couldn’t explain.

“Can we gather up some of his things?”

Delaney asked the question of Jessie, but he replied. “A few things, Doc. He’ll be at Child Services just until they find a family member to come pick him up.”

She nodded and whispered to the boy. He watched as the child picked out a hoodie, a book, and a grimy, bedraggled stuffed animal. Rory had no clue what the critter had once been. Now it was a dirty gray lump, but the kid clung to it like a lifeline. When they were ready, he escorted Delaney and the boy out to the command post vehicle to wait. He slipped inside the truck and dug around in a box under one of the seats. The box was filled with donated toys the cops could hand out when a child was involved. When he found the stuffed dog he was looking for, he stepped out and located the doc standing next to the open back door of a cruiser.

"His name is Andre," Delaney said as Rory walked up. "His mother works the night shift at a nursing home, and he stays with his brother."

Feeling a little stupid, Rory held out the fuzzy dog. The frown lines between Delaney's eyes melted as she smiled at him. She stepped back to give him room, and he felt even more awkward. With one hand on the top of the police car, he leaned into the backseat.

The boy wiped his nose with the lump of fuzz he clutched to his chest. "What's gonna happen to my brother? If you take him to jail, I'll have to stay home alone. Don't arrest him, 'kay?"

"I wish we didn't have to, Andre, but he's done some bad things. Child Services will help your mom."

The boy gulped and nodded, his big, haunted eyes filling with tears. "That cop tried to shoot me, didn't he?"

Rory swallowed his anger and inhaled deeply. Several times. "That cop was stupid, Andre. He'll be dealt with." The boy noticed the floppy dog he carried, and Rory held it out to him. "Here. I thought you might like this."

Andre reached for it but didn't quite touch. His

eyes stayed glued on Rory. “To keep?” He sounded so hopeful, Rory’s heart broke a little.

“To keep. He’s yours, if you want him, but you have to give him a name.”

The boy smiled and dimples creased his round cheeks. “Boss. That’s what that lady cop called you.” Andre took the stuffed animal then and folded the dog into his arms, squished in with the lumpy critter.

Rory straightened and his gaze met Delaney’s.

“That was a very nice thing you just did,” she murmured.

Feeling awkward again, he wanted to dig his toe in the dirt and do some stupid “aw shucks” thing. “The kid was scared. And not all cops are bad guys.”

She offered him a tentative smile. “No, not all cops are bad guys. Some of them are heroes, especially in the eyes of an impressionable boy.” She held out her hand. “Let me see.”

He narrowed his eyes. “Let you see what?”

“Your hand. You smacked that officer really hard.”

Rory placed his hand in hers and did his best to ignore the feeling of his skin touching hers. He couldn’t call it an electric shock, but there was a sense of hyper awareness. She explored his fingers and knuckles with gentle probes.

“Be sure to put some ice on it when you get back to the police station.”

He nodded, struck dumb for the moment. She chuckled, almost as if she knew the effect she had on him. Delaney glanced around before she suddenly leaned in to kiss his cheek. “Andre isn’t the only one who thinks you were a hero tonight.”

Chapter 7

The front of the swanky restaurant reeked of class. Gatsby's. He'd had to read *The Great Gatsby* in high school—didn't understand it then, sure didn't understand it now. Despite feeling out of his element, Rory held the leaded glass entry doors so Jessie and the rest of the team could enter. Since it was her birthday, Jessie got to pick the place. Who knew she was such a girlie-girl deep down? Tough, dishing out as much as she took, and able to take down any guy on the team, he sometimes forgot she was a girl—and quite an attractive one now that she was dressed in a black mini and wearing impossibly spiked heels. How the hell did she balance on those things? Scott's nudge in his back kept him from the unconscious whistle building against his lips as Jessie walked away. Man, but she had some legs.

"Close your mouth, Rory."

He did as his best friend requested. "When did she grow those?" The muttered question drew a deep chuckle choked off by a cough as the object of their speculation turned around to glare at them.

"I've even been known to wear perfume." The twinkle in Jessie's dark eyes belied the smirk she favored them with.

"So that's why Hoss always wants to team up with you!" Scott fired off the zinger before Rory could.

"Huh?" The big man had stopped and turned, waiting for the three of them to catch up to the group and only caught the mention of his name.

"Never mind, Big Man. C'mon. You can buy me a birthday drink." Jessie looped her arm through Hoss's, and they headed toward the bar. Rory and Scott followed, still chuckling.

The team grouped around a tall cocktail table, comfortable in their skins and with each other. Rory assessed the men and woman he trusted with his life on a daily basis. New Boy had canceled on them, not that Rory had wanted to invite the jerk. Hot date, New Boy explained. It was one more tick mark in the negative column as far as Rory was concerned. Dean Carter would always be called New Boy since he didn't know how to be a team player. His actions two nights ago just confirmed Rory's suspicions.

He flexed his right hand, the bruised skin pulling across his knuckles. The pain reminded him of his own stupidity. Captain Davis would make damn sure he ended up behind a desk for the rest of his career if he pulled another stunt like that.

"Hot date, my ass," he muttered. Carter was obviously too wimpy to show his face.

Scott patted him on the shoulder. Jessie flashed a little smile and added some verbal encouragement. "Hey, the big boss wasn't happy with New Boy either. He won't be around long, especially if he pulls another stunt like that one. He's already on report." She glanced up at Hoss, towering on her left. "Besides, he's lucky you got to him before Hoss did.

The normally reticent giant growled. "He coulda killed that kid. Or you or the doc. You 'n' Jessie had things under control, Boss. New Boy's dangerous. I told cap'n that." He glanced down at Jessie. "He coulda hit you, too. And mighta missed your vest."

The conversation continued, but Rory lost interest as he fixated on a woman sitting in the restaurant area. Dr. Delaney Burns in the flesh. What was the doc doing here? And alone? She glanced up and a smile transformed her face. She waved and he waved back then wanted to cut off his hand. She hadn't even noticed him. Her gaze was fixed on the man coming through the door. His gut churned and bile rose in his throat. With effort, he unclenched his fists and shook his hands down by his sides to loosen them. Too bad his nerves wouldn't relax as easily. He could only see what the doc's date looked like in profile. The way their table was positioned, he could see her face, see the way her eyes lit up, how animated she looked when she replied to something her date said, leaning closer to the guy, touching his arm with an intimate gesture. Jealousy reared its snarling head as his heart hammered.

MINE! The emotion was so powerful he almost choked on it as the word burst in his brain.

Yours. The affirmation whispered in his ear. A voice as sweet as spun sugar soothed him with its slight lilt. *Bide your time, Riordan. She'll be knowin' yee soon enough.*

"Stop scowling." Jessie punched him in the shoulder.

"I'm not scowling."

"Yes. You are. If the doc looks up and sees that expression on your face, she's going to put you on mental health leave."

"I'm not scowling."

"Oh yeah. Whatever. Who's she with?"

"No clue. Never seen the guy before."

"I know she's not married."

Rory cut his eyes to her. "How do you know that?"

Jessie laughed and gave him a friendly shoulder bump. "Because she doesn't wear a ring on her left hand. Any ring. You've been in her office. Does she have any pictures stuck on her desk?"

His brow furrowed as he thought about it. After a long moment, he gave a curt shake to his head. "Nope. In fact, her office is sort of generic. Not much of anything personal there." Not to mention that when he'd all but kissed her, there'd been none of the righteous outrage one might expect from a married woman.

Jessie turned to face him, shock registering on her face. "Seriously? No knickknacks or art or anything?"

"Not that I recall. Why? Is that weird or something?"

Laughing, she nodded. "Like d'uh. We girlie-girls usually feather our nests with all sorts of crap. Odd that the doc doesn't. I bet there's some dark, psychological meaning to that. I wonder what her house looks like."

Rory wondered the same thing. And he wondered if the guy sitting at the table with Delaney, the guy who even now reached for her hand and squeezed it had ever seen her house. More specifically, her bedroom.

"Dude, if looks could kill." Jessie chided him so he took a moment to put on his poker face. "Oh, yeah. Like that's gonna work. You're still shooting lasers in her direction. Chill out, Rory. I mean, it's not like you two are..." Her voice trailed off and she stared up at him. She blinked once. Twice. A third time before she continued. “You aren’t, are you?” Disbelief colored her question. “Oh, jeez, Rory, tell me you and the doc aren’t seeing each other.”

“We aren’t.” She continued to stare at him. He felt her gaze burning into his cheek until he finally glanced at her. “We aren’t, Jessie. I’ve never seen her outside of her office or on a scene before tonight. And since she doesn’t know I’m here...” His gaze locked back on Delaney just as the doctor looked up. She looked startled before puzzlement radiated in her expression. A hesitant smile bloomed on her lips before fading.

“Dang it, Rory.” Jessie elbowed him. Hard. “You’re going to scare the woman to death scowling like that.”

“I’m not scowling.”

She didn’t answer him, raising her hand to wave to the couple across the room instead. The man with Delaney angled his head to see what was going on. He raised a hand in an uncertain wave, as if he thought he should know the people Delaney acknowledged. Rory studied him like a target. Tall. Broad-shouldered. Probably about six feet two or three inches tall and around one hundred and ninety pounds. The guy looked fit enough though with the tailored suit he wore, Rory couldn’t really tell. Tanned, he likely played golf or tennis and skied in the winter. Thick, dark hair with a slight wave styled in a longish-cut. Blue eyes narrowed as the man assessed Rory in much the same way. He pushed his chair away from the table and prepared to stand before Delaney’s hand on his arm settled him back into his seat. She said something, glancing Rory’s way before her gaze returned to her escort.

“Rory, this isn’t the place to get into a pissing

contest."

Scott's calm voice was meant to soothe him. But why the hell did he feel the need to whip it out to prove his was bigger. "Because mine is, dammit."

"Because yours is what?" Jessie flashed him a fish-eyed look with her trade-mark lopsided grin.

"Did I say that out loud?" Jessie and Scott both nodded. "Look, I'm...Hell, I don't know what I am. Way off base for one thing. I'm only seeing the doc because the department says I have to. I don't plan to ask her out."

Liar.

He glanced around, looking for whoever had voiced that opinion. He didn't recognize the voice and no stranger stood close enough to overhear the conversation. Had that been his conscience?

Yours. The word crooned in his ear, every bit a love song.

"Mine," he growled.

Scott's hand curled around his biceps and yanked. Hard. "Come with me, ol' son. Now." It wasn't a request, it was an order. He didn't give Rory a chance to argue or pull away. His grip tight enough to leave bruises on someone not as well-muscled as Rory, Scott pulled him toward the back of the bar and the hallway that led to the restrooms.

With his back to Delaney and her date, he could breathe again. He sucked air into his lungs and let it out before swiping the back of his free hand across his forehead to wipe the sweat that had formed there.

"What the hell happened back there?"

He stared at his best friend, read the worry and concern in his expression. Unable to explain, he simply shrugged, one shoulder rising a bit higher than the other. "I have no idea."

Scott's eyes narrowed and Rory knew what he was going to say.

Rory held up his hand. "I don't know, Scott. I..." He shook his arm loose and scrubbed at his cropped hair with both hands. "I...It was the damnedest thing. I...man, I was jealous! So jealous I wanted to march over there, grab that poor guy, and pound his face in."

Scott shook his head in disbelief. "Jealous? But...Rory, it's not like you two are dating or anything. Why would you be jealous?"

He shrugged again, feeling both hopeless and helpless. "I don't even like her. Why should I care who the hell she sleeps with?"

That rocked Scott back on his heels. "Sleep with? Man, are you listening to yourself?"

He closed his eyes and rubbed his face with the heels of his hands. "Scotty, I don't know what to say. I...I don't feel like I'm crazy. But maybe I am?" The pitch of his voice climbed on his last sentence, making it a question. He needed affirmation from the man who knew him best that he was still sane. He didn't get the immediate reaction he sought.

"We need to talk, Rory. But not here. Not now. This is Jessie's birthday. We're here to celebrate with her. Right? I'm asking you to keep it together for Jessie. For the team. Okay? Can you do that?"

Rory couldn't stop his mouth from dropping open. "I'm not crazy, Scott."

Scotty patted him on the shoulder. "Good. But we still need to put on a happy face for Jessie. Now, go into the men's room. Wash your face or something. Take some deep breaths and then come back and get a drink. Beer. Nothing hard. You got that?"

He nodded. Scott was right, as he usually was. "Order me a Guinness. I'll be out in a sec."

Inside the bathroom, he leaned against the lavatory staring at his reflection. This was definitely a high-dollar place. The room smelled of pine with no undertone of ammonia or the other odors usually associated with the men's room. The mirror had been wiped clean not long ago so there was no grime to soften his view.

"You almost lost it out there." His mirror self nodded. "We can't let that happen again, right?" He nodded. "Right." Convinced he was okay, he headed back out to meet his friends. Rory jerked the door open and all but collided with the man coming in. Their eyes met and recognition sparked in both their expressions, only for Rory, that spark burned deeper. Yes, this was the dude out with Doc but there was more—some gut level instinct he couldn't pin down. He *knew* this man. His brain sorted things out even as he brusquely apologized.

"Sorry."

"No problem. Hey, aren't you one of the cops Laney works with?"

He nodded. "Yeah."

The younger man appeared amused by his reticence. "She's a great gal."

"Yeah." Rory did not want to stand here jawing with this guy, but his ego got the better of him. "You been dating her long?"

"Connor. Connor MacDermot."

Something uncurled in Rory's gut, some hint of a

memory obscured by smoke and shadows. "Rory MacDermot." He didn't offer his hand but tilted his head, studying Connor. "Have we met before? I know we aren't related."

Wearing a jovial grin, Connor looked younger than he'd first appeared. "I don't think so—met or related either one, unless you testified in one of my cases. I'm an attorney."

"Yeah, that figures." He muttered the words under his breath then added louder, "Which side?"

Connor laughed. "Oh, the dark side in your view, I'm sure. I'm a defense attorney."

"Definitely the enemy." Why did this cocky pup have to be handsome *and* congenial? And why did Rory want to like him? Like a curious kitten paw batting the back of his subconscious, memories shifted but nothing coalesced.

"Weird, though, that we have the same last name. You ever been to Ireland?

Rory shook his head. "Not this lifetime."

His rival grinned, still brash and boyish in his demeanor. "My folks are Irish. Well, my dad anyway. He's the MacDermot clann chieftain. Mum's American, though. I spent a lot of time here in the States growing up, so I shed the accent, got my JD, passed the bar, and here I am." He tilted his head. "I should call Dad, tell him I met a long-lost MacDermot. You do spell it with the 'a', right? M-A-C not M-C? Irish, not Scottish? And only one 't'?"

Rory held up his hand to stop the flood of information and questions. "No wonder you're a lawyer. You never shut up, do you." He managed not to roll his eyes. "That wasn't a question." Before he could continue, his phone beeped. Snagging it from his pocket, he turned and walked away. He left Connor standing flat-footed and holding the door to the men's room open.

"MacDermot." He listened for a moment then grabbed a passing waitress. Rory gestured for her pen and pad. He jotted down Connor MacDermot's name, tore off the page, and stuffed it in his front pocket. "The team is here with me. We're headed to the station now." He returned the waitress's things and strode deeper into the bar.

"Head 'em up, move 'em out, cowboys and cowgirl. We have a briefing down at the station. Captain wants us there an hour ago."

Amidst grousing and grumblings, the group paid their tabs and headed for the door. Rory made the mistake of glancing over at Delaney. She stared back at him, anxiety etched on her face as she watched the quick departure of his team. He offered a reassuring smile even as she dug in her handbag for her phone. She glanced down at it then looked up, puzzled.

He couldn't risk crossing to her table to explain. He'd never leave if he inhaled her perfume. His groin tightened just thinking about it. Instead, he flashed a wink and pulled out his phone as he pushed through the doors.

She answered on the first ring, her voice breathless. "Hello? I mean...Dr. Burns here."

"Take a breath, Doc. We're going in for a briefing. And no, it's not an incident. Routine stuff. Okay?" Was that a little sigh from her? His chest tightened.

"Oh. All right then. Uhm...thanks for letting me know."

"G'night, Doc." He broke the connection before his voice gave anything away. "Dammit. What the hell is wrong with me?"

"Nothing getting laid won't cure," Scott assured him.

"Crap. I said that out loud, didn't I?"

His best friend nodded. "Yeah. You got it bad, buddy. I know you have a roster of girls on speed dial. Call one. Get it out of your system."

Rory slowly unfurled the fist he clenched around his cell phone, a bit surprised the plastic had survived his death grip. His free hand was also fisted and he forced it to relax. When had that happened? He didn't remember clenching it. Why was the thought of sleeping with a woman who wasn't the doc upsetting? He shook his head. No, not upsetting, downright revolting! His libido always ran hot. Once. Before meeting Dr. Delaney Burns. While he could appreciate Jessie all dressed up, in a big brotherly way, he hadn't considered going on a date in a long time. Not since meeting the doc, if he was honest with himself. Man but she had him whipped. And he didn't like the feeling. Not one bit. Maybe he'd take Scott up on his advice and call one of the girls he had on speed dial after the briefing. Yeah. That's what he'd do all right.

Maybe.

Chapter 8

Delaney slipped the phone back into her purse and offered Connor a relieved smile. Their date wouldn't be disrupted, despite her worry when Connor had called asking her to meet him at the restaurant because he was hung up with a client. His request had stung more than she'd wanted to admit. She had to arrive on time or they would have lost their reservations. Delaney had dressed with care, and then debated whether to drive herself or call a cab. An abundance of caution sent her to her car. Luckily, Gatsby's had valet parking. She'd been seated almost immediately. She declined when asked if she desired a cocktail. If she didn't order anything and Connor didn't show up, she could leave without fuss or calling attention to the fact she'd been stood up.

Watching the door like a proverbial hawk, she'd waved madly when he stepped inside and then dropped her hand feeling like a complete fool. The big smile and immediate apology as he dropped into the chair closest to her went a long way toward soothing her nerves.

"You are such a good sport, Delaney. That guy is a big client, so I was stuck. I swear, if he said 'And to make a long story short' one more time, I was going to stuff my tie in his mouth." The waiter approached, and he paused to order two glasses of wine by vineyard name and year.

Now she sipped her second glass of a very

excellent pinot noir as they waited for their food and listened as Connor told her about his encounter in the men's room. "The guy reminded me a lot of my dad."

"Oh?" Delaney knew next to nothing about Connor's family and she hoped to glean some information.

"Dad is this big, military kind of guy. He walks in and everyone knows he's arrived. Of course, my mum has the same sort of presence. They were Olympians. That's how they met."

"Really?" She worked to keep her expression from looking crestfallen. No wonder he looked so athletic.

He chuckled. "I hate horses. They still ride, though they just breed and train now instead of competing. Sadly, neither my sister nor I followed in their footsteps."

"Oh! They're equestrians."

Connor rolled his eyes. "Don't tell me you're one of the horsey set. Mum will love you."

She shuddered and shook her head. "I've never been on a horse. I'm actually terrified of them, but I love to watch the equestrian events on TV. Your dad is military?"

"Retired. He was an Irish Army Ranger. Now he's the *Taoiseach* of Clann MacDermot."

Delaney stumbled over the word. "Teeshock? What's that?"

"That's the Gaelic word for clann chief. For our branch, it's mostly hereditary."

"Does that mean you'll be…whatever that word is someday?" Oh, the romantic fantasies that thought created—living in an Irish castle with her very own sexy clann chief at her side.

Her question evoked another roll of Connor's eyes. "Not if I can help it. If Dad ever decides to step down, I'll put it up to a vote of the Clann. I'm too American now. I have no desire to move back to Ireland. A cousin can hold the spot just as easily. And Dad is on an aggressive hunt for long-lost cousins. I don't know why. My parents have some…odd ideas."

"Odd?"

Connor looked uncomfortable and his gaze roved around the room instead of focusing on her.

"I'm sorry. It's none of my business."

"What about your family?" The question was sincere, but he definitely shifted the subject away from his parents' odd ideas—whatever they might be.

Now it was her turn to roll eyes. "Mine is almost text-book dysfunctional. I have an older brother who is a perpetual Peter Pan and my older sister is…" How did she explain Nessa? "Nessa is a bit ambitious and sometimes she's not too polite about stepping on toes to get what she wants."

He chuckled. "Sounds a bit like Ciara, my twin."

"You have a twin? Wow. That's rather cool."

"Really? I always thought it was a pain having to share birthdays and other important events." He laughed at the shocked expression on her face. "Don't get me wrong. I love Ciara, but we're both attention whores. When we're together, it's just a big game of one-upmanship." He leaned back in his chair and sipped his wine. "Is your brother attached?"

Delaney's brow furrowed. "Keegan? Ha. He can't keep a girlfriend."

"We should introduce him to Ciara. She loves a beta male. I get the feeling Keegan might be right up her alley."

She laughed and had to stifle her mirth with a napkin. "Beta male describes him perfectly. He doesn't have an ambitious bone in his body. He's brilliant, but he's working in retail sales at a computer store. He'd still be living in my parent's basement if they had one. As soon as I left for college, they sold their house and moved into a condo."

Connor winked. "He sounds perfect for Ciara. She's got enough ambition for ten people. Maybe we should double date one of these times."

She worked to keep her surprise from showing but inside, she did a Snoopy dance. He wanted to ask her out again. He liked her. Now she regretted driving her own car.

He reached over and stroked his index finger down the back of her hand where it rested on the table. "Thanks for being such a good sport tonight. I really am sorry I had to babysit that client. And I'm glad that phone call you got didn't pull you away. I've enjoyed dinner."

The phone call. She'd totally forgotten. "Oh…yes. I told you I'm a consultant with the police department, right? When the SWAT team all left, I was worried there'd been a call out."

Connor didn't quite jerk his hand back, but he no longer touched her. "I figured you did employment screenings or the like. What exactly does your position entail?"

She inhaled slowly, the knot in her abdomen expanding until her tummy ached. "I work with the SWAT team after an incident. I help debrief them and provide counseling if it's needed. I also act as a negotiator sometimes."

Connor folded his fingers around her hand and gave it a little squeeze. "That must be fascinating, though I certainly hope none of my criminal clients ever end up on the wrong side of that deal. Interesting coincidence some of the people you work with were here."

"One of the team members chose here to celebrate her birthday. Too bad they didn't get to stay. They were called into a meeting at the police station."

He tilted his head and studied her for a long moment. Nervous under his scrutiny, she wet her now dry lips with the tip of her tongue before reaching for her wine glass. Interrupted as the waiter arrived with their entrées, Delaney grabbed a moment to regain her equilibrium. Connor MacDermot made her feel light-headed. And hot. And shivery. And just a little bit out of control. For a woman who prided herself on self-control, it was an uneasy feeling.

The conversation paused as they ate a few bites. She sighed happily over the taste of her steak. The garlic and mushroom crust melted on her tongue, as did the tender beef. Connor watched her, intent on her mouth and the movement of her throat as she swallowed.

"Good?"

"Excellent. Thank you again for inviting me here. I've wanted to try it but…"

"But it seemed wasted on a best friend?"

She laughed. "Exactly."

"So tell me more about your work with the police department. Are you close to anyone in the group who was here?"

Delaney swallowed her food and reached for her glass, sipping before answering. “I’m getting to know them better.”

“That explains things.” He offered a knowing smile topped by a quirked brow.

“What things?”

“The big guy staring daggers at me—the one I bumped into in the bathroom and who might be a long lost cousin even though he has red hair. That’s rare in my clann.”

“Rory?” She blinked several times, unable to hide her surprise. “Rory MacDermot. Of course. He’s one of the snipers on the team.” Puzzled, she stared at Connor. “Wait. He was staring at you?”

Connor chuckled. “Indeed he was. If looks could kill, the EMTs would be doing CPR on me even as we speak. I think he might be a little sweet on you.”

“Oh good heavens, no. That’s not possible. He’s a—” She snapped her mouth shut. She didn’t know what to call him. Colleague, yes. But he had secrets, too. Secrets she wanted to understand, and she was appalled that she’d almost spilled information about him. Delaney’s chest hurt at the thought of betraying Rory.

Connor wisely backed away from the subject. “So, dessert? The Chocolate Decadence is supposed to be fabulous.”

Thankful for the gracious out, she agreed. She felt so comfortable with Connor, like she’d known him forever rather than this being a first date. His hand on hers felt warm and… She tamped down on the shivery feeling in her middle and had to admit she had a major crush on him. But what woman wouldn’t? He was gorgeous, an attorney, sweet, caring, yet with a dash of devil-may-care flair that appealed to her on every feminine level. She couldn't wait for her goodnight kiss and made a mental note to actually eat the after-dinner mint.

When the bill arrived, Delaney was pleased to note that Connor snatched one of the mints and surreptitiously popped it in his mouth. She sucked on her mint and decided that she'd just leave her car in the parking lot so she could ride home with Connor.

****

Manannán mac Lir stared at the white-capped waves marching relentlessly toward the strip of beach where he stood, feet braced against the wind racing to land in front of the storm churning out at sea. His emotions roiled, every bit as potent as that tempest. The Irish wolfhound at his feet whined softly. Beside him, a black stallion tossed his head and neighed in challenge.

"Am I as bad as Abhean, then, Arien?" The horse pawed at the sand. "I condemn him for meddling yet did I not do the same? I took Riordan before his time and even now history repeats itself. She is there and he senses her, but she makes the same mistake time after time." Arien whickered and nibbled at the mantle draped over the fae's arm. "I would bring them both home to find their peace, but I smell the harper's magic stench in this. I must let the game play out, I fear."

The dog sat up, staring at something off to the right. The ruff on the back of the animal's neck rose in a silent growl. "Yes, Broc, I know he watches. I expect his mournful tunes to whip the tempest to a frenzy any moment." Manannán dropped his hand to the big dog's head and ruffled his ears, the gesture providing comfort to fae and animal alike.

Almost on cue, wailing pipes rode the storm winds and fat drops of rain splattered on the wet sand. With a heavy heart, Manannán vaulted onto the bare back of the horse. The horse turned away from the source of the music and cantered off, his hooves kicking up foam and sand. Broc, the wolfhound, stood watching the opposite direction, the hair on his neck still ruffled, his whole body tense and ready to hunt. The fae whistled and the dog followed with reluctance.

Abhean finished the dirge, the smirk curling his full lips not mournful in the least. He knew what path to tread. He might now have a chance to repay mac Lir for a millennium of slights. He whistled a jaunty tune as he walked up the beach in the opposite direction. A large gray dog appeared from the waves and shook the saltwater from his fur. The animal galloped up to Abhean, tongue panting. "And did yee have a bracing swim, Bród? Come m'friend, we have mischief to make.

Chapter 9

Delaney did her best to contain the flutters in her tummy. Around Connor her palms always felt damp and…needy, like she had to touch him. His presence alone made her light-headed to a point she felt like she'd been drinking champagne for days. And he'd invited her to lunch. Lunch! In the middle of the work day. She'd arrived early and now tried not to fidget as she waited for his arrival. She'd ordered raspberry tea because plain, old mundane ice tea just didn't fit the occasion.

The moment Connor appeared at the entrance, every female in the restaurant turned to stare. Delaney reminded herself to breathe as he strode toward her—handsome, self-confident and oh so very male. His deep blue eyes twinkled and his jet-black hair glinted like ebony. He paused at her chair and dropped a little kiss on the top of her head. She bit back a gulp and plastered what she hoped was an alluring smile on her face.

Connor dropped into the chair next to her and the waitress arrived to hover and flirt while he gave his drink order. Delaney didn't blame her. Women flocked to Connor like moths to a porch light on a hot summer night.

"I'm glad you could slip away to join me, Delaney."

She mmmhmmm'd, lost in the sparkle of his gaze.

“Luckily, my court appearance was postponed this afternoon. If you don’t have to rush back, we can take a long lunch.”

“Mmmhmmm.” He laughed and she flushed, blinking rapidly and straightening in her chair, appalled she’d been leaning, chin on palm, as she’d all but drooled on him. “I don’t have any appointments this afternoon.” Her voice only squeaked a couple of times. She grabbed her tea and gulped to give her ego a chance to catch up with her id even as she tried to squash her libido. Where was Dr. Freud when she needed him?

“Excellent. I’ll take you somewhere special for dessert.”

Her id did a happy dance as her libido rubbed its hands and *bwa-ha-ha’d* at her. His devilish grin only fueled the mutiny. Delaney had never been a fall-in-love-at-first-sight kind of woman, but there was just something about Connor, some connection she’d felt from the moment they’d met. While she didn’t want to rush into things, for fear of scaring him off, she found herself wishing and hoping for a happy ever after with this man.

Their salads arrived with an unexpected guest. “Laney!”

Her heart plummeted at the sound of her name. Nessa. What was her sister doing here? Effervescent, Nessa looked like a Miss America contestant. Where all the women had followed Connor’s progress, now the men all watched Nessa flow through the aisle of tables like water over stones—all liquid grace.

Delaney turned to Connor to introduce them but he only had eyes for her sister. Of course he did. Nessa was sunlight. The golden highlights in her hair danced in the sunlight filtering through the windows. Her sister's green eyes sparkled like stained glass and her smile? The wattage should have caused a power outage in three states and it was all for Connor. As far as Delaney was concerned, neither remembered she existed.

Nessa offered her hand and her mouth formed a pouty little smile as her eyes turned sultry. "Well, hello there. I'm Nessa Burns."

"Of course you are."

Nessa chuckled, a throaty sound that made the hairs stand up on Delaney's arms. She felt like a voyeur.

"Connor MacDermot." He rose and offered her his chair. In moments, the waitress appeared with another chair and place setting. "Please join us, Nessa."

Much to Delaney's dismay, Nessa did, settling into the chair just vacated by Connor. She waved her hand airily at the waitress. "I'll have whatever he's having."

Delaney's heart sank. Her sister was a year older but she seemed so much younger…freer. And Nessa always got what she wanted, which at the moment appeared to be Delaney's boyfriend. She bit back a growl. It's not like she and Connor were an exclusive couple. She'd dreamed. She'd planned. But in retrospect, she'd read way more into Connor's motives than she should have. All the clues were there, like a slap in the face. He preferred to meet her places for their dates, claiming their schedules as an excuse. He'd only picked her up and returned her to her door a handful of times. And while his kisses thrilled her, he'd never made any move to get more intimate with her.

She leaned back in her chair, forgotten by the other two as their animated conversation bounced across the table. Their entrées arrived but Nessa and Connor ignored theirs, too busy learning about each other. Delaney picked at hers, her appetite having fled.

Her eyelids prickled with the salty sting of tears. Clearing her throat, she pushed her chair back from the table. “You two don’t mind me.” They didn’t. She headed to the ladies room.

Twenty minutes later, she could stall no longer. After several fortifying breaths, which did nothing at all for her nerves, she headed back. In her absence, a pianist had appeared at the baby grand piano tucked into a discreet corner of the restaurant. The stage might as well have been front and center. Everyone—well, all but two *everyones*—watched and listened. Delaney stopped at the entrance, bracing a shoulder on the wall as she waited for the song to end.

A memory tickled her subconscious. The musician seemed very familiar but she was positive she’d remember him. The man was flat out gorgeous. Tall and lithe, a mane of blond hair flowed across the broad shoulders of his black shirt. His long, nimble fingers teased the tune from the instrument. His voice crooned a love song so sweet she could almost taste cotton candy on her tongue. She licked her lips. No, not cotton candy. Crackerjacks. Or both. She looked up to find him watching her. His eyes fixed on hers, knowing and wise as if he read her very soul. Disconcerted, unsettled, she couldn’t look away.

The song ended and applause erupted. She glanced toward Connor and Nessa. Their heads remained close together, and Delaney got the distinct impression there was a bubble surrounding them, forming a world of their own within the world around them. Jealousy twisted in her gut, and she swallowed the bile rising in her throat.

Her gaze returned to the musician. He still watched her, his expression shrewd. He knew. The man stood and, with the grace of a dancer, he waltzed toward her. Halting right in front of her, he offered his hand. She lifted her hand in a reluctant response and he gripped it. Staring into his eyes, she toppled into the kaleidoscope of colors swirling there.

The world tumbled around her like clothes in a dryer. She felt warm and oddly safe for all that her body felt boneless

Close your eyes, little one, a voice as sweet as spun sugar crooned in her ear. Arms circled her, held her close against a muscular chest. *You'll be safe so long as you're with me.*

"Where are we going?" Did she say the words out loud or only think them?

To a place far, far way. To a time when men still believed in magic.

"But I don't want to."

Doesn't matter, child. Yee've lessons to be learned and 'tis time you did so.

****

Delaney stretched but didn't open her eyes. Her sluggish body responded under protest so she burrowed deeper into her pillow, only something scratched her cheek. Her nose twitched and she fought the sneeze building, especially after she heard someone scream. Trapped between her desire to help and her fear, her body remained paralyzed. She couldn't see, her eyes blocked by…hay? Nearby, a child whimpered and a dog growled but outside? Out there, even though the sounds were muted by whatever building she was in, the noise and racket sounded like a slaughter.

She caught a soft noise, like footsteps shuffling through something soft. Carpet? Dirt? Straw? Two men, talking in gruff voices. Their language might be unfamiliar but the crude sounds sent shivers down her spine. Instinctively, she knew they searched for the child. More shouts outside and the men fled.

Silence descended. Delaney strained to hear. More shuffling steps. The dog growled. Was he protecting the child? She heard a man speak to the dog in that strange language, but this time, she almost understood the words. The effect was similar to watching a foreign film with subtitles. By the time the movie ended, she could almost understand the dialogue.

"Ah, cailín, 'tis safe you are now. I have you," the man said, and she heard the child gasp.

Delaney exhaled slowly. The little girl would be okay, but she needed to see the child's rescuer. She tried to move again but couldn't, and in a panic, she fought her paralysis. Desperate now, she had to see what the man looked like.

"Shhh, Delaney."

She calmed, though her heart still thudded in her chest. This voice she recognized. The singer at the restaurant.

"You need only to see with your heart. Open your eyes to what it knows, cailín."

She struggled again until a gentle hand cupped her cheek. Moments later, her vision cleared and with it, the strange paralysis. Disoriented, she clutched the wall behind her as the room swam in circles before her eyes.

A man sat at the piano, but not the mysterious musician who'd held her hand. Flatware clinked against china plates. A buzz of conversation hummed beneath the bright notes flowing from the piano. She glanced toward her table. Nessa's hand covered Connor's where it rested on the pristine tablecloth. He speared a strawberry from the fruit plate she'd ordered and offered it to her sister. She wasn't sure what was worse—losing Connor to her sister or having a psychotic break over it.

Crushed, Delaney choked back a sob, turned to run. Only to collide with a hard body. Strong arms circled her shoulders and waist, and she buried her nose in a soft, cotton tee shirt. Inhaling deeply, her nose twitched. The man smelled like new mown hay, leather, and an underlying musk that made her knees wobble.

"Whoa, Doc. You okay?"

Rory? She fought to control her turbulent emotions as they smashed into her raging hormones.

I told you he would come. The musician's voice melted in her memory, like buttercreme icing on her tongue.

Delaney fought the urge to wipe her nose on his shirt and prayed it wasn't dripping as she raised her head. "Uhm…fancy meeting you here?"

His big hand cupped her face and he brushed his thumb across her cheek. "What's wrong?"

"Nothing. Nothing's wrong."

"Little liar. You've been crying." His gaze tracked across the restaurant and settled on the table where Connor and Nessa sat oblivious to anything but themselves. "Ah."

That one syllable carried the weight of his disapproval and she felt the need to defend Connor. “It’s not like we were an item or anything.” She hated that her voice sounded whiny. And that she’d automatically used the past tense in regards to her relationship with the other man.

“But you had a lunch date with him. What happened? Who’s the chick?”

“My sister.” She blurted it out even as her mind whirled. “Wait. How did you know I had a date with Connor?” Her brow furrowed as she glared up at him.

“Mandy.” He dropped the name of her receptionist like that explained everything. Which it pretty much did.

“I really need to talk to that girl.”

“In her defense, I wheedled it out of her.”

“Wheedled?” One eyebrow arched in amusement.

“I’m quite good at it.” His lips quirked in a not-quite smile.

“Yes, I imagine you are. You seem like the kind of man who can pretty much *wheedle* whatever he wants out of a woman.”

Now the crooked smile formed and reached his brown eyes—his amazing amber gold eyes. She blinked and dragged her gaze from his face to glance over at Connor. Midnight and sunset. That’s what they reminded her of.

“True and right now, I’m turning my charms on you. C’mon. I know a great burger place just around the corner.”

She watched Connor and Nessa for a wistful moment and her heart ached. Then her stomach growled. “Can I get onions on it?”

"You bet."

His hand on her elbow felt strong yet gentle, and she was reminded again of the dichotomy presented by this man. She'd seen him comfort terrified hostages. Heck, he'd comforted a terrified doctor after her first full-blown incident. But she also knew he could stare into the eyes of a criminal through the scope of his sniper's rifle and pull the trigger without hesitation. The scientist wanted to dissect his psyche. The woman wanted to be saved by him. She almost snorted at her thoughts. She'd worked her whole life to be a woman who didn't need saving.

"Do you need to tell them you're leaving?"

Delaney studied the couple across the room. She lifted one shoulder in a negligent shrug as the corner of her mouth dragged down in a half-frown. "No. I took all my things to the ladies room with me, and they'll never know I'm gone. Besides, Connor is feeding my lunch to Nessa." Turning, she caught a fleeting expression she couldn't decipher before his face settled into a blank canvas.

"I'll feed you fries and onion rings. C'mon." His hand pressed against the small of her back, urging her toward the exit.

The hostess offered a puzzled look, and then she gave Rory the onceover. Three times! Delaney bristled, glaring at the young woman. Outside, she had to wonder at her reaction. When the hostess escorted Connor to the table, she'd been bright and chirpy and obviously interested until the waitress swooped in and took over. Delaney took that in stride. Connor was GQ gorgeous. Rory was… She cut her eyes to the man. Rugged. Square-jawed. Auburn hair flamed above his brown eyes. She hadn't noticed his body before. Not like this. During his therapy sessions in her office, she remained focused on the job and his emotions, not the package they came in. In fact, the only other times she'd been this close, he'd been in full body armor. He'd always projected a sense of strength but in the tight tee shirt and form-fitting jeans, she could see the muscles. All his muscles. Oh yes. Tall, wiry but oh-so-very muscled.

She felt heat rush into her cheeks as Rory glanced down at her. His eyes danced with humor, and she'd bet money he'd read her thoughts. Mortified, she broke eye contact by looking down.

"Don't do that."

His voice whispered across her embarrassment and compelled her to glance up at him. "Don't do what?"

"Doubt yourself."

She stared at him, her mouth slightly agape. "I wasn't!" She blinked several times and pursed her lips, thinking. "Was I?"

He nodded and then steered her into a little hole-in-the-wall café. He pushed the door open, waiting for her to precede him. Odors rolled over her—grilled onions, hot grease, baking bread. The place had the vibes of a neighborhood bar. Construction workers in hard hats knocked elbows with guys in three-piece suits. Rory grabbed a table next to the front window as two banker-types vacated it. He stacked the dirty dishes on one corner. A waitress sailed by, dropped two menus, and grabbed the dishes.

Moments later, she was back to wipe down the table and put tall plastic glasses with ice water in front of them. She pulled out flatware rolled in napkins from her apron pocket, placed the rolls on the table and had her ticket book ready for their order. And she didn't flirt with Rory. Delaney decided right then to slip her an extra tip.

About half-way through her burger, she swallowed and said, "I don't, you know."

"Yes, you do."

She huffed a breath. "You don't have to sound so positive."

He tilted his head and watched her. Delaney did her best not to fidget under the intensity of his gaze.

"I don't do things by half measure, Doc."

Her appetite pacified for the moment, she leaned back in her chair and studied him. "True. You are a man of action."

"Nothing wrong with that."

"Especially given your job?"

"This isn't a therapy session, Doc."

"You don't like therapy, do you?"

"You always ask questions."

She chuckled. "Guilty. But while you are a man of action, I am a woman of words."

"Mars and Venus."

"Something like that. What are you afraid of?"

He shook his head. "We're here for lunch, Doc. If I want you poking around in my psyche, I'll come to your office and stretch out on your couch." Devilish lights glinted in his eyes. "Though I have a better plan for that couch."

Heat flushed her cheeks again and she choked. "Stop that."

"Stop what?"

"You know what." She glared at him. "We have a

professional relationship. I am not crossing that line."

His grin matched those glints in his eyes. "Then sign off on my psych profile. We won't have that problem, and I can ask you out without treading on your sense of professional responsibility."

"You are feeling pretty darn sure of yourself, Rory MacDermot." Once again, his last name registered, and she stared at him, wondering. "Wait. Are you two really related?"

Rory shook his head. "He thinks we're long lost cousins or something. His dad is some Irish clann guy. Never been to Ireland, have no plans to ever go."

"Oh, that's right. You've met." Her voice squeaked and she grabbed her glass and gulped, hoping he hadn't noticed.

"Yeah. A couple of weeks ago at that fancy restaurant where you met him for dinner. The team was there to celebrate Jessie's birthday."

She nodded, remembering. "You were called into the station." She blushed, remembering that Connor had mentioned Rory…and his suspicion that Rory had more than a professional interest in her.

"Yeah."

"When you called me to explain, you only said it was for a debriefing. If it was for an incident, I would have been included."

His eyes slid away from hers, and he stared out the window as if trying to decide what to say. "There was a small problem with the new boy."

"Dean Carter?"

"Yeah."

Delaney leaned forward, resting her forearms on the table. "You aren't going to explain?"

“It’s a personnel matter, Doc. The captain took care of it.”

She wasn’t satisfied, but his closed expression and the way he folded his arms across his chest left no room for further questions. She watched him for nonverbal cues and pushed with another question anyway. “Did it have to do with the night the team served that warrant? If there’s a continuing problem, Rory, it could affect the efficacy of the team.”

His face twisted into what could only be described as a “Really? D’uh” expression, but he didn’t respond verbally.

The implications of that night hit her. “Wait. You didn’t get in trouble did you? For punching him?”

He still didn’t respond. Instead, he dragged an onion ring through a puddle of catsup and dangled it in front of her. She bit, nibbled, chewed. And her eyes watered. She managed to swallow and grabbed her glass, gulping long swallows.

When she could speak without gasping she waggled her finger at him. “You did that on purpose.”

“Really?”

She scowled. “Really. I didn’t see you mix any hot sauce in your catsup.”

His gaze shifted to the bottle of Tabasco next to the red squeeze bottle of catsup. “I put Tabasco on everything I eat.” His eyes darkened as he gazed at her. “Well, almost everything.”

Her breath caught in her chest, and she swore her heart was beating so loud the whole restaurant could hear it. She attempted a smart retort, but even though her mouth hung open, no words witty or otherwise spilled forth. Half of her wanted to wipe the smirk off

Rory's face. The other half wanted him to prove his point. The waitress arrived with the bill, saving Delaney further embarrassment. To hide her blush, she picked up her glass to finish her iced tea.

Rory fished in his pocket and pulled out a couple of bills. He handed them and the tab to the waitress, his eyes never leaving her face. He stood and offered her his hand. "You coming?"

Delaney coughed and sputtered as she tried to swallow that last mouthful, her brain going someplace it shouldn't. He pounded her on the back.

"Talk."

"No." The word came out strangled but it came out, and she sucked in a breath.

He appeared to relax a bit, but still looked like he was ready to perform the Heimlich—or hold her in his arms. Her mind drifted. Would he give her mouth-to-mouth? And how much would she enjoy it? She blushed. Technically, she was his therapist so he couldn't kiss her. Yet. Ever. She wouldn't risk her license for a fling. Oh, but he was temptation incarnate. Was he really a "patient?" She shut down that line of thought, not wanting to cross it. But what if he weren't?

Chapter 10

Rory sat beside the bed and listened to the beeps and hisses that issued from the array of medical equipment. He came every day, picking a time when the family was absent, to sit with Nelda Whitson. He talked to her. Told her he was sorry. He even read romance novels to her. Because her daughter said in a television interview that her mother loved reading them. But not today. Today he'd come to say goodbye. The family was meeting with Nelda's battery of doctors—all the specialists who'd worked so diligently to keep her alive. He knew what the meeting entailed. The doctors wanted to pull the plugs, to stop the machines that breathed for her, pumped her heart, fed her. He knew whatever made her "Nelda" was no longer here in this bed. Her spirit was gone, leaving only the husk of her existence behind.

Like mourners gathering around a granite headstone, her family had clung to this last vestige of wife, mother, friend. Now, they'd had time to say their goodbyes. The time had come to move on. For him, too.

Rory squeezed her hand, stood, and bent to place a kiss on the cheek that remained mostly intact. His lips brushed her withered skin and his belief was confirmed. A husk. That's all that was left.

"I'm sorry," he murmured. His nostrils burned from the tears threatening to swamp him.

“I thought you were the one.”

He whirled.

Nelda’s twelve-year-old granddaughter stood in the doorway.

“Everybody’s still talking and I got bored. I don’t like that Nana is alone. But she’s not. You’re always with her.”

“Not—” He ahemmed to clear the lump in his throat. “Not always. I come by when I can.”

“She would have liked the book you brought her.”

He glanced at the book on the bed table. “I’m sorry.”

The girl walked over and put her arms around his waist, pressing her cheek to his chest. Rory stood stone still for a long moment and then his arms, of their own volition, curled around the child.

“You don’t have to be.” She raised her head to look up at him. “You didn’t mean to shoot her.”

His heart stopped beating. How did she know? His name had never been released. Reflexes took over, restarted his heart, and forced air into his lungs.

As if she didn’t notice his shock, the girl continued. “You wanted to take out the bad guy, before he hurt anyone. And he would have. He would have hurt everybody there. He picked my nana because he thought she was old and wouldn’t fight. Nobody knew her like I did. She would have wanted those people to be safe. You and my nana, you rescued them.”

Rory’s throat closed and he closed his eyes against the moisture filling them. Her arms tightened around him in a fierce hug.

“You came to say goodbye. That’ll make Nana happy. She’s ready, you know.”

He nodded, still unable to trust his voice, and then the girl stepped away from him. She stood on her tiptoes and placed her hands on his shoulders for balance. She kissed his cheek. "I wish I was old enough to go out with you," she whispered. "You remind me of one of the heroes in Nana's books."

Rory stifled the groan but couldn't stop the tear that trailed down his cheek. The girl brushed it away. "Don't be sad. I'm not. Nana's in a better place."

A better place, he mused sometime later. He'd stayed to confirm the decision and ended up meeting the rest of Nelda's family. The men shook his hand. The women hugged him. And they all told him he'd been a hero. He hadn't killed their loved one, the man who took her hostage had by his actions.

Alone in his truck, he gripped the steering wheel so hard his knuckles turned white and cracked from the squeezing pressure. A song came on the radio. Something gravelly. And he gave in to emotion as the refrain washed over him. "If today was your last day..." Tears flowed unheeded and his throat ached from the sobs he swallowed.

****

Delaney leaned back in her chair and crossed her legs. She fiddled with the pen in her hand, twisting and spinning the silver cap, as she studied Rory. His eyes appeared red-rimmed like he hadn't slept—or had been drinking. She suspected the former. He'd never given any indication of being a heavy drinker. When dealing with PTSD, many of her patients self-medicated with alcohol. Rory? He was Type A all the way. He'd confront things head on, for better or worse.

He stared back at her, as still as a predator. She

shivered when the light bulb turned on. He was a predator. And his prey consisted of other predators, so he was a hunter, too.

"How many?"

Rory didn't blink. But he didn't reply either.

"The sooner you talk to me, the sooner we can work through this, and the sooner you can get on with your life."

His smile curled like a lazy river across his face but didn't reach his eyes. "I've already gotten on with my life, Doc. You're the one who is stalling. Why is that?"

Delaney swallowed. Hard. His smile grew colder—the predator sensing his prey's weakness. "You—" She coughed to clear the constriction in her throat. "Have a maddening habit of ignoring my questions." She narrowed her eyes and glared at him. "You've killed people, Rory. And…injured others." His brown eyes turned the color of burnt coffee.

"Killed, Doc. All of them."

"But I thought Mrs. Whit—"

"Her family pulled the plug this morning." He spit the words out, short, succinct—a sound bite delivered with no emotion.

His blood-shot eyes. So much became clear for her now. Vulnerable. Off balance. Now was the time to press home her advantage, get him to open up, and purge all the baggage he swore he didn't lug around.

"How can you sit there and insist that those lives mean nothing to you?"

His eyes narrowed. His nostrils flared. His fingers curled around the arms of his chair in lieu of forming fists. "I'm sorry Nelda Whitson got in the way, Doc. But I didn't kill her. The man holding the gun to her head did that. He sealed her fate and his own the minute he walked into that bank and tried to rob it."

The righteous outrage rolled off him in waves. Delaney was missing something, some important clue. "I don't understand."

Rory pushed out of the chair, paced to the window and stood, feet braced a shoulder's width apart, his hands fisted at his sides. Stiff. Proud. Deadly. This was not a man she ever wanted to cross.

He turned, regarded her with dispassionate eyes. "Exactly, Doc. You don't understand. You're…prey. A victim waiting to happen. You'll never understand."

She suppressed the cold shiver clawing up her spine. "Then do us both a favor and try to explain it." Her voice sounded sharp in her ears, but his expression didn't change.

"Explain it. Okay."

He stalked toward her, stopping when his shins bumped her knees. Rory towered over her. With the sinewy grace of a natural hunter, he bent, his hands gripped the arms of her chair and caged her between his arms and body. His face, within inches of her own, looked like a mask. She swallowed hard. Again. And hated herself for showing the weakness and fear he'd just accused her of.

"You need to understand, Doc. At an incident, the only person with absolutely no choice is the hostage. Me? I can quit. I can put down my rifle, stand up, walk away. I can go grab a hamburger. Drink a beer with my buddies. Sleep." His breath hitched in his chest. "Make love to a beautiful woman."

His exhaled breath whispered across her skin, and she recognized the flare of heated passion in his eyes.

Her tongue peeked out between her lips and tucked her bottom lip between her teeth. Rory was aware of every movement she made. He stared, holding her gaze for a heartbeat. Four. Ten. He straightened and strode away from her returning to the window. He continued speaking, still staring out across the city.

"The bad guy. He chose to be the actor, Doc. He willingly placed himself in the situation. He holds the power. He can walk away. He can choose to end it." His shoulders stiffened and his head jerked as he raised his chin. "But the victim? The hostage? That's the only person who has no choice. Take Nelda."

That he referred to the victim by her first name was telling. Delaney made a note on her pad, the scratching of pen against paper loud in the quiet of her office.

"Nelda went to work. Like she had for countless other days. She was living her life. A nice lady with a family. Getting ready to watch her granddaughter's piano recital next month. And she had all her choices taken away the moment that asshole walked through the doors and pulled his gun. The minute he grabbed her as a shield, her choices ended. The bad guy made the choices for her, Doc."

He inhaled deeply, his shoulders rising and falling. His fists loosened and he worked his fingers to ease tension before fisting them again. He turned.

"Do I feel guilty when I put a bullet through the bad guy? Not one shred, Doc. He had every chance to change his mind, to make a different choice. But he didn't. He forced the action."

"But you made the choice to end his life." Her voice quivered.

Rory spun around, stalked back and glowered

down at her. "No. *He* made that choice, Doc. Every one of the choices was his. He chose to enter the bank. He chose to hold hostages. He chose to grab Nelda. He chose not to put down the gun. He chose, Doc. Not me. He looked at me knowing I watched through the scope, smiled and tightened his trigger finger. I was faster. Yeah, I hit Nelda. But a heartbeat later, I killed him, too. Do I feel bad about Nelda? Hell yeah. She was a victim. But she was the criminal's victim, not mine. That asshole will never hurt anyone else, Doc. I can live with that. If he'd killed all those people? *That's* when I would need the rubber room. I did my job. I'll do my job again."

Her fingers curled against her palm, the sudden need to reach out and touch him, to wrap her arms around him palpable within her. Delaney held herself rigid. But she knew the minute she gave herself away by the look in his eyes. He smiled. Cold, almost cruel, but for the heat blazing in those incredible amber eyes. He bent. His face softened and then his lips touched hers.

"Prey, Doc, but I'll never let you be a victim."

He whispered the promise across her mouth, and hungry need pooled low in her body. She fisted her hands, willed them to stay still on the arms of her chair. She steeled her expression but her heart pounded, tripping like a snare drum. His eyes focused on her throat.

Betrayed again by my stupid romanticism and raging emotions.

What was it about this man that stirred her so? Was it that he kept kissing her—okay, it wasn't a real kiss—

His lips sealed on hers, not asking. This time he

took. His rough hands cupped her cheeks with a gentleness belying his strength. He devoured her, hungrily thrusting his tongue against the seam of her lips, demanding to be let inside. Her lips softened and he swept inside, tasting and teasing her. Her hand uncurled from the armchair, only to curl around his biceps. Her chest rose, lifting her torso away from the chair, her breasts seeking contact with him.

Rory pulled her up then his hands surrendered her cheeks to wrap around her, clutching her to his chest with searing need. His erection nestled against the vee of her thighs, and she pressed against him, rubbing shamelessly until he groaned. One hand dropped to her butt, cupping that cheek like it had cupped her face just moments before.

"I want you."

Her heart hammered at his words. She wanted him, but one small, rational portion of her brain poked her psyche. Hard.

Patient. Well, he's supposed to be a patient. Ethics, woman!

She pushed away from him, and stumbled backward when he relinquished her. Rory quickly steadied her, though, and she glanced up at him. He appeared as stunned by events as she did.

"We can't."

"We could."

"No. You're a patient.

"Yes. Because I'm *not* a patient. I never have been. I'm only here because regulations say I have to sit in that chair until you sign off on my CISD paperwork."

Delaney huffed. "No." God she hated that she purred that word, her voice husky as she flirted with him. She cleared her throat. “No. I mean it.” Oh that devilish grin that reached his eyes and made them twinkle. She just managed to stifle the deeply feminine sigh threatening to escape.

“Yes.” He quirked a brow and leaned in to kiss her forehead. “Maybe not now. But someday, Doc. Someday soon. I’m going to take you to bed. And when I do, it’ll be a night you’ll never forget.”

She arched a brow in response. “Pretty darn cocky, aren’t you?”

“Nothing cocky about it, ma’am, when it’s a promise.”

She sighed. Despite her best efforts to hold it back, that sigh whispered from deep in her chest. Before she could retort, he kissed her again. On the lips. Just as fervently, if not so demanding and hungry.

“This was just a taste, Doc. When I get you in my bed, I’m going to kiss you like that all over. And I do mean all over.”

She flushed and trembled in places deep inside. She had to clench her thighs together to keep from swaying toward him. She reached for the one defense she had. A question. “Why?”

Oh, that lazy grin, and the devil behind it. “Because.”

He eased her back into her chair. With what seemed like reluctance, his hands dropped from her arms but one palm cupped her face and he tilted her head up to look at him. “That’s a promise, Doc, and I always keep my promises.”

His thumb teased her lips as sweetly as a kiss, and the shadows she’d always associated with him withdrew for a few heartbeats. She closed her eyes and breathed for a moment. When she opened her eyes, the door to her office clicked shut. Rory was gone and she wanted to cry. For just a moment, she wanted to cry. She felt his loss with an intensity that rocked her.

After long minutes, she managed to get up and walk to her desk, only to sink into the chair there. With shaking fingers, she reached for her digital recorder to dictate her notes on today's session. With an unconscious gesture, her fingers grazed her lips. They felt hot and swollen and as she shifted uncomfortably in her chair, she realized other lips felt the same. She couldn't breathe for a moment, had to clench her thighs together, and rock her hips to ease the pressure down below. Cold shower. She needed one desperately. But she didn't want cold, she wanted heat. The heat of his arms around her, his mouth on her, tasting her, licking her, suckling her like she was some delicious treat.

"Jeez, Delaney. Get a vibrator!"

Chapter 11

"Don't you believe in knocking, Nessa?" Delaney's cheeks flushed with a combination of embarrassment and anger.

"I did knock, Laney. But you were obviously too involved in your fantasies to hear me. I mean, really? You were moaning. You need a boyfriend. Bad. Or a good vibrator."

She bit her tongue, despite the fact she wanted to rail at her sister, to spit out that she'd had a boyfriend until Nessa stole him. If she were fair, she'd admit that Connor had been just as smitten with her sister as Nessa had been of him. "You're the one into the kinky stuff, Nessa. Why are you here?"

Delaney watched her sister's expression transform from superior know-it-all to wheedling entreaty. Nessa was nothing if not the consummate actress.

"I need a favor, Laney."

She settled back into her chair and schooled her face. This did not bode well. She didn't say anything, simply waiting for Nessa to move the next chess piece. This was a game they'd played all their lives.

Nessa flounced into one of the desk's side chairs and settled what Delaney labeled her "pretty-please look" on her face. "I know you're probably still upset about Connor and me."

Ya think? Delaney gave no indication of her

internal dialogue. She waited for the next move.

"Look, I suppose you have every right, but it's not like we planned it. It just…happened. He's like my…soul mate or something." Her sister inhaled deeply and a dreamy look transformed her expression. "We plan to introduce his sister to Keegan. And Mom and Dad to everyone. That's why I need you."

Without meaning to, Delaney rubbed her temple where a throbbing headache threatened. "What? You've lost me completely, Nessa."

"It's a family get-together. Connor's parents are flying in from Ireland. To meet me. To meet…us. The whole family. I need you there to help run interference with Mom and Dad." She sighed dramatically. "You know what they're like."

Delaney's throat closed off for a minute. "His parents are coming?" Something fluttered in her chest, a feeling she couldn't define. *To meet you.* The accusation ricocheted in her head, but she maintained the sterile expression she wore with her patients.

Nessa continued to babble about the clothes she needed, the time off she'd scheduled, and how excited and nervous she was because she positively, absolutely knew Connor would ask her to marry him once his parents approved.

Her sister's words washed over her like waves creeping up on the beach, tickling her consciousness with wet foam before dragging back out to sea, pulling her along. Nessa's voice closed over her head, drowning her in an ocean of emotions. How easy it would be to just let go, to close her eyes, and breathe in the numbness welcoming her with its clammy embrace.

"So what do you think?" Nessa beamed at her,

clueless about Delaney's internal struggle. "Surely you can find someone to bring. Or I'll have Connor coerce one of his friends to escort you. Keegan will be with Ciara, of course. Connor is convinced those two are a perfect match. Delaney? Delaney!"

She blinked slowly, her vision finding focus as she stared at Nessa's face. Amazed she didn't wince at her sister's choice of words. Delaney inhaled and swallowed to give herself another moment to keep her composure. She sat up a little straighter and wrapped what dignity her sister's babbling had left intact around her like a security blanket. "I'm quite capable of finding my own escort, Nessa."

"But he has to be someone Mom and Dad will like. And Connor's parents. Thank goodness his mom is American. That will make things so much easier. His dad, though, scares me. I've seen a picture of him—dark and brooding like some hero in a romance book. Very stern, but since he's a big deal in their clann—"

"*Taoiseach*."

The word stopped Nessa dead. "What?"

"*Taoiseach*. Connor's father is *Taoiseach* of Clann MacDermot."

"How did you know that?"

"Connor told me. On one of our dates." Oh, the perverse joy she derived in saying that and creating the look of consternation on her sister's face. "We did go out for some time, Nessa, before you appeared on the scene." Well, they'd had a handful of dates and no matter how petty that made her or how tenuous her relationship with Connor had been, she smiled because she'd left her sister flustered. For once.

Nessa blinked hard, as if she had tears in her eyes,

and she provided a credible sniffle to accompany the flutters, but Delaney knew her sister too well. Those tactics might have worked on her once but no longer. She wondered what had been the last straw—briefly—but knew Connor was tied up in the rivalry between them. A rivalry Nessa always seemed to win.

"Well—" Nessa sniffled and hitched the deep breath she drew into her lungs just for effect. "You don't have to come if you want to be all mean and bitchy."

Delaney laughed, the sound a snorting giggle she made no attempt to hide. "Me? Mean and bitchy? Really? You want to go there, Nessa?"

She shouldn't feel such satisfaction at the flush staining her sister's cheeks. Anger, not embarrassment. Nessa didn't know the definition of embarrassment.

"If you don't want me there, fine. If you do, please keep me informed of dates and time so I can ensure I have an escort. I'd hate to create a seating problem by being the odd one out." She glanced at her watch. "I have work to do, Nessa."

At least her sister recognized the dismissal and pushed to her feet. "I don't know what's gotten into you, but I don't like it very much."

"What? You don't like that I'm no longer your doormat? Tough, Nessa. Life is too short to live in your shadow and at your whim. You want Connor? Go for it. I hope the two of you will have your happy ever after, but don't expect me to feel all warm and fuzzy that you've never recognized a personal boundary in your life."

Delaney clamped her teeth around the words wanting to spew out. Years of hurt and suppressed resentment boiled inside her. She tamped down the feelings, curious they would explode now. Looking at her motives dispassionately helped her regain control. She eyed Nessa, waiting for her next outburst.

"You've always been jealous of me, Delaney. Admit it."

Laughter bubbled out again but sounded a bit more hysterical than Delaney was entirely comfortable with. "Whatever, Nessa. I still have work to do and I'm sure you have somewhere you'd rather be."

Her sister sniffed one last time, turned sharply, and marched to the door. She jerked it open at exactly the same moment someone shoved it from the other side. Nessa stumbled backward, howling and cradling her nose with her hand. Bronwyn stood in the doorway looking much more satisfied than she should given the circumstances.

"Oh, I'm sorry, Nessa. Did I bust your nose with the door?"

Delaney pressed her lips together and bit them to keep from laughing out loud. Bronwyn didn't sound sorry at all. In fact, her best friend looked as pleased as she sounded.

"Just stay away from me." Nessa growled the words around her hand and exited with as much dignity as she could muster—which wasn't much.

Bronwyn waited by the door until she was positive Nessa had gone then she closed the door, turned to Delaney, and giggled. "I'm really sorry I didn't break her nose. Without her looks, maybe Connor would see what a bitch Nessa actually is." She waggled her brows and skipped over to drop into the chair Nessa had just vacated. "I'm sorry."

Delaney's brow furrowed as she tried to figure out Bronwyn's comment. "For what?"

"For introducing you to Connor, the asshat. I can't believe he dumped you for Nessa. That's just…wrong on so many levels I can't even begin to count them. I want to scratch his eyes out every time I see him in the office."

Delaney couldn't help but smile. Bronwyn was every inch the outraged friend, and she appreciated the show of solidarity. Something stirred in her memory—brown eyes watching her hungrily, lips brushing across hers. Rory. Not Connor. Maybe she wasn't as heart-broken as she once thought. The smile on her face shifted, and she knew the moment Bronwyn realized her thoughts had shifted.

"I know that look. You wore it every time you thought about Connor. But you aren't thinking about jerkface now." She glanced around the room and even sniffed, as if she could suss out the reason for the change in Delaney's demeanor. "Oooh…" Bronwyn's eyes widened and she leaned closer, bracing her hands on the desk and looking conspiratorial. "Was *he* here today? You know who I mean—tall, muscled, and sexy as all get out?"

Heat flushed her cheeks, but she didn't look away. "I can't talk about him. I'm a professional."

"Then you need to go all unprofessional on him ASAP, girlfriend. That man wants you as much as you want him. And—" Bronwyn snapped her mouth shut, as if she'd been about to say something she'd regret.

"What?"

Bronwyn shook her head, a decisive and adamant motion.

"You know you're going to tell me." Delaney wheedled and wagged her finger.

"Well…okay. I think you need to go out with that guy. The cop." There was nothing teasing about Bronwyn now.

"Rory."

"Yeah. Him. And I think that if you'd been going out with him and Nessa had tried to steal him away? I think he would have laughed at her. And kissed you. Right in front of her."

Delaney tilted her head to study her friend, considering what she'd said. Her fingers brushed her lips, the gesture unplanned but very telling.

"Oh. My. God. He's kissed you!" Bronwyn bounced in her chair. "When? Where? What was it like?"

"Shhhh. Don't say that so loud. Technically, he's…" Her voice trailed off. She'd almost called him a patient but was he really? He didn't consider her his therapist. Her contract stated she was to conduct a critical incident stress debriefing and either sign off or recommend counseling. She'd done neither with Rory. "I could be breaking all kinds of ethics and rules to even consider going out with him. I shouldn't see him personally."

"But you kissed him!"

"No, he kissed me." There. She'd admitted it.

"And?"

"And what?" Delaney bristled, remembering once again that getting involved with Rory was all kinds of wrong. "I told him not to do it again."

Bronwyn stared, disbelief etched all over her face. "Are you kidding me? Delaney, you're crazy! The man is drop-dead gorgeous, and he has the hots for you. I'm telling you, you need to sign off on whatever bullshit paperwork you have to sign off on, get him off your professional list, and sign him up on your date list. Invite him to this thing Nessa and Connor are doing. Make them both jealous. And enjoy the hell out of yourself while doing it."

Delaney pursed her lips and stared at Bronwyn. "Such language, young lady. Shame on you."

"You know I'm freakin' right, Delaney Burns. Don't wag that finger at me. And I'll say bad words if I want to. So there." She stuck out her tongue. "You need to wag your finger in your own face, Laney."

She sighed, unwillingly admitting that Bronwyn was right. But she'd stood up to Nessa today and that was a step in the right direction. "I have a better idea. Retail therapy. After dinner?"

Bronwyn nodded like a bobble-head. "Deal. We are going to find you an outfit that will make Connor really sorry he ever laid eyes on Nessa."

Delaney inhaled slowly. "No. That's not necessary, Bronnie. I appreciate the sentiment. but you know something? Deep down, I really think this is all for the best. Connor and Nessa, I mean. When they're together, nobody else in the world exists. You can't fight that kind of attraction. Like Nessa said, you'd think they were soul mates if such a thing existed."

The other woman snorted, the sound derogatory and inelegant. "I know you're the scientific one, Laney, but really? You don't believe in love at first sight either. I'm telling you, sometimes there is such a thing. I don't know if Cupid exists, or love potions, or anything else that's all woo-woo stuff, but if you'd ever stop to look around you with optimistic eyes, you might just learn a thing or three."

"The next thing you're going to try to convince me about is reincarnation, or déjà vu, or…voodoo dolls."

Bronwyn's eyes glittered with malice. "Ooh, now there's an idea! I have a friend in New Orleans. I bet she'd buy us a voodoo doll with Nessa's name on it. She and Connor might be destined for each other, but that doesn't mean we can't be a pain in her ass. Literally."

She had to laugh. Bronnie always knew how to make her feel better. "Naw. Leave them alone. They deserve each other."

"They really do. Just wait until she goes all PMS on his ass. Connor'll never know what hit him."

Despite her best intentions, a devilish smile curled her lips and crinkled her eyes. "I hadn't thought of that. Nessa is a real beast during that time of the month. It'll serve him right. Now get out of here so I can finish up my dictation. I can't leave until it's done."

Bronwyn huffed, but did as asked. "I'll be out in the waiting room reading those old magazines. You really need to get new ones, Laney. Just sayin'."

As the door closed, Delaney flipped open Rory's file and read through her notes. Despite her misgivings—and perhaps some misconceptions on her part—she had to admit he made sense. Every time they talked, he remained grounded and resolute. He was an alpha male with a capital "A" but one who carried a protective streak bigger than Texas.

She'd seen the pain in his eyes when he talked about Nelda Whitson and her granddaughter. And she'd seen the acceptance of Nelda's death and that of the man who'd taken her hostage. Rory's arguments made reluctant sense to her and as she sat there, she questioned her own perceptions of his job. Was he right?

She touched her lips again and her thighs clenched reflexively. Was he right about everything? She seemed to be the only one who thought of him as a patient. He certainly didn't. So, if he wasn't a patient, there were no ethical lines to cross. What was she afraid of? Maybe it was time for the "physician" to heal herself—and the first step to that was acknowledging she was the one throwing up roadblocks.

Chapter 12

For about the thousandth time, Rory wondered what the hell he was doing. The house—mansion if described accurately—teemed with people. He managed to get close enough to the bar set up in the massive, open living area to order. The bartender pulled him a draft Guinness from a tapped keg and with negligence born of experience tipped a bottle over a wine glass. Rory carried the fragile crystal stem filled with a white wine of some sort—Sauvignon Blanc or something like that—as if the glass was a live bomb. He located Delaney across the sea of humanity and with single-minded purpose, wove and dodged through the revelers to reach her side.

His heart tripped a couple of beats as her face lit up when she saw him. Her smile touched every inch of her—her shoulders and chin lifted, the frown on her brow relaxed, and her eyes warmed but still twinkled. And her mouth. Art critics raved about the Mona Lisa. That dame had nothing on Delaney Burns. Her full bottom lip beckoned him with wanton disregard despite her admonishments to keep things professional between them.

She'd been in need of an escort to this shindig. And she trusted him to be a gentleman. He felt his cheeks crinkle as his mouth curled into the wicked grin that mirrored his thoughts. He'd be professional, a colleague only during the party, but once he got her in his truck, Rory had every intention of taking her home with him. To his bed. He'd waited long enough to claim what was his.

Mine. The word echoed in his mind but he no longer fought the sensation, nor the voice which replied, *Yours*. He wasn't crazy. And maybe, just maybe, he'd find the woman he was meant to love for the rest of his life. His heart already knew that woman's name was Delaney. His body craved hers with a need bordering on pain. He just had to convince her of the…rightness of their being together. He liked the way that sounded in his head. He felt *right* when he was in her presence.

"Sauvignon Blanc for the lady." He almost had to shout the words as he handed her the glass with a flourish. Her fingers touched his as she retrieved the drink, and the hum of strident conversation faded to the pastoral buzz of bees. All his senses went hyper, like the moment when he first sighted a target through the scope of his sniper rifle. His hearing seemed so acute he swore he could hear the sound of her heart beating. His nostrils flared as her fragrance washed over him—a blend of orange, cinnamon, and sweet cream that reminded him of Christmas. He wanted to wear her scent, rubbing against her to get it on his skin so he could smell her always. Her fingers on his felt like silk rubbing against suede—fingers that were long and slender, nails, pink with white tips. He wanted to feel those nails digging into his shoulders, scratching his back as he pushed into her over and over until her breath hitched and she screamed out his name.

Delaney's eyes widened, and he wondered if the

same thoughts occurred to her. His gaze dropped to her lips, and he wanted to run his tongue over them, to fasten his mouth on hers and kiss the breath from her. He hardened, painfully so, and wanted to press against her, rubbing his erection against her abdomen to show her the effect she had on him. Her nostrils flared and her chest rose and fell as she all but panted. Her breasts strained against the soft drape of the material covering them, and his hands itched to cup them, to feel her pebbled nipples pressing into his palms.

The ebb and flow of the crowd didn't touch them. They'd created their own little eddy in the corner, and it was as if a bubble surrounded them, cutting them off from the noise and notice of the other party-goers. Intent on Delaney and his feelings for her, Rory ignored the prickle of warning on the back of his neck. He felt reckless, daring, and he wanted this woman with his entire being. He couldn't remember a time in his life when he'd wanted anything more. He would live or die by her smile, her touch.

"Jeez, Delaney, what's gotten into you? You might as well be screwing the guy right here in the corner."

He jerked like someone had hit him and only the iron grip he maintained on his self-control kept him from throwing his beer in the face of the offender, Nessa, Delaney's sister. They'd met briefly, upon their arrival, and the woman had grated on his nerves even then. Delaney flushed and he turned, shielding her from Nessa's probing glare. With a cold smile and narrowed eyes hinting at the predator he was, he stared at Nessa like she was his next prey until she looked away, her eyes sliding to the side.

"Did you need something, Nessa?" He

intentionally growled the question, to reinforce their positions.

"Connor's parents have arrived. They want to meet Delaney."

Nessa wouldn't meet his gaze and her tone of voice irritated him. It was pure negligence—as if introducing Delaney to her future in-laws was strictly an afterthought, a formality to be dealt with before sticking Delaney in a corner. Nobody would ever ignore Delaney again if he had anything to say about it.

He turned and offered his hand to Delaney. She set down her untouched wineglass and took his hand. Her fingers felt cold. He rubbed his thumb over them to add warmth. "Let's get this over with."

They'd taken maybe half a dozen steps, with Nessa leading, when Connor appeared at her side. He planted himself in front of Rory and bristled like a…hedgehog. Rory choked back laughter at the image. The pup looked like he wanted to fight, and while Connor might be in good shape, he'd lose in a heartbeat.

Between one heartbeat and the next, Rory's whole body stilled. His expression went blank as he narrowed his eyes, regarding the younger man. They might be only a year or two apart in actual age but the other man *felt* like a kid to him, as if his experience far outstripped Connor's. Everything about his demeanor screamed menace. The people standing nearby felt it, too. As their conversations tumbled into silence, the whole room seemed to hold its collective breath.

"This must be your sister, Nessa." A woman appeared, and she extended her hand toward Delaney.

Rory studied Connor's mother when Delaney extended her own hand. "Delaney Burns, Mrs.

MacDermot."

"Oh, heavens. Please call me Becca. We'll be family soon and I've never been one to stand on formality."

The woman's gaze flicked to him and lingered, as if she found him an interesting specimen. The intensity of her scrutiny made him want run his finger under his collar to loosen it. This woman had presence, regal and serene. She'd dominate any company around her. Except him. He shook the image of a recalcitrant schoolboy being chastised out of his brain and raised his chin just a hair meeting her gaze dead on.

"This is my…friend, Rory MacDermot." Delaney tripped over how to label him.

If he hadn't been watching the woman so closely, he would have missed the flicker in her eyes and the momentary shock that registered on her face before she recovered her equilibrium. Now that was interesting. She acted almost as if she knew his name—or him. The woman held out her hand to him, and out of habit he took it.

"I am *very* pleased to meet you, Rory MacDermot."

Something in her mysterious smile and her voice made him believe she meant that sincerely. Her hand felt fragile in his, but as she gripped back, her strength belied the delicacy. Her unwavering gaze met his, and she even smiled just a little when his poker face dropped into place. It was as if she knew the reason for his mask.

Becca slipped her arms through those of Connor and Nessa and turned them. "Come, children. I know Kieran is looking forward to meeting Delaney and…Rory." She glanced back over her shoulder before she added his name, and again her smile hinted she knew something no one else did. He reached down and reclaimed Delaney's hand before he started after them.

Delaney tugged on his hand and he stopped. She rose on tiptoes and whispered in his ear, "You make good cop face." Then she giggled.

That sound loosened the bands in his chest, and the constrictions on his breathing eased. As long as he could make her smile, could make her laugh, he'd be complete. He grinned and the change in his expression caused his cheek to brush against hers. "I do what I can," he whispered back. He slipped his arm over her shoulder and urged her through the crowd again. They caught up to the other three. Like a queen, Becca strode through the crush, and as if she projected some sort of force field, people parted to let them pass. Rory figured this woman pretty much got whatever she wanted, and if she didn't, she wasn't afraid to take it herself.

Becca led them through some open French doors, and they stepped outside to a covered patio area with a sparkling pool. A man held court near the brick outdoor kitchen. A head taller than anyone in the bunch gathered around him, his neatly trimmed black hair glinted with blue highlights every time he moved his head. Rory was immediately reminded of a raven. Kieran MacDermot's dark blue eyes tracked his wife's progress and heated as she neared. The sexual energy ramped up more than a few degrees as she slipped under his arm and he dropped a kiss on the top of her head.

"I have some very *interesting* introductions to make, darling."

Rory caught the inflection and wondered about it, given the woman's own reaction to him. Why would they find him interesting?

"Kieran, this is Nessa's lovely sister, Delaney. And her friend, Rory MacDermot." Becca wasn't looking at them as she made introductions. Her eyes remained glued to her husband, watching for his reaction.

What the hell was going on here? He saw a flicker of recognition in Kieran's eyes, the slight narrowing of his brows, and the tightening of his mouth. The expression was fleeting, quickly replaced by one well schooled.

"May I call you Rory, Mr. MacDermot?" Kieran extended his hand.

Rory gripped it and a profound sense of déjà vu settled on him. He knew this man. And more troubling, this man knew him. They stared into each other's eyes, neither blinking, in a silent communion. Once again, sound retreated and he was encased in a bubble insulating him from everyone but Kieran MacDermot. No. Not everyone. Becca remained inside the bubble, there beneath Kieran's arm. Aware of warmth at his own side, he realized his arm still circled Delaney's shoulders as she slipped her arm around his waist.

He shook his head, feeling like a dog emerging from water and shaking off the excess. Sound returned. Music. Laughter. The clink of glasses.

"I've waited a long time to meet you, Rory."

He tilted his head, studying the other man and almost smiled as Kieran mirrored the attitude.

"You are well?" Kieran's eyes flicked toward Delaney.

Rory pondered the odd question. "I am."

Kieran nodded then and his expression relaxed as he released Rory's hand. "Connor tells me you are a police officer?"

"And he told me you were an Irish Army Ranger."

The other man chuckled. "Aye, that I was. Among other things, then and now. You saw military service as well, I suspect."

"I did. United States Marine Corps."

"Always the warrior and protector, Rory."

Cold fingers skittered up his spine, and he wondered if someone walked across his grave. He had the distinct feeling that Kieran wanted to say more but was worried he'd think the man crazy. He was more concerned about his own reactions. They *were* crazy—this sense of familiarity, of loss, of…kinship. Becca and Kieran exchanged glances again before they both studied him, waiting for a reaction or comment. He offered neither. Until he knew the angle of this slippery slope, he wasn't climbing it.

Any further introspection ended with the announcement that dinner would be served as soon as the guests were seated. Uniformed staff herded everyone to a huge tent set up on the expansive lawn. Rory's vision wavered as he ducked through the flaps. A hint of peat smoke and roasted meat bullied his senses. The head table presided over the rest of the room. Kieran and Becca led the way, ushering Delaney's parents with them. Connor escorted Nessa, and a young man he didn't recognize, but guessed from his looks to be Keegan Burns, escorted a beauty with long black hair. Anyone could tell the young woman had to be Connor's twin. As folks milled about the tables looking for the place cards with their names,

Rory realized that Kieran kept the two seats next to him open. The older man caught his attention and waved him forward.

"Looks like we have a command performance, Doc. You ready for it?" Her hand trembled in his and he squeezed gently. "C'mon. We'll do this together."

They took their places at the table, Rory seated at Kieran's right hand, Delaney to his right, and her parents next to her. Becca sat on Kieran's left, with Connor, Nessa, Ciara, and Keegan, next to them. As people took their places, Delaney quickly introduced him to the rest of her family. After a great deal of milling about, people sorted out and settled in. Wait staff filled wine glasses, and Kieran raised his in a toast to the upcoming nuptials. Rory managed to hide the shudder that word created, but didn't bother to suppress the righteous outrage he felt for Delaney's situation. She'd warned him her family was classically dysfunctional, but it took a stone cold bitch to move in on the man your sister loved.

Rory glanced at Delaney and wondered how she felt. She'd made it clear he was simply a substitute for Connor. He didn't mind. For the moment. Being close to her like this gave him a chance to prove her wrong. He wasn't a substitute for Connor or any other man. Each time he held her hand and gazed into her eyes, or made her nostrils flare and caused her breath to hitch in her chest, he moved that much closer to making her his.

Yours.

Yes, she was his, finally. And he would spend the rest of his days proving that to her. He covered the laughter the thought caused. No one in his unit would believe he was sitting in a starched shirt that chafed his neck, wearing a monkey suit and bow tie, while contemplating loving one woman for the rest of his life. He'd always been a "love 'em and leave 'em" kind of guy. But he'd also been honest with the women he'd dated. He told them going in he didn't believe in long-term relationships, love, or marriage. Until the first time he'd laid eyes on Dr. Delaney Burns. Until the first time her voice whispered in his earpiece. Until the first time he'd leaned across her desk and brushed his lips across hers.

Mine.

Chapter 13

"You don't like getting wet, Doc?" Dinner had finally ended, and they stood near the pool as the evening wound down.

"Only in the shower."

The corner of his mouth twisted into a wicked grin. "Not even a hot tub?" He waggled his brows and winked.

She shivered and backed away from the pool. "Not even a bathtub." She jerked her gaze away from the sparkling water and stared up at him.

"You don't swim at all?" He cocked his head to one side, curious about her reaction.

"No. It's odd, especially given that my brother and sister swim like fish, but..." A delicate shiver shimmered through her body. "I've always been terrified of water."

The chill of déjà vu wrapped around him like an ice pack. A memory, as nebulous as a dream, hovered in stark contrast to the woman standing in front of him. "Any traumatic event as a kid involving water?"

She shook her head, quite adamant in her denial. "None. My mother says I would never even go near the wading pool, and she bathed me in the kitchen sink because I'd freak out in the tub. Keegan and Nessa teased me unmercifully, but I didn't care." Her gaze slid from his, inexorably drawn to the water just a few feet away.

Delaney's chest rose and fell as if she struggled to breathe and the hair on the back of his neck prickled. Not for the first time, he wondered if someone walked over his grave. He didn't believe in déjà vu or reincarnation—none of that New Age bullshit. But something weird was happening. Something he couldn't define and didn't understand. Rory curled his fingers into fists to keep from reaching out and touching Delaney. Everything that made him who he was screamed that she was his—that he needed to protect and cherish her.

"Do you believe in soul mates?"

Rory couldn't breathe for a minute. How did she know what he was thinking? He shook his head but didn't speak.

She looked pensive and dipped her chin in a gentle nod. "Me either. But sometimes…" Her brow furrowed as she considered what to say next. Unable—or unwilling—to look at him, her gaze remained riveted on the ripples glittering on the surface of the pool. "Sometimes, I feel like I know someone, like we've met before even though I know there is no possible way."

"Like when we met Connor's family tonight."

Delaney nodded, the motion absent-minded. "Yes. Like that. And…" She glanced up at him then. "You felt it, too?"

Was it time for him to 'fess up? "Sort of." That was a wimpy answer. He cleared his throat. "I know it sounds weird, but I felt like I knew his parents, especially his dad. Like we'd been friends for a long time." He wasn't about to admit the feelings she engendered.

"It is weird." She held up a graceful finger. "It's weird because…I felt very close to them. I felt closer to them than I do to my own parents." She laughed, the sound forced and a little choked. "I won't describe my classically dysfunctional family. Suffice it to say that I was always the odd duck. But when I met Kieran and Becca, I just…I wanted to crawl into his lap for a bedtime story, like I was a little girl or something. Talk about weird! I never felt that way about my own father. Ever."

His chest burned as a bolt of jealousy seared his psyche. She'd sit in no man's lap but his own! Then the gist of her words cooled the flames. Bedtime story. Like a little girl in her father's lap. Kieran had to be in his early sixties, though he looked fit and trim. As a former Irish Army Ranger, the man would be. Even though he was old enough to be Rory's father, Kieran felt like more a peer. Unsettled, he reached for Delaney's hand and snagged it. Lacing his fingers through hers, he pulled her a step closer.

"I only believe what my senses tell me—what I can see, hear, smell, taste, and touch, Delaney. But here, lately? I'm beginning to wonder if there's not more out there. Stuff that makes no sense, stuff that can't be explained away."

She stepped closer and leaned in. While he continued to hold her hand, he also wrapped his other arm around her shoulders and pulled her against his chest. This...this felt…right. She belonged in his arms, her body pressed against his. He rested his chin on the top of her head. Somewhere in the distance, a voice crooned a love song. Something vaguely Celtic sounding. He couldn't make out the words.

He didn't know how long they stood there, the music sheltering them from the world around them. People walked past, laughing and chatting, but the sounds remained faint echoes. Like before, inside the house earlier in the evening, a bubble seemed to surround them, muting the outside world, narrowing focus down to just the two of them. Rory tilted her chin up and dropped his head so their lips met. A gentle kiss, exploratory, almost innocent. Heat would come later. Heat generated by their bodies rubbing together until flames erupted. He deepened the kiss, gratified when her hands slipped around his neck and she rose on tiptoes to meet his kisses.

Later, when they both needed to breathe, Delaney stepped back and cleared her throat. "I…uhm…little girl's room." She offered a slightly embarrassed smile before darting away through the crowd.

Rory found a darkened corner where he could watch without being seen.

Kieran appeared a few feet away and his wife slipped up behind him but he gave no notice until she slipped her arms around his waist and pressed her cheek against his back. "How are you feeling, darling?"

Kieran lifted his shoulders in a negligent shrug but the deep breath he sucked in gave away his tightly controlled emotions. "Becca, I never understood how it happened, you know. That bloody night has haunted me all these years. The accident was such a shock. Riordan could drive anything and he wasn't careless. Not when he needed to be in control."

Rory felt like he was intruding but he couldn't leave. He sensed these people knew something—

something important—and he wanted find out what it was.

She slipped around and fitted herself under her husband's arm. "You are convinced then?"

"As are you."

"Why now?"

A wry chuckle erupted from Kieran. "Why not now? They were never bound, Becca. Not like us. But the damned fae keep throwing them together. There must be a reason."

Becca turned her head and Kieran followed her gaze. At the other end of the pool, Ciara and Connor held court at a table, Keegan and Nessa at their sides. "Abhean's hand is all over this. He's here, hiding somewhere."

Becca brushed her cheek against her husband's shoulder. "Yes. I heard him singing earlier."

Kieran stared at his children. "They're the reason, I think. Their lives are tied with hers somehow."

"And his."

He sighed at his wife's statement and Rory caught a hint of remorse in the sound. "I am not a wistful man, Becca. But ever was Riordan at my side. Always. Until that terrible day thirty plus years ago."

Rory caught a glint of light in Kieran's eyes and wondered if tears formed there. The other man cleared his throat and continued.

"That telephone call in the middle of the night, the dispassionate voice explaining that Riordan's Land Rover had been found crumpled on its top, my cousin's lifeless body inside." Kieran rubbed his chest, an unconscious gesture to ease the pain that still lingered in his heart. "He was so much more than just my cousin. Brother. Best friend. Conscience. Confidant. My life has been so much bleaker without his laughter to illuminate the dark corners. As much as I love you, Becca, as much as you are my life, my light, he still had importance." The man rubbed his chest again and turned his gaze to his wife.

"Do you think he'll finally find his place?"

"His place has always been by your side, Kieran. And you both felt it tonight. The easy camaraderie, the way you both fell into old habits. I knew him as soon as I looked in his eyes. They haven't changed. His looks might be different, though I admit I like the way he fills out that tux."

He growled and she laughed. "There's no man for me but you, Kieran MacDermot, though you can't blame a girl for window shopping."

"Of course, I can."

She laughed and stretched to kiss his cheek. He turned his head to kiss her lips and hugged her tightly. She pushed away to gaze at him, her demeanor serious. "Whatever game Abhean plays, there's nothing we can do, love. Be glad we've found Riordan again. Be glad that maybe, this time around he'll find the other half of his heart."

"And this time you can be bloody sure I will teach him the binding vow."

****

They moved off but Rory remained in the shadows, mulling over that conversation. When Delaney reappeared, he stepped out of the shadows and strode to her side. He pulled her close and kissed her, unsettled by the conversation he'd overheard.

Delaney offered a bemused smile."Well, I guess

you missed me."

"I did." He circled her waist with his arm and tucked her into his side. Rory didn't care that Connor's parents stood in the shadows nearby and watched him with Delaney. Nor did he care that Connor, his sister, and Delaney's siblings occupied a table near the pool drinking and laughing like they'd been friends all their lives. He did care that Delaney gazed at the quartet with something akin to hurt in her eyes. Or longing. She wanted to belong to that group, to be included. She wasn't—and never would be. The four of them closed ranks the moment they all met, shutting out Delaney and anyone else. He controlled the outrage he felt on her behalf.

"You're three times the person any of them are, Doc."

She jumped, as if he'd hit her with a jolt of static electricity and rubbed her hands up and down her bare arms. "But they look so…happy. So…complete. Like they own the world." She sighed. "I know I'm petty."

"Petty? You?"

She breathed a couple of times, still watching them, her expression melancholy. "I'm jealous. That's pretty petty if you ask me."

Rory laughed, his amusement bubbling out. "Jealous? Of them? What the hell for, Doc? When I look at them, I see a bunch of self-absorbed, smug asses. They have nothing on you, Delaney, and frankly, I think they're fools for ignoring how wonderful you are." She blushed, and he could feel the heat radiating from her cheeks. He softened his voice. "You are, you know. Wonderful. And beautiful. Sexy."

She sputtered. "Sexy? Me? Not likely!"

He arched a brow, glanced around, and then edged her deeper into the shadows. When he was sure no one could see them clearly, he reached for her hand and pressed her palm against his erection. “Feel that, Doc? That’s what you do to me. I want to kiss you. Touch you. Worship your breasts and bury that hard-on so deep inside you I can touch your soul. I want to make you come so many times you see stars. And then I want to sleep with you in my arms so that when I wake up, I can slip inside you again. I want to watch you wake up knowing you make me feel impossibly hard and it’s only for you.”

Her breath quickened and he pulled her against him, rubbing his erection against her tummy. “Come home with me, Doc. Let me undress you and worship you with kisses and touches. Let me show you how beautiful you are. How sexy you are. How you make me feel like the luckiest man in the world because you’re in my arms.”

His mouth claimed hers, his tongue tickling the seam of her lips until she opened to let him inside. He deepened the kiss, hungry to claim every part of her. *YOURS.* The word roared in his head and he let it wash over him as the thought sent even more blood south, swelling his erection until he thought the head would explode if he didn’t get inside her soon.

“Please.” The word was both plea and promise.

Delaney sighed into his kiss and he knew. He had her. But he had to get her out of there, away from her family, away from prying eyes so he could claim her. For once, Delaney’s anonymity worked to his favor. No one would miss them if they snuck out. He knew they could skirt going through the house by slipping around the outside corner. With luck, his keys would be in his truck, and he could bypass the valet parking attendants as well. He was about to whisper his plan in her ear when the soft clearing of a throat froze him in place. This was bad. Very bad. His job was to remain situationally aware, yet someone had gotten the jump on him.

"Easy, Rior—Rory."

Kieran. He breathed again and plastered his cop face on as he turned to the other man. Something dangled from Kieran's fingers.

"You'll need these, Rory, to take the cailín home. As you've already scouted your way out, I'll leave these with you." He reached into his pocket and pulled out a crisp white business card. "Along with this. I hope you'll decide to stay in touch, Rior—Rory."

He reached for both keys and card, staring at the print for a few moments though the hesitant light made the words difficult to read. He glanced away with a tilt of his head and then cut his eyes back to other man. "Who was he?"

His question caught Kieran off guard. "Who?"

"This Riordan guy."

A momentary flicker of sadness touched Kieran's expression, and he gazed at something over Rory's shoulder for a long moment. The man cleared his throat before his gaze returned to focus on Rory. They stared at each other for several heartbeats. "My cousin. My brother. My best friend."

"What happened to him?" Rory thought he knew from eavesdropping, but he wanted the other man to say it to his face.

"He died. Automobile accident in Ireland."

Kieran's blue eyes bored into him. "Thirty-six years ago in April. And not a day goes by that I don't miss him. That I don't mourn him."

Rory's vision wavered for a moment. He saw a younger Kieran on a big red horse. And him on a gray. What the hell? He shook his head, fighting the double vision and forcing air into his lungs. What was happening to him? This was like some bad B movie. He didn't believe in reincarnation or any of that bullshit. But something about this man called to him—reached out to him like a long, lost friend. Like Kieran before him, he had to clear his throat to speak. "He must have been very special."

Kieran clapped him on the shoulder and smiled at Delaney standing behind him. "'Twas a pleasure to meet you both. Please don't be strangers." The corner of his mouth quirked in a wicked grin. "Not that my wife would be lettin' ya now." He turned and took two steps before he paused and glanced back, his eyes once more boring into Rory. "He is, Rory MacDermot."

With that cryptic parting, Kieran rejoined his wife and they disappeared into the crowd of revelers. Rory half turned and gathered Delaney under his arm. "Let's make a run for the border," he teased, and was pleased when she offered a wink and a conspiratorial grin.

He led her around the house, using the mini-maglite on his keychain to guide her over the flagstone path. When she stepped off the path and her high heel sank into the grass, he simply picked her up, despite her protestations. He ignored her futile thumps against his chest and stopped walking for a minute so he could kiss her into silence.

"Hush," he murmured against her lips. "This is

easier."

"Barbarian."

"Yeah. I am." He laughed and started walking again. "At least I'm not a caveman, otherwise you'd be thrown over my shoulder."

He managed to find his truck—not that it was all that hard to spot in the sea of sleek luxury cars—and deposited Delaney safely on the passenger's seat. Rory kissed her again for good measure and sprinted around to get behind the wheel. They'd made good their escape. While they waited for a break in traffic at the end of the drive, he turned to her. He didn't smile. He couldn't. He had to ask her one more time, and her answer had the power to kill him if he let it.

"You're wearing your cop face again. Why?" She reached over and smoothed her thumb between his brows, as if to ease the furrow there.

"Will you come home with me?"

Chapter 14

"You're afraid I'll say no."

There it was. A knot of fear tied around two little letters. N. O. No. The word had the power to take Rory's breath away. His tongue felt like sandpaper against the roof of his mouth and he couldn't work up enough spit to swallow. No words came. So he watched her, cop face in place, and said nothing.

Her hand smoothed the skin on his forehead before she cupped his cheek in her palm. "I've never been in charge before."

"You've always been in charge." The admission whispered across the distance between them.

Delaney tilted her head, a curious chickadee in search of a grain of truth to feed upon, and her hand dropped back to perch on her lap. "Why do I feel so out of control? So…reckless?"

"Don't you want to feel that way?"

She glanced away to stare out the windshield. "I don't know. I've…I've always been the responsible one. Mom and Dad are…old hippies. That's the nicest way I can describe them. And you've met Nessa and Keegan. I'm the one who got up and made my lunch. But as often as not, I was late to school because everyone else was in charge. I couldn't walk to school alone or I'd get in trouble. Then one day, I did it anyway. And nobody cared."

He shouldn't have been surprised, knowing her as he did, but he was anyway. "How old were you?"

"Six." Delaney cut her eyes to glance at him before returning her stare to the traffic zipping past them. "I might be the youngest, but I've always felt like the oldest. The responsible one. I wanted to go to school. And I wanted college, so I worked my way through. But even then, I wasn't in charge. I wasn't in control of things."

"Yes, you were, Doc. And you still are. You might not have felt like you were, but you've always been in charge. Being in control and being in charge are two different things, Delaney. You can be reckless and be in charge. All you have to do is let go."

"I…" He watched her breasts rise and fall as she inhaled deeply and sighed. "I can't let go. I'm too afraid."

Rory reached for her hand. Her skin felt cold and smooth, like satin, to his calloused fingertips. "I'll catch you."

She turned to face him again, her eyes shining with unshed tears that glistened in the headlights flashing past. He tugged her closer and met her halfway.

"I'll catch you." He reiterated the promise. "I'll always be there to catch you."

Her lashes shuttered her eyes, dark lace shadowing her cheeks as she ducked her chin. "Why do I get the feeling that you've always been there to catch me when I fall?"

Rory brushed his lips across her forehead. "I'll always keep you safe, Delaney."

"You always have."

"Will you come home with me?"

"Yes."

The knot in his gut unraveled and he kissed her again, slow and sweet and filled with promises. "Home," he agreed.

****

Delaney bathed in the pool of moonlight spilling across the floor of his bedroom. Rory's hands shook as he tugged on the zipper of her dress. His fingers brushed the straps off her shoulders, and the silky material skimmed her skin. She crossed her arms over her breasts, trapping the dress's bodice before it fell away. He circled her body with his arms, his hands cupping hers where they fisted against her shoulders, and he bent his head to kiss the nape of her neck. She sighed, her pleasure evident in the sound, and he smiled against her skin.

"I'll catch you."

She shivered at his words, but her fingers loosened on the material of her dress and it slipped away, caressing her body with silky touches. His palms itched to mimic the dress, but he kept them on her hands and continued to kiss her neck and shoulder.

"You are beautiful." The words hitched as he uttered them. He released her and tore at the buttons of his shirt, the studs pinging against furniture as he ripped them free. He wanted to be naked so his skin could relish the touch of hers. He needed to feel her skin sliding against his with a desire so fierce he was choked by it. Rory peeled off the starched tux shirt, forgetting the cuff links at his wrists.

Delaney turned at his muffled curse and smiled. "Here. Let me."

He held up an arm, helpless to do anything else.

She unhooked the link with deft fingers, and he obediently offered her his other wrist. Her palms traced his chest and abdomen. “Oh. My.” She sounded full of awe, and he puffed up like a high school kid on his first date. He managed the fly of his trousers without incident and kicked them off. The moonlight painted Delaney’s skin a delicate shade of creamy silver, and his erection strained within his briefs.

“I want you.” He whispered his need into the dark. “I want to back you against the wall. I want your legs around my waist as I drive into you over and over.” He pushed her hand down from his chest until her palm cupped him She gasped and his erection throbbed. “But I’ve wanted this for so long, I can wait.”

Delaney shuddered, and he sensed the raw emotion in the action. “I don’t want to wait.” The words dragged out of her mouth, teasing his skin with the moist heat of her breath.

“Shhhh. Let me do this for you, baby. Let me show you how much I want you, how much I need you.”

She nodded, mute but for another sighing breath. He smiled and carefully picked her up to carry her to the bed. He’d never been a lingerie man, but in her bustier, panties, and stockings, Delaney could turn him into a lingerie kind of guy. He settled her against the pillows at the head of the bed and stood, simply staring at her, devouring every inch of her body. His shaft throbbed again, and he laughed, the sound not much more than a brief gust of summer wind. “I’ve never been known as a patient man, baby, but God I want to take my time with you.”

Every inch of her skin flushed with pleasure. Delaney started to cover her breasts, but he grabbed her hands, staying the gesture.

"Don't. Please. I just want to look at you. So beautiful."

He ran one palm down her side and hip and traced the outside of her leg. He brushed his fingers between her legs, stopping just short of the moist heat at the top of her thighs. With reverent fingers, he unhooked her stockings. Rory lifted one leg and rolled her stockings down the length of it. He paused to kiss her inner thigh, behind her knee, along her calf, and finally her ankle as his hands revealed each bit of bare skin. Then he did the same with her other leg. He hid his smile as her hips squiggled against the bed.

Sitting beside her hip, he examined her bustier with eyes and fingers both. That ribbon there was just decoration. Tugging it would get him no closer to his goal. But that lacing and the hooks hidden beneath—those would lead to paradise. Rory dipped his head and kissed first one breast and then the other through the lacy cups. Her breath whispered across the top of his head and then hitched in her chest as she inhaled sharply. Pride swelled inside him. He made her do that. Not Connor. Not any other man. Him. He ripped his briefs off, one less barrier between them.

Impatience made his fingers fumble, but he managed to get the lacing undone and the delicate hooks and eyes separated. His hands shook slightly as he parted the bustier and got his first look at her. He glanced up to meet her worried gaze. "You are so beautiful, Delaney. I…I want to kiss you and touch you but first, I just want to look at you and…damn, darlin'." His admiration coated those last two words, thickening his voice.

Delaney offered a tentative smile, relief warring with pleasure in her expression. He dipped his head to kiss her lips—but only briefly. His lips trailed along her jaw, found soft skin and her pulse point. He left a lingering kiss there before following the arch of her throat so he could kiss his way across her collarbone. Her hands grabbed the coverlet on his bed, and she wrapped her fingers in the suede material as her chest swelled. Her nipples kissed his chest each time she inhaled, and he exhaled sharply as his shaft pulsed in time with her breaths.

He flicked his tongue over a nipple and Delaney moaned. She pressed her shoulders into the pillows and arched toward him. Rory smiled as he sucked her breast into his mouth. A perfect handful when he cupped the other in his palm. She moaned and her hips squirmed from side to side. His free hand roamed across her stomach and dove under the scrap of silk alleged to be her panties. Fingertips brushed through the soft curls at the vee of her thighs before one finger pushed between those lips and found her nub. She stiffened but he ignored her hesitancy and rubbed with gentle pressure. Delaney stiffened again, but this time, it was to push against him. His hand spread her thighs and, as his thumb continued to rub, his fingers sought the moist heat of her entrance. One finger dipped inside and then two. Her inner muscles clenched around him.

With swirling fingers, he pressed inside her before withdrawing over and over to set up a rhythm matched by the thrust of her hips. Rory suckled her breast, flicking his tongue in counterpoint to his thumb on her nub. Her hips arched off the bed and she gasped, her thighs shaking with tension.

"Come for me, baby. Just let go. I'll catch you." His words got lost against her creamy skin and the puckered nipple of her breast, but she obeyed him anyway. With a last frantic flutter of her inner muscles, her release coated his fingers. Hungry for her, he pounced, spreading her legs and settling between her thighs. With her knees over his shoulders, he could still tease and caress her breasts while his mouth devoured her core. His tongue replaced his finger, probing her channel as his teeth and lips teased her nub.

She let go of the coverlet and fastened her hands around his forearms, squeezing him with fierce need. "No…" The fervent denial trailed off.

"Yes." He blew the word against her and she shivered. "Again, baby. Come for me again."

He drove her higher and felt the growing tension in her muscles. He lapped at her, delved deep with his tongue, teasing her nipples and nub with his fingers and lips. And wound her up higher and higher. Tighter and tighter.

"No." She moaned the word. "Please. No. I want you inside me this time. Please. Oh, please."

Her whimpered plea stilled his hands and mouth. He raised his head, watching her. Delaney opened her eyes, closed them again as if the effort to look at him was too much. A deep breath made her breasts swell against his palms, and then she opened her eyes again.

"Kiss me."

Rory crawled up her body and braced on his hands and knees. Her inner thighs brushed against his, and he was struck by the way his wiry hair felt against her smooth skin. With infinite care, he lowered his head and his lips brushed across hers. His gaze never left her face. She watched him in return, her eyes dark with need. He broke off the kiss and hovered above her, stiff and anxious.

"I feel like I'm made of glass. Like I'll shatter if you touch me. Shatter if you don't..."

He stilled, holding his body away from the welcome hers promised. Waiting. As much as he wanted her, he would not take her until she surrendered, until she felt ready to accept him. He winced as her fingers wrapped around his shaft and Rory called on everything within him to stop a shudder before it wrecked him and he lost all control. Brittle. He knew exactly how she felt. Breathing shallowly through his nose, he waited in agony for her verdict.

"I'll catch you and put you back together again if you do." His promise was reckless. If she shattered, he would break. And then who would make them whole?

Delaney spread her thighs wider and guided the head of his erection toward the hot, moist welcome her body offered. As soon as his tip touched her sweet spot, he was almost lost.

"No," he said. Denying her was like being gutted. She whimpered as he pulled away from her.

He dragged open the drawer on the nightstand and grabbed a silver packet. Using his teeth, he ripped the package open with a savagery born of desire. He got the condom on despite his shaking hands and positioned his body between her thighs once more.

"I said I will always keep you safe," he promised. With one surge of his hips he thrust into her, sliding deeper and deeper as hot silk greeted and cocooned him. And when he was buried as deep as he could go, he froze. Afraid he'd lose it. Afraid he would shatter into a million pieces before he could fulfill his promise to her.

A little moan wrapped around her breath as she exhaled. And she lay quietly beneath him except for the jump of her pulse in the hollow of her throat. He buried his face there, kissing her and wanting to laugh and cry in the same moment. But he did neither. Instead, he slowly moved his hips, withdrawing his shaft until only the tip remained surrounded by her warmth. Slowly this time, he pushed back inside and smiled as her inner muscles greeted him with silken caresses. He pulled out again, and Delaney matched his actions, surging to meet him as he thrust inside her.

This dance between man and woman, as old as time itself, needed no lessons. Rory knew exactly what to do, where to touch, when to kiss, speed up, slow down, how to lead them in this exquisite communion of bodies and hearts. Delaney's arms circled him, her fingers clawing at his back and shoulders.

He drove her up and up, spiraling ever higher until neither of them could see or breathe, just feel. Lost in her passion, he surged into her time and again. And when she came in his arms, moaning and crying, her whole body shook with her orgasm. His body soon followed...his shaft throbbing and jetting his release into her tight, hot core.

Rory collapsed on top of her, panting and sweating, shudders racking his body as her inner muscles coaxed the last bit of life from his shaft. Delaney sniffled and he opened his eyes to find her face slick with tears. He kissed them away as her legs and arms held him cradled to her.

"Never," she gasped, panting to get her breath

back. “Never like that.”

His heart felt like it might burst. Pride. He was so damn proud he didn’t care he grinned like an idiot. He kissed her forehead. “No,” he agreed. “Never like that.”

Chapter 15

Rain. Huge splattering drops that did nothing to wipe away the fog. He'd left the warm bed of sweet Alice why? Duty. The headlamps on the big Land Rover did little to pierce the roiling mist. The engine growled as he down-shifted the gearbox to take a climbing turn out of the valley. Barely illuminated gaunt figures lined the road. Trees. Not giants. He chuckled at his own imagination. 'Twas a spooky night and he wouldn't be at all surprised to find the Wild Hunt riding the road with him.

He thought of the drowsy woman he'd left in a warm bed. A few pints at the pub could make any woman warm and willin' but Alice was a beauty. He'd bedded her time and again when he was in camp. She worked the bar at his favorite pub in Kildare and always greeted him with a hug and a kiss. He'd met his mates and they'd watched the football game on the telly hanging above the bar and he'd walked Alice home after.

But duty called, so he'd left her snug asleep, with tousled hair and well-kissed lips, to make the drive to Curragh Camp and a day of training the new recruits. 'Twouldn't do for the OIC t'be late. He'd be glad when Kieran returned to duty and took his job back. He had no desire to be Officer in Charge a day longer than necessary.

The road leveled out but fog collected in patches. The air'd be clear and a moment later, the sturdy SUV would plunge into a swirling world of white. Vertigo teased his senses despite his best efforts and he gripped the steering wheel until his knuckles turned white.

"Silly bugger." He flexed his fingers and reached for the radio. He punched a few buttons searching for a station and he caught the strains of U2's newest single. He glanced up just in time to see a large dog standing in the center of the road. Reflexes took over. He jerked the wheel even as his feet pumped brake and clutch as he down-shifted. The rear of the Rover skidded on the wet pavement, hit gravel, and dipped into the drainage ditch beside the road. Off-balance, the vehicle's front end flipped up. The damned thing was going to roll. All he could do was brace. His stomach turned as metal scraped against the roadway. Sparks shot across his vision. And then the force of the accident tossed the Rover end over end. Someone screamed. That couldn't possibly be his voice, but the sound bruised his ears. Even though the screams were in his head. His world turned black.

Searing, crushing pain.

Something warm dripped into his eyes. Something smelling of salt and copper. Blood. His.

A voice. One that sounded like the sea colliding with the boulders strewing the shore at the Giant's Causeway.

Dark. Pain. Blood. His world narrowed to those. Fight. He had to fight.

For a long, terrifying moment, Rory couldn't move. Couldn't breathe. Couldn't see. Paralyzed but for the pounding thud of his heart and the surge of bile clawing its way up from his gut. *Breathe.* He ordered his lungs to expand. Air filled them and then he exhaled slowly. His fingers tingled and then one foot jerked. Feeling returned. Covered in sweat, he willed his body to function.

Delaney had turned away from him, sleeping on her side, the peaceful sounds of her breathing and her warmth an anchor. When he felt capable of moving, he slipped out of bed, hesitant to disturb her. He wanted to gather her in his arms, to hold her against his fevered skin and let her touch and voice soothe him. But how would he explain the nightmare? If that's what it was. So real. Like he'd been in that vehicle. He brushed his fingers across his face expecting to see them covered in blood. They weren't.

Snagging a pair of gym shorts, he crept to the French doors opening to the balcony off his bedroom. He glanced over his shoulder as Delaney stirred. She'd simply rolled over and nestled into the warm spot he'd left behind. His hand shook as he reached for the door handle. *Breathe.* Why did he have to keep reminding himself to do that? He sucked in a deep lungful of air. Exhaled. Drank in another. His thudding heart eased, slowed, and his fingers tingled again with the last vestiges of adrenaline in his system. He stretched out his right hand. Rock steady now. Rory grasped the handle and flipped it down. With a soft click and a little creak, the door opened.

He stepped outside, and shivered as the night wind kissed his heated skin, drying the sweat enough to leave him chilled. He stared at the moon as it inched toward the western horizon, watching as clouds skittered across its full face.

"What the hell." This was no question to the universe. This was a demand, albeit a whispered one. Rory rubbed one hand across his head, his short hair barely ruffled by the action.

He jumped when two arms slipped around his waist. Delaney. "I'm sorry."

"For what?"

"For waking you."

"Nightmare?" She laid her cheek against his back and tightened her arms in a gentle hug.

"No. Yes. I'm not sure what it was." He rubbed his palms along her arms and hands where they clasped him, finding solace in the motion. She'd found his tux shirt and put it on, but hadn't buttoned it.

"About the shooting?"

"No." He felt her stiffen slightly. "No, Doc. I don't dream about that. If I want to replay that day, all I have to do is close my eyes. I only dwell on it for training purposes. I know what I did. I know what happened. I'm at peace with it."

"Then what?"

Rory tried, but the shudder escaped before he could clamp down on his muscles. Delaney felt it, too, so there was no hiding his reaction. "What is it called when you know you are dreaming but you feel like you're part of the action, that you're there, and you can't stop the dream, can't change what's happening?"

"Lucid dreaming?"

"Yeah. Something like that."

"Will you tell me?"

"There's not much to tell, Doc."

"Something upset you."

Breathe. He inhaled again. Why was it so hard to

remember to do that? And why was he so cold now? Delaney's warmth pressed against his back seemed like the only thing keeping him grounded.

"Just a dream, Doc. That's all."

"Rory."

Breathe. He opened his mouth to inhale but words rushed out, tumbling over each other. He told her about the dream—nightmare—whatever the hell it was. His voice didn't sound like his, not to his ears. It carried a lilt that was foreign, a turn of phrase that wasn't his. And in the dream, he'd been someone else. But not. He'd been himself as well. He finished and the silence stifled him. *Breathe.*

Delaney said nothing, but she continued to hug him. His muscles ached from holding so stiff, but his lungs seemed to be working a little easier. The sky to the east lightened. Dawn wouldn't be far away now. He'd often wondered why Man was so afraid of the dark. Darkness had always been an ally. He no longer questioned. He knew the answer. Things lurked in the dark—thoughts, emotions, fears. But that was good, his knowing this. Now he could face them. Conquer them. And survive.

Loosening her arms with a careful tug, Rory turned to face her. He cupped her face in his hands and dipped his head to taste her lips. "Thanks." He whispered the word but she heard him.

Delaney smiled, moonlight teasing her features and creating lights in her eyes that made her look mysterious and otherworldly. "I don't think I can get back to sleep…" Her expression left no doubts as to her intentions.

He swept her up into his arms in a princess carry

and kissed the tip of her nose. “Good, because I’m definitely a morning kind of guy.”

She giggled, dropped an arm, and brushed her fingertips across his growing erection. He stumbled and she squealed. With both arms wrapped around his neck she chided him with a breathless kiss. “You did that on purpose.”

Rory dropped her on the bed and pounced, burrowing his hips between her thighs. He flicked the plackets of the shirt she wore open and inhaled deeply. “So beautiful, Doc. I could look at you for hours.”

She arched her hips and rubbed slowly against his hard shaft. “I am not a patient woman, Rory MacDermot. You should remember that.”

He chuckled, the sound almost a growl rumbling low in his chest. “Yes, ma’am. I’ll remember that, ma’am. Anything else I should know?”

Her expression turned wicked as she reached for him. “Shut up, Rory, and make love to me.”

Chapter 16

Despite an afternoon at the combat range shooting the hell out of pretend bad guys, Rory still felt restless. He snagged a bottled Guinness from the fridge, popped the top and poured the beverage into a glass. He favored the dark body and rich foamy head of the Irish beer over American and other imports. Outside his condo, heat waves shimmered on the parking lot pavement. He considered heading to the community pool for some laps—for about a minute. Instead, he headed for the shaded patio at the rear of his place.

Rory dropped into one of the comfortable chairs and propped his feet on a matching ottoman. Bees buzzed in the honeysuckle vine one neighbor had planted while the cat belonging to the neighbor on the other side sat atop the privacy fence steadily ignoring the human intruder. He and the damn cat had a love-hate relationship. Very much a dog person, Rory missed having one around but his lifestyle and schedule precluded pet ownership. If he ever got a dog, though, he wanted a big one. Like a German shepherd or… He thought about it as he sipped his beer. An Irish wolfhound. They were huge but not bulky. Graceful. Loyal. Independent. Yeah, he liked that idea. He finished his beer and once again contemplated a swim.

Ten minutes later, Rory launched from the side of the pool. He knifed into the cold water and surfaced, blinded for a moment by the hair hanging in his eyes. Treading water, he shook his head and almost put out an eye as long locks whipped across his face.

"What the hell…" He brushed the hair back and wiped water off his face. Blinking, he glanced around and swallowed a mouthful of water in surprise. This wasn't his pool. This was a river. With a current. And banks with trees and rolling hills beyond.

"HELP!"

He knew that voice. Delaney! He kicked hard and used his arms to turn in a circle. There. A splash. And a hand thrusting out of the water. With sure strokes, he swam over to her and grabbed for her hand. He missed as she sank beneath the surface. Before he could react, she disappeared. He sucked in a deep breath and dove after her. The water, cold and dark, blinded him and sucked the strength from his muscles. Out of air, he kicked to the surface and gulped air before diving again. A shaft of sunlight highlighted a dark shadow off to his left, toward the middle of the river where the current was strongest. He swam hard. Delaney. He grabbed her arm but almost lost his grip as the current sucked at her body. She wore long skirts and they dragged her deeper. He reeled her into his body, turned her so that he held her back against his chest, and kicked with his legs until their heads broke the surface.

Rory realized she wasn't breathing and he panicked. Figures waved from the shoreline as he towed Delaney toward them. A part of his brain acknowledged the arrival of a group of horsemen. Two of them leaped to the ground and waded out to help him. The biggest of the two, a bear of a man with dark blond hair and massive hands, swooped in to pick up

Delaney. He fought the man for possession until the second man touched his shoulder.

"Riordan! Let loose. Niall's trying to help. C'mon, man. Cease."

"My name isn't—"

"Ciaran, hurry!"

He realized a woman rode with the men. He stared at them all as he waded out of the river and stumbled to the bank where the big man laid Delaney in the grass. Five teens stood off to the side looking worried while the adults gathered around the still body. Rory pushed them away and dropped to his knees beside her.

He rolled Delaney to her side and thumped his hand between her shoulder blades. Water dribbled from her mouth but no inhalations followed. He placed her on her back, checked her pulse and started chest compressions when he found none. He paused to start rescue breathing but was stopped by Becca, Connor's mother…no, not Connor. This wasn't Connor of the three-piece-slick-lawyer suit. This was a teenager wearing homespun trousers and rustic shirt. Conor. This boy's name was Conor. Somehow, his brain sorted out the difference.

Rory stared at the woman, knowing her somehow. Her face wavered, like a badly tuned television, two faces not quite lining up—the ghost of a ghost. She stared back. He recognized surprise in her expression—surprise that he'd know CPR, and then he saw the dawning realization in her eyes. She knew. She knew he didn't belong here, that he wasn't Riordan. Still other memories overlaid his own—but the new memories felt like…his.

"Out of time." The words were out of his mouth

before he could define their meaning.

She nodded, bending to begin mouth-to-mouth resuscitation on Delaney.

Rory continued chest compressions, almost on autopilot as his brain chewed over events. Out of time. Those afraid of Becca had whispered that. A woman out of time. A woman sent back by the fae to marry their beloved clann chief. Ciaran. His cousin. As close as any brother.

"One, two, three, four, five." He counted the beats. He'd seen Manannán mac Lir take Becca away on that fateful *Lughnasadh* night, seen Finvarra and Onagh of the fae court arrive and gift Ciaran with the MacDermot Knot. And he'd watched his cousin fade away, willing himself to die in order to join Becca in Tir Nan Óg. He'd sworn never to love a woman that much, even as he celebrated Becca's return on *Samhain*.

And then the O'Neill raided the small O'Beirne keep. And he'd rescued a little girl. Delaney. He'd waited for her to grow up, despaired as she loved Conor, and knew in his heart that he was never meant to be the man of her heart.

"One, two, three, four, five."

"Riordan. Cease, man. She's gone." Ciaran's hand rested heavily on his shoulder, fingers digging in to pull him away from the lifeless girl.

"No." He continued the count in his head. The water was cold. He'd read about drowning victims coming back because the water had been so cold. Mammalian Dive Response. That was it. How could his brain be so clear when his body felt so numb? "One, two, three, four, five."

Someone sobbed and moaned. Bronwen. Delaney's

friend. The others exchanged guilty looks. “What did you do?” he demanded even as he kept up the count in his head and pressed rhythmically against Delaney’s unresponsive chest.

Neasa dug her toes in the grass and refused to look at anyone. The twins, Ciara and Conor, glanced at their father and then bowed their heads. Keegan looked uncomfortable before his gaze slid to his older sister. And Bronwen continued to cry.

“Ciara?” Becca’s voice brooked no argument. “Answer Riordan’s question.”

“’Twas only a prank, Mama. We meant nothing by it.”

“Conor?” Ciaran growled his son’s name.

“Delaney is such a scaredy-cat.” He sounded sullen and wouldn’t meet his father’s glare. “As Ciara said, we meant no harm.”

“They grabbed her and threw her in the river, and her screamin’ the whole time.” Bronwen spit out the accusation between her sobs. “Neasa pulled my hair when I tried t’help. An’ then Riordan came. He jumped right in t’save her.” Big, fat tears rolled down her cheeks. “Is she dead?”

The other four teens looked horrified as the implications of their actions sank in. Ciaran’s hand shook where it still gripped Rory’s shoulder.

“’Twas an accident, Uncle Ciaran.” Neasa’s chin rose stubbornly as she faced the adults. “If she’d learned t’swim she’d have been fine. But she was too scared t’get her feet wet.”

A mournful dirge, played on the pipes, wafted on the breeze. Abhean. Rory knew the fae was near. The damn fae had a habit of showing up when least expected and never wanted. He gathered Delaney's lifeless body in his arms and stood. Throwing back his head, he roared the fae's name. The music died. He didn't see the look Ciaran and Becca exchanged behind his back.

"What do you, cousin?"

"What I must. ABHEAN! Show yourself, faerie."

Not far away, the air shimmered and a form appeared. The girls gasped and then sighed. The being who stood there radiated beauty. A playful wind teased his long, blond hair and he looked nothing if not amused. With all the arrogance of his kind, the fae harper strode forward. "Beware what you demand, mortal."

"Bring her back."

"I cannot. Only mac Lir has that power."

"Then summon him."

The fae threw back his head and laughed. "You know not what you ask, mortal fool." He shifted the bag pipe he held and squeezed the bag under his arm, his slender fingers dancing over the holes on the chanter.

"I know exactly what I ask."

"What conceit yee MacDermots enjoy." The fae's gaze rested on Ciaran and Becca. "'Twas not enough to get the *Taoiseach*'s mate back?"

Color rose to tinge Becca's cheeks. "I'd not be casting aspersions, Abhean. Has Manannán forgiven you yet for telling me the secret?" That wasn't embarrassment painting her pink, but anger, and Rory tried not to smirk. Becca backed down from no one.

The harper pursed his lips and the color in his eyes swirled. "Come then, Riordan MacDermot. Let us strike a bargain." He turned on his heel and walked away.

Still holding the lifeless girl, Rory followed. His chest tightened, as if iron bands bound him round and round, and he couldn't draw a deep breath.

Out of earshot of the others, Abhean stopped but didn't turn. "What is it you wish, mortal?"

"Bring her back."

"What do you give in return?"

Rory stared at the fae's back, trying to breathe as his thoughts tumbled. He stared down at Delaney's face. "What do you ask for?"

"Do you know who she is?"

"We don't have time for twenty questions."

"Answer me, Riordan MacDermot. Do you know her?"

"In my time in the future, she's the woman I want to love."

The fae turned and the kaleidoscopes in his eyes slowed. "Time keeps you apart life after life, mortal. And always will if she never recognizes you for what you are. Do not allow her to make you the fool. Let her life pass now so time catches up."

"She's done nothing to deserve death."

"She was born mortal. As are you all. Death comes to each of you in its time. This is her time."

"I don't believe that. I think this is some game you and Manannán continue to play."

"A bargain must be struck, Riordan MacDermot, if she is to stay."

"I ask again, Abhean, what do you want?"

"Your life, mortal. At a time of my choosing."

Rory didn't even take the time to breathe before he answered. "Yes. Bring her back and take me."

The fae laughed again, the sound bending the

leaves of grass around him and rattling the leaves of the nearby trees. "You wish it so, mortal. But this time is not my choosing. You must watch her pine for another until she realizes what she has lost. Time after time."

Lightning danced overhead and thunder reverberated. A jagged bolt split the air and when the ensuing sparkles stopped dancing like glitter in Rory's vision, an imposing figure towered over him and the fae harper. Manannán mac Lir, the King of Tir nan Óg himself.

"What havoc have you wreaked, harper?" Thunder echoed in the fae's words.

"I simply return a life taken before its time, my king."

The king regarded Rory with eyes the color of a sunlit sea, unblinking, unemotional and he fought the urge to blink under the other's scrutiny. Standing his ground, Rory met Manannán's gaze.

"You know the consequence of your actions this day, Riordan MacDermot?" Where Abhean's voice reminded him of spun sugar, Manannán's voice roared like waves crashing on boulders.

"So long as Delaney lives, it doesn't matter."

The two fae watched him silently for long moments. "Every action matters, Riordan." Manannán's voice rumbled like far-off thunder now.

"As long as Delaney lives, I'll deal with the rest." Rory listened to the thud of his heartbeat even as he wondered at the sadness on Manannán's face.

"So be it, mortal." The King of Tir nan Óg clapped his hands.

When Rory could see again, he stood alone holding Delaney.

Ciaran appeared beside him. “What have you done, Riordan?”

Delaney stirred and the other man gasped. “What I had to do.” Rory’s voice sounded hollow in his own ears.

“Yee’ve made a deal with the dark, cousin.”

The girl opened her eyes and stared up at him. He offered her a smile before he glanced at Ciaran. “And so I have.”

****

Rory braced his feet on the bottom of the pool and pushed off. He broke the water’s surface and knifed upward like a dolphin. What the hell? He spit out a mouthful of water and with sure strokes swam to the edge of the pool. Palms flat on the rock surround, he hoisted his body from the water. Two women he didn’t recognize occupied loungers nearby and they both admired him openly over the tops of their designer sunglasses. He ignored them. Snatching his towel, he strode away from the pool, headed back to his condo.

Inside, he grabbed another beer from the fridge. As the door closed, he saw the white business card stuck to the door with a Bugs Bunny magnet. Kieran. A lump settled in the pit of his stomach. If he called, what would the man tell him? Hell, what would he say to Kieran? Maybe the Doc was right and he was more screwed up than he thought. He’d never had any doubt about his job, his abilities, or his sanity. Never. Not until Delaney Burns walked into his life. Not until memories of other places—other times—left him sleepless and pacing the floor every night. He stared at the card until the name and phone number branded his retinas. He’d shower first. Put on some clothes. And then he'd decide what to do.

****

Rory occupied his favorite booth in the rear of Celtic Crossroads. He'd gravitated to the pub soon after it opened and was a fixture now, it seemed. He arrived early and the foamy draft Guinness appeared even as he settled into the booth. From this vantage point he could see the front doors and windows, the cash register, the bar, and the shadowed hallway leading to the restrooms and rear exit. He couldn't see into the kitchens unless someone went through the swinging doors next to the bar. Situational awareness—his stock in trade.

The bell above the door clanged. The bartender glanced over to the newcomer and shouted his standard welcome. "Have a seat anywhere. If yer in a hurry, order at the bar. Otherwise, a waitress will be around in a bit."

Kieran MacDermot paused just inside the door but he'd taken a step to one side so he wasn't silhouetted in the entryway. He nodded to the bartender, his gaze roaming the room, sliding over Rory until he'd fully assessed the place. "I'll have a Guinness to that table in the back, then."

The bartender's expression lit up at the sound of Kieran's voice and anyone could read his thoughts. *A true Irishman. In my pub.* "Aye, sir. Comin' right up."

He dropped onto the bench opposite Rory and leaned back into the corner. Rory took his time assessing the man, taking an occasional sip of his beer.

"Rory."

"Mr. MacDermot."

"Nay, Rory. You know your tongue trips over calling me that. Kieran, please. I think we're beyond the formalities here." He leaned back, one arm resting along the back of the booth bench. Kieran MacDermot might be in his sixties but he was still a warrior—would always be a warrior.

Just like him. Rory knew that with a certainty that left him shaken. He acknowledged the other man's words with a brief dip of his chin. Equals. But not quite. He might be a leader in his own right but Rory knew with certainty that he would follow Kieran into battle without hesitation.

Kieran's beer appeared, delivered by the bartender himself. "I hope all is to yer satisfaction, sir?" He bobbed and fidgeted, obviously not going away until something was said.

"'Tis bang on. Thank you."

The bartender backed away, still bobbing his head in supplication. Rory choked back his snicker. "Do you always have that effect on people?"

Kieran rolled his eyes and settled deeper into the shadows of the booth. "'Tis a curse I'm destined t'bear."

Rory let the snicker escape. "And no ego either."

"None."

They both laughed and it was as if a breath of fresh air swept through the room, clearing it of smoke and fog. He knew he should but Rory didn't want to examine the easy camaraderie too closely. Sitting here with Kieran, even drinking in silence felt…right. Something eased in his chest. Maybe he could talk to Kieran. Maybe. Eventually.

"I'm glad Delaney chose to bring you to the party, Rory."

"Are you?"

"I am, yes. And while you might not think so, you are a member of Clann MacDermot. You always have been."

Rory didn't react to the other man's words. They seemed laden with hidden meanings he didn't want to explore. Not yet anyway. "Connor told me you were on some sort of mission to find missing cousins."

"Aye. I was." Kieran sipped his beer, watching Rory for a reaction. A rueful smile appeared on his face. "Delaney is right. You do give good cop face."

He hoped the negligent lift of one shoulder conveyed his feelings well enough—at least the feelings he wanted Kieran to see. Inside, emotions roiled and churned until he almost couldn't breathe again.

Now Kieran's smile looked almost sad. "You've questions, Rory. I'll answer what I can. Truthfully. And tell you my suppositions when I'm not sure of the truth."

"I don't believe in reincarnation." There. He'd said it.

"I'm not surprised."

Rory waited, to see if Kieran would add anything. He didn't. "There's no such thing as karma."

"Not in the sense most people believe."

"For a man who offered the truth, you aren't saying much."

"I'll answer your questions, Rory. But until I know what they are, I can't offer you the truth. What's happened?"

He laughed, a short bark of harsh sound that held no mirth. "What hasn't?"

Leaning forward, Kieran's face moved from

shadow into the flickering glow of the faux gas lamp lighting the booth. His features wavered, short hair becoming long, blue-black shadow beard defining his rugged jaw, the sharp eyes of a hunter peering at him, before Kieran's face settled back into its normal demeanor. He watched Rory with a knowing expression. "I see."

"What do you see, Kieran? What the hell is going on?"

"Abhean."

"What about him?"

"You know him?" Kieran answered Rory's question with a question.

"No."

"But you know the name."

Rory glanced away, taking a moment to get his cop face back in place. "Who is he?"

"You know, Rory. Deep down. But what do you remember?"

"You still want to call me Riordan."

"I do, yes."

"Abhean doesn't exist."

Kieran laughed, also without mirth. "We both wish that was the truth but it isn't. He exists, though he's been quiet these thirty years past. I suspect he had other lives to muck up." He blinked slowly, studying Rory, his expression still sad. "I've missed you, odd as it sounds."

"It was a dog."

Kieran looked confused.

"In the road. That night."

"You remember?"

"Sort of. I had a dream. Doc called it lucid

dreaming. Sure felt real. So did the blackout I had while swimming."

Now the other man looked concerned. He leaned forward, his forearms bracing on the table, his beer long since forgotten. "You blacked out in a pool?"

"Sort of." Rory felt odd explaining all this but he forged ahead in hopes Kieran could help him make sense of things. "I dove in, and when I surfaced I was…" He closed his eyes and rubbed his forehead. "I was someplace else. Some…when else."

"Ah. Up to his usual tricks then. Where and when did Abhean fling you? And I have t'say, you're damned lucky he let you come back." Kieran's accent thickened as his emotions swelled.

"No idea, really. As to the where, probably Ireland though no clue to the when. You were there. And Becca. The kids." His heart tripped as he remembered those heart-stopping moments when he held a lifeless Delaney in his arms. "Delaney. She…uhm…she drowned. The kids teased her, threw her in the river. She couldn't swim."

"Aye, and that'll explain a lot of things."

"Abhean was there. I summoned him." He raised his eyes and his gaze collided with Kieran's. "I made a bargain."

"Foolishly."

"Maybe."

"Will y'tell me the bargain?"

He shifted his gaze to the front and watched shadow figures pass outside the pub, their shapes obscured by the frosted glass. "My life." He breathed. "For hers."

Chapter 17

The conversation with Kieran went downhill after his admission. They'd parted soon after, with the other man promising to stay in touch. Oddly comforted by that, Rory at least knew he wasn't crazy. He'd been seriously worried about that the past few weeks. The hairs prickled on the back of his neck, as if someone watched him. With the wall to his back, he had the whole pub laid out in front of him. No one could get the drop on him but the feeling persisted. Part of him wanted to call Doc. Talk to her at least, if he couldn't hold her in his arms. His shaft hardened just thinking about her. He backed off. No woman had ever affected him like that. Why this one?

"D'uh." He almost pulled the literal action of banging his forehead on the table. Soul mates? Really? Suspicious now, he shoved thoughts of Delaney to the rear of his memory. Maybe he'd call Hoss, meet the big guy at the gym for some sparing. A good hard workout. That's what he needed. And a cold shower.

****

Several hours later, his hands were stiff and sore from working over the heavy bag. Rory danced on his toes, still restless and unsettled. His muscles ached but not from the workout. Delaney. He wanted her near. No, he needed her near. Where he could see her. Smell her. Touch her. Hear her laughter. Kiss her lips and fit his body into hers. Lost in the sensations, he didn't hear the stealthy footsteps, didn't sense the man creeping up behind him until too late. Two hands planted in the middle of his back and shoved him up against the lockers.

"What the hell?"

"You think you're so damned good, MacDermot. You aren't shit compared to me. I just got the drop on you."

New Boy. "What do you want, Carter?"

"I want your damned job, MacDermot. I want everyone to know what an asshole you are. I want you on suspension instead of me."

Breathe. "You'll never be as good as me, New Boy."

"Wanna bet?"

Footsteps. Someone else was in the gym. Question became was it a friend of his or a friend of Carter's? Rory could take more than one, even tired and sweaty from his workout. His training kicked in and the OODA loop played in his head. Observe. Orient. Decide. Act. He planned out his moves. Relax. Drop. Turn. Shoulder to gut. Drive Carter over the low bench running down the center of the locker room. A pretty boy, Carter on the defensive would protect his face. You didn't go for the face in a fight. You went for the gut. And lower. You fought to win. Didn't matter if the win was dirty or clean so long as you won. Rory almost hoped Carter had reinforcements. He was spoiling for a fight. Beating the crap out of a heavy bag wasn't near as satisfying as the sound of flesh meeting flesh.

"I'm gonna make you pay, MacDermot."

He laughed. "How? By talking me to death?"

Carter's fist twisted in Rory's tee shirt. There. That's what he'd been waiting for. He relaxed, let his knees collapse. The move caught New Boy off balance and his face slammed into the locker over Rory's left shoulder. Twisting, he squirmed out of the tee shirt and drove his shoulder into Carter's solar plexus. The oomph of exhaled air was exactly the sound he wanted to hear. He wrapped the other man up in a bear hug and pushed him backward toward the bench. Once on the ground, he'd be able to handle Carter. Anger fueled recklessness and recklessness could be used to advantage when you kept your cool, stayed in control.

The force of Carter's legs hitting the bench sent the two of them over and to the floor on the other side. Rory rolled and came up on top. He straddled the other man's chest and scrabbled to grab Carter's flailing fists. He really wanted to beat the guy until he was bloody but didn't. Cool. Calm. Collected. He was in charge. Carter forgot everything. Everything but his anger at Rory. The guy screamed and cursed, spitting at him. He simply kept his mouth shut, squinted, and squeezed his thighs tighter around Carter's chest. He snagged one wrist and hung on. Grabbed the other and wished he'd had time to grab a set of cuffs from his locker.

"Ahem."

Rory looked up at the polite cough. Captain Davis. How long had he been standing there?

"Good to see your training is up-to-date, MacDermot."

"Yessir."

"Nice reversal there. I thought he had you for a minute."

"Thank you, sir, but no way was that going to

happen."

Davis raised his right hand to shoulder level and waved it forward from the wrist. Three uniformed officers appeared from behind him. One each grabbed Carter's arms and Rory slid off, rising to his feet in a quick upward surge. He backed away to let the three uniforms finish subduing Carter. They handcuffed him and marched him out. Carter didn't say a word, but the stare he offered Rory promised things weren't over between them.

Davis said nothing until the others cleared out. He favored Rory with a long look. "If Dr. Burns hadn't signed off on your release already, I would have after witnessing this little altercation."

Rory laughed, a sharp bark of sound. "Little altercation, sir?" He didn't hide the sarcasm.

"You kept it small, MacDermot. You handled him with the full intent to control the situation and not let it escalate. Another man with the same history attacked like you were? The outcome could have been far different. Carter will be discharged, pending a hearing. It could easily have been both of you up on charges."

How did someone reply to that? Rory simply kept his mouth shut but nodded, one brief, emphatic dip of his head.

"Get a shower, MacDermot and come to my office."

"Yessir."

****

Delaney stared at her best friend. Bronwyn had been avoiding her for weeks now but she'd finally tracked the other woman down and dragged her to lunch. Bronnie refused to look at her.

"What's wrong? Have I upset you?"

Bronwyn's eyes filled with tears. "You upset me? Oh, Laney!" She wailed Delaney's name, turning the last syllable into at least twenty undulations—a vibrato any opera singer would be proud of. "I figured you hated me."

She wondered what it was about the long "e" sound that made it so ripe for bawling modulation? Doing her best not to wince, she shushed her friend. "Bronnie. Listen to me. Shhhh. It's okay. Why would I hate you?"

"Because I introduced you to Mr. Scumbag of the Year." She sniffled and swiped at her nose with her napkin. "I can't believe he turned out to be such a total jerk. I thought you two were perfect for each other." Her face screwed up and she was about to utter another wail.

"Bronwyn, hush! Seriously. People are staring." Delaney glanced around the restaurant furtively. "I'm not mad at you, okay?"

More sniffles and a hiccup later, Bronwyn heaved a deep breath. "Thank you. I really thought you'd hate me forever. I know how you feel…felt about him. And he was perfect."

Delaney shook her head. "No. He wasn't perfect. At least not for me. Nessa? Yeah. They deserve each other. But he wasn't perfect for me." She touched her mouth self-consciously, remembering the touch of Rory's lips on hers. "No, he definitely wasn't perfect for me."

Bronwyn added a second huge sigh and then gulped her appletini. She waved toward their waitress, holding up the glass in a silent order. "Well…good then. I guess."

"Yes, hon. Very good." She glanced around again to make sure people's attention had reverted elsewhere. "Want to know something really weird?"

Bronwyn's eyes widened and she leaned forward with a conspiratorial whisper. "Well, d'uh. What?"

The waitress appeared and Delaney held her thoughts until she'd delivered Bronwyn's drink and disappeared with the empty glass.

"What?" Bronwyn demanded again.

Delaney leaned forward, too, adding to the feeling of secrecy. "I think Connor and I were supposed to meet. But not so we'd be together."

"What? What does that mean?"

"Shhh. Keep your voice down. I mean, I think Connor and Nessa were meant to meet and be together. And they wouldn't have if you hadn't introduced me to Connor. But it's okay because…well…"

Bronwyn's eyes widened and she clapped her hand over her mouth. She hissed around her fingers, "Who? Who have you met?"

Delaney checked for eavesdropping ears once more. "Rory."

"YES!" Bronwyn jumped up and fist-pumped. "I knew it! Details, girl. I want the details."

Cheeks flaming with embarrassment, she admonished her friend. "Bronnie, please! Shush." Delaney waited until Bronwyn sank back into her chair, even though the girl continued to bounce in excitement. Inhaling to steady her nerves, she continued. "Rory took me to the engagement party."

"He did? I bet he totally rocks a tuxedo."

She grinned and glanced down, heat still radiating from her face. "He absolutely rocks a tux. I thought the evening would be a total bust and second guessed myself the whole time. At least until we met Connor's parents." She leaned forward and dropped her voice to a whisper. "That's what was weird, Bronnie. Connor's father? It's like he and Rory were long lost friends. I know they'd never met before, and Kieran is old enough to be Rory's father. Even so, they acted much more like peers than say…Connor and Rory. And I know there's only a year or two difference in their ages."

"Bizarro."

"Exactly! At the dinner? Kieran insisted that Rory sit next to him. The caterers completely rearranged the head table to accommodate him."

"Dude!"

"I know, right? And they talked all through dinner."

Bronwyn hummed the theme from the *Twilight Zone*. "What did they talk about?"

"All sorts of stuff. Guns. The military. Kieran. MacDermot was in the Irish Army—some sort of special ranger or something. And Rory was a Marine before he joined the police department." Delaney leaned back in her chair. "But it was more than that. I don't really know how to explain it."

Bronwyn offered a crooked grin. "Sort of like us? I mean, we were like BFFs five minutes after we met in Mrs. Nigh's second grade class. Right?"

She chuckled. "Right. We were. I think it might have been something like that, though I'm not sure men connect that way. Bronnie? May I ask you something really off the wall?"

"Sure, hon. Always. Best friends forever, right?

You can ask me anything."

"Do you believe in reincarnation?"

The other woman gulped her appletini and sputtered. "Really? You're asking me this? Miss Queen of New Age Tarot-reading SCA Costume Role-playing me? Seriously?"

Delaney giggled. "I forget you dress up and play wench at the Renaissance Faire."

"I swear I was a witch or fortune teller or something in a former life." Bronwyn waggled her finger. "Don't laugh at me. I'm serious. There are times during faire season that I'm way more comfortable there, talking to knights and knaves, than I am stuck in traffic on my way to work."

"I'm not laughing at you, Bronnie. Promise. I just can't believe I forgot. You know the feeling then. I have another weird question for you." At her friend's encouraging nod, Delaney continued. "Have you ever had a dream…or a daydream you thought was real? Thought you'd actually lived and done that action before?"

Bronwyn tilted her head. "Not sure what you mean, babe."

Delaney sighed as she worked up her courage. "Here lately, some things have happened. Sort of."

"What sort of things have sort of happened?"

"Dreams. Sometimes lucid dreams where I'm transported somewhere else."

"What? Like Kansas, Dorothy?"

She shook her head. "No. And I'm being serious, Bronnie. It's happened a couple of times. I'll be somewhere…normal and the next thing I know, it's like I'm tumbling through space and when I open my eyes,

I'm someplace else. Like in the past someplace else. And I'm me…but not."

"Whoa-ah. Dudette. Out of body astral projection time! That's too cool. I've always wanted to be able to do that but I've never been able to."

"I don't do it on purpose, Bronnie! It just happens. And it's freaky. Really freaky. I can't tell anyone but you."

"Why not?"

"Because people will think I'm crazy."

Best friend or not, Bronwyn glared at her. "Oh? So I'm crazy, too, and therefore that makes you the sane one."

Sighing, Delaney reached over and patted Bronnie's arm. "That's not what I meant and you know it. You're the only one who might come close to understanding what's happening to me. Bronwyn, I'm seriously scared of what's been happening."

"Déjà vu all over again, right? Maybe you've found a worm hole or something and you're doing some temporal displacement."

"I'm pretty sure wormholes only exist in space, not here on Earth. And it's not so much déjà vu as it is…I don't know." She twisted her napkin in her hands.

"Okay, so tell me about the first time it happened. Where were you? Where did you go? And what happened while you were there?"

The waitress appeared with their food, giving Delaney a few moments to marshal her thoughts. When was the first time? If she were honest, there'd been incidents in her childhood, though fleeting. Her parents admonished her to stop daydreaming. Assured their food was fine, they needed no more drinks, or anything else, the waitress left them alone again.

"The day Connor and Nessa met."

"Ouch. You never did tell me about that."

"Connor invited me to lunch and Nessa showed up. I still don't know how she found us. She just appeared at the table, sat down, and…took over. Though to be honest, Connor was as…I don't know. Enamored? Spellbound? He took one look at her and it's like I no longer existed."

"Dang. That's gotta be murder on the ego. So what happened to you?"

"I didn't realize the place was a piano bar but this guy…" She closed her eyes and breathed deeply, remembering. "You would have been all over him. Long hair, gorgeous, and this yummy Irish accent. Anyway, I went to the ladies room, not that Nessa or Connor noticed."

"Wait! What? He followed you to the bathroom? That's like way creepy, Laney."

"No, I wasn't in the bathroom anymore."

"He dragged you out?"

"No. I mean I came back to the dining room and the guy walked up to me. I didn't move but I was suddenly in a barn, and I was watching this scene—like a movie—play out in front of me. There was a little girl hiding and some men hunting her, but then they ran off and another man came. He rescued me. Her. I mean her."

Bronwyn's gaze felt like laser beams boring into her. "What do you mean he rescued you, but it was her? You were the little girl?"

She lifted her head to stare out the window. People passed on the sidewalk. Cars and trucks trundled along on the street. Inside the restaurant, glasses clinked in counterpoint to the soft buzz of conversation. “Yes.” The admission fell into a silent void as the room fell into a hush. “And the man who saved me looked like he should have been one of your SCA buddies. He looked like a warrior, complete with a sword. He looked like he could have killed those two men if he’d caught them. But…” Her breath hitched as she remembered the tenderness in his touch, the compassion displayed by his expression when he retrieved the little girl from the pile of straw, holding her in his arms, safe.

Bronwyn snapped her fingers in front of Delaney’s face several times. “Yo, Laney. Yoohoo. Come back, girl.”

She blinked several times, shocked by the brightness. Her eyes refocused on the woman across the table. “Sorry.”

“Nothing to apologize for, hon. Who was the guy? The warrior dude?”

Ah. Now that was the rub. Her heart knew what her brain couldn’t wrap around the facts. She said his name anyway. “Rory.” Shaking her head, she stared at Bronwyn. “But not. He didn’t look like he does now, and his name was Riordan, not Rory. But he *felt* the same. If that makes any sense?”

Bronwyn nodded, a sage expression on her face, as if she knew exactly what occurred but she made no comment. She took several sips of her drink, forked some salad into her mouth and chewed, all the while waiting for Delaney to continue.

“There was another time, too. Only Nessa, Keegan, Connor, and…” Her mouth gaped as she stared. “Oh my gosh, Bronwyn! You were there, too. I swear you were. We were like best friends."

"Whoohoo! See? I knew we were destined to be best friends forever." She giggled and waggled her fork in Delaney's direction. "You realize that some people pay really big bucks for regression hypnosis so they can explore past lives. You? You walk out of the bathroom with an Irish hunk and get the experience of a lifetime. So not fair!"

Goosebumps pimpled Delaney's arms and she smoothed them down with her palms. "That Irish hunk isn't... There's something weird about him, Bronnie. Like bad weird. He has this voice that is amazing. When he talks you can taste... Well, you know when we used to go the state fair when we were kids? And we'd share that huge glob of cotton candy? Remember how it feels melting on your tongue? *That's* the way this guy's voice sounds."

Shivering, Bronwyn rubbed her own arms. "So...he's the bad guy in all this?"

"I don't know. I...I don't trust him, I know that much."

Bronwyn nodded, still wearing what Delaney called her Faire Face, the one she wore when reading Tarot cards and telling fortunes at the Renaissance Faire. "You want my opinion?"

She rolled her eyes. "Well, d'uh. Why do you think I've been telling you about my bouts of insanity?"

"Nope. You aren't insane. I really do believe in reincarnation, Delaney. No kidding around, okay? I mean, jeez. You, Keegan, and Nessa have some major issues and the way Connor and Nessa are acting—"

"Not to mention Keegan and Connor's sister, Ciara."

"Wait. What? You haven't told me about this."

Holding up one hand to slow down the tirade before it started, Delaney jumped in to finish. "At the engagement party, Keegan took one look at Ciara and it was love at first sight. What's weird? She reacted the same way. She's gorgeous, Bronnie. I mean like Miss Universe gorgeous. And she's all gaga over Keegan? My scrawny, dorky brother? Really? I mean, either there's drugs involved or something otherworldly. There has to be."

Neither of them said anything for a few minutes. Bronwyn chewed over that bombshell like she chewed her food. Delaney forced food into her mouth but she didn't taste it and after swallowing, each bite contributed to the lump sitting in the pit of her stomach. She finally put her fork down and squared her shoulders.

Bronwyn flashed a cheeky grin. "I know that look. You need chocolate. In dessert. Like a big ol' piece of chocolate volcano cake. With ice cream. Trust me. It'll make everything right again."

When the waitress appeared, Bronnie cheerfully ordered the restaurant's signature dessert and two spoons. Neither of them spoke again until the treat arrived. Even then, Delaney picked at her side while Bronnie attacked the cake with gusto. She licked her spoon and used it to point at Delaney.

"Here's the deal. I think you are one lucky duck. You have the chance to get it right. I think you have met a man most women would kill to get. You, m'dear? You have this guy wrapped around your little finger. Nessa is safely out of the way, not that I'd give her a snowball's chance to come between you and your cop, but she'd certainly try. So… Go out with Rory. Fall in love, get married, and have his babies. I think the two of you will be happy for the rest of your lives." She dipped her spoon into the dessert, filling it with cake and ice cream and relished the bite for a long moment. She swallowed, leaned forward, and held Delaney's gaze. "You know I'm always right about these things."

Chapter 18

Haunting music wafted down the hallway. Determined to discover who was singing, Delaney stomped toward the shadows at the end of the corridor. As she was alone on this floor and it was long after closing hours, this was not the smartest thing she'd ever done. At the moment she didn't care. Feeling reckless, she pushed open the stairwell door. Nothing. Silence blanketed her.

"What the heck?" She listened, her head cocked so her right ear angled toward the gloomy stairs. She held her breath but only heard the soft beat of her own pulse thrumming in her ears.

Delaney exhaled. Completely baffled, she let the heavy fire door close. It whispered into place with a hiss of hydraulics. The music had been so clear, so compelling, she knew it couldn't be her imagination. Besides, she was a psychoanalyst. She didn't have an imagination. Just ask anyone who knew her. Deciding she must have heard someone's radio, she turned back toward her office. And smacked into a man. A man with a hard chest and strong hands that gripped her biceps. She opened her mouth to scream but nothing came out—not even a squeak.

"Shhh, cailín."

She swallowed a few times and tried her voice again. "Who are you?" At least her mouth worked and she thought the words came out though hardly any sound whispered from between her lips.

"'Tis hardly important."

She had to lick dry lips to open her mouth. "It's very important to me."

He smiled and she got lost in the swirling colors of his eyes. "Aye, 'twould be now wouldn't it. Most call me Abhean, though I have many names."

"Ay-veen? What sort of name is that?"

"A very proper sort for one such as me, cailín."

Delaney blinked, breaking the hypnotic spell spun by the man's eyes—and gasped. She no longer stood in the corridor outside her office. Stone walls closed around her and she choked back a sense of claustrophobia. Ghostly figures bustled around her. The sweet, yeasty scent of baking bread tangoed with the pungent, greasy odor of roasting meat. Her stomach growled. She stood in the corner of a kitchen, but a kitchen unlike any she'd ever seen before.

"Delaney!"

Startled, she stared at the girl who'd called her name. An overwhelming sense of familiarity swamped her. Delaney *knew* this girl and though she didn't look like her sister and the voice was wrong… "Nessa?"

The teenage girl shoved a bowl into her arms. "Why are yee standin' there starin' into the corner like a moonstruck calf? The troops'll be arriving all too soon. We've food t'get on the table and I want to put on a fresh dress. Get yer chores done. I'll be back in a nip."

Her arms automatically supported the bowl. Filled with some sort of stew, her nostrils flared and her stomach growled as the scent wafting from the bowl enveloped her. Delaney stood as still as a statue while people, both women and men, bustled around her. Their clothing matched that of her sister's—if that girl was indeed Nessa. Homespun materials, long skirts, boots or slippers and the occasional pair of bare feet.

"Delaney!" She whipped her head around at the demand.

"What's got yee dreamin' so, cailín?" The older woman had laughing eyes that didn't match the frown on her lips or the fisted hands braced on her hips. "Get that food to the table and come back here. I need yee to stir up the black puddin'." The woman grabbed her shoulders, rather more gently than Delaney thought she would, turned her around and gave her a little shove toward an arched doorway.

She walked through the door, her feet shuffling through the layer of straw on the stone floors. Delaney just thought the kitchens had been busy. This room boasted a vaulted ceiling, a massive fireplace and rows of sturdy wooden tables and simple benches.

"A dream," she muttered. "I've never had such a lucid dream but there is no other explanation. No matter what Bronnie says." She approached the first table and a woman brushed past her with a trencher piled high with roasted meet.

"Don't be dawdlin', cailín. Put it there on the main table."

Her gaze followed the woman's pointing finger. A single table angled across the rows and sported high-backed chairs instead of benches. She ducked around and through the bustling…servants? Interesting that she would dream about being a servant and that Nessa would be in the dream with her. "Ha. Talk about comeuppance." She snickered but decided to play out the dream, curious as to where it would lead her.

A few moments later, she was back in the kitchen and the pretty woman who someone called Siobhan handed her a large wooden spoon and pointed her toward a heavy metal pot hanging from a chain near one of the hearths. She gamely stuck the spoon in and tried to stir the contents before realizing it would take both hands. The stuff in the pot really was some sort of black pudding, but it didn't look or smell like chocolate—more like blood and something she didn't' want to think about. As she churned the spoon in the pot, Delaney assessed her surroundings. No student of history, she remained clueless as to time or place. The accents sounded lyrical to her ears, though some of the words didn't make sense. The human mind was an amazing place, as she well knew from both her studies and her practice, but that her own imagination could create such a layered and realistic dream space astounded her.

Shouts from the other room cleared the kitchens as people rushed to the great room. She had the presence of mind to grab a rag and push the big pot further from the fire so it wouldn't scorch. Once again, she boggled a bit at the intricacies of her brain. She was so not a cook in any way, shape, or form. Still clutching the rag, she reached the archway just as the massive front doors banged open.

She gaped. Her jaw dropped and her eyes felt like they might pop out of her head. The man who strode through the open doorway looked like a god surrounded by a golden nimbus. She gulped and worked to close her mouth and keep it closed. Raven black hair, tall, handsome, and even with the backlighting she could see the color of his brilliantly blue eyes.

"CIARAN!"

Whipping her head around, she watched a woman dash down the stairs, her feet barely touching the treads. She launched into the man's arms. Becca? She shook her head. No. This wasn't possible. What were Connor's parents doing in her dream? Stunned, she stepped behind the arch and leaned against the cold stones, gulping in air. From her hiding place, she watched other women greet their men. Men? No, these were warriors, complete with swords belted to their waists.

"Keegan!"

At her brother's name, she jerked her head back and forth between the tall boy who had just entered and a lovely girl descending the stairs. Ciara? That sort of made sense, since Connor's parents peopled this dream. Why not his sister?

"Conor!"

Nessa flew past her, knocking her against the arched doorway so hard she banged her temple on the corner of it. Stars danced across her vision for a moment. When they cleared, she found herself staring at…Rory. Only…not. Oh, this man was just as tall and well-muscled, but flowing auburn hair brushed his shoulders and he looked wild. Untamed. And she wanted him, the need to feel his arms around her an actual physical ache that pierced her heart.

His gaze seemed to slide right past her and his warm amber eyes lit up as a small woman threw herself into his arms. He lifted her so he could kiss her without bending over and Delaney doubled over as a pain, sharp and intense as a razor slicing her skin, pierced her heart. Rory. Kissing another woman. Sick to her stomach, she turned away and stumbled back to the safety of the kitchen.

Another man sat on one of the benches drawn against the wall. He fingered a small harp-like instrument, and the notes he plucked from the strings were so achingly sweet tears welled in her eyes.

"Yee've missed so much, cailín."

Ohhhh. The sound sighed in her heart. His voice was a sweeter sound than even his music. She wanted to cry. And laugh. And doubt her own sanity. This was the same man from the restaurant—the one who sang to her, who… She blinked, returning to the whole question of her sanity. "Who are you?"

"Aye, now 'tis a telling question, that one. Mortals call me Abhean."

"I saw you in the restaurant." She tilted her head, a curious bird. "And in the corridor at my office. Just now."

"Yee did. Yee've seen me many times in each life, Delaney, though yee've hidden from the memories."

"Where are we?"

"Long ago, this was your home, though yee've had many in the course of your lives."

Delaney furrowed her brows, mulling that over. "Lives? What do you mean?"

He laughed. At her. And she shivered as the dulcet tones caressed her cheeks and an unseen hand teased her hair.

"Ahhh, cailín. Yee've forgotten so many of the lessons yee were supposed to have learned. Time is running out, though. The king himself has declared it so. Yee have one last chance t'get it right. You and him."

"Him who? The king? And who is this king?"

He strummed the harp and hummed a tune she didn't recognize. "Why the King of Tir Nan Óg, himself, cailín. Manannán mac Lir ."

She backed away, shaking her head in disbelief. "You're crazy." She blinked. "Or I am." Delaney couldn't help but wonder if she was having some sort of psychotic break. This man couldn't be real. This *place* couldn't be real.

She clapped her hand over her mouth to stifle the moan welling in her chest. "I want to go home."

He tilted his head, a half smirk twisting his full lips as he watched her. "Yee are home, Delaney."

"Delaney?"

The hand on her shoulder felt warm. And real. Even so, she whimpered and refused to raise her head despite the realization she'd curled up in the corner at the end of the corridor.

"Doc? What's wrong?"

Doc. Only one person called her "Doc." Rory. She raised her head and his face swam in her vision for a moment while she blinked away tears. Rory. Not that other man, that…warrior who only resembled him. Close-cropped hair, eyes the color of the topaz ring on her pinkie finger, and a worried frown. Without thinking, she touched his mouth with trembling fingertips to smooth his anxiety away.

"Are you okay?" The words whispered across her fingers, and his lips brushed her skin.

No. Yes. What could she say? He'd found her curled in all but the fetal position in the hallway outside her office. And she wondered about her own mental condition. She inhaled slowly through her nose, the breath hitching in her chest though she fought through it to fully expand her lungs.

"I am now." The tightness in her chest eased, and she discovered that statement was the truth. With Rory kneeling before her, his strength and concern radiating like an aura, she was okay. She offered a sheepish smile. "I suppose I should explain…"

He shook his head. "Not unless you want to. C'mon." With the fluid grace of an athlete, he stood. Reaching for her outstretched hand, his fingers wrapped around hers and she jumped as an electric jolt raised the hair on her arms. She stared up at him and licked her lips, her mouth suddenly so dry she couldn't speak. He looked as stunned as she felt. Even so, he tugged her to her feet and steadied her while she regained her balance.

"May I buy you a drink?"

He arched a brow as he stared at her, one corner of his mouth quirked in a quizzical smile. "No, but I'll buy you one. Do we need to stop at your office?"

Delaney shook her head. "No. I-I was leaving for the day. Before…" She waved her hand in a vague gesture.

He nodded as if he understood exactly what she meant. Still holding her hand, he led her toward the elevators. She almost balked but held her tongue. It was bad enough she'd had something of a psychotic break. To admit she was claustrophobic, among other fears, was more than she could own up to. Her own phobias were one reason she'd gone into psychotherapy. The elevator doors slid open, Rory tugged her inside, and guided her to turn around. He let go of her hand but his arm circled her shoulders, and he tucked her in close to his side.

Twenty minutes later, a hostess had them installed in a back booth at Celtic Crossroads. The place had the feel of an authentic Irish pub—no blaring TVs with 24/7 sports, no loud music, and the guy behind the bar who called out a greeting to Rory had a voice full of Ireland. She sat across from him in the booth and immediately missed the warmth of having him close. When a glass of dark, foamy beer arrived, Delaney chugged about half of it.

"Whoa, Doc. This stuff is a little more potent than what you buy at the store."

She licked the foam off her top lip. "I should explain."

Rory leaned back against the faux leather banquette and waited. His face remained perfectly blank, and Delaney made a mental note never to play strip poker with him. She gulped another swallow and almost choked. *Strip poker? What the heck am I thinking?* That at least got a reaction from him. Concern showed in his expression as he reached for her hand.

"Can you breathe?"

She coughed and sputtered but managed a nod.

"Can you talk?"

Delaney nodded.

"Then say something."

She coughed again and dragged in a ragged gasp of air. "Something?" The word came out strangled. Her throat hurt as it worked to force air back out, but she didn't think she was going to die now. After several attempts, she managed a few pain-free breaths.

"Thought I might need to do the Heimlich. And you don't need to explain."

"Yes, I do. A person shouldn't find their therapist curled up in a ball."

He released her hand and leaned back, putting both physical and emotional distance between them. "I thought we were past that. I don't need a therapist, Doc. And after the other night, there's no way you could treat me."

She bit back her protestation and chewed her lips. Who was she to say whether or not he needed a therapist? He appeared to handle his trauma far better mentally than she was dealing with her own fantasies. And she had signed off on his full reinstatement to duty—not that he'd ever actually taken off. After several deep breaths, she forged ahead despite her misgivings. "That remains to be seen." She held up a hand to stay any comment he might make. "I have to ask you something that will probably sound totally off the wall." She watched him watch her. "Okay. I take that back. This will sound crazy. Reincarnation."

He blinked but that was the only change in his expression.

"Yes? No? Do you believe in it? Believe in soul mates? In past lives?"

Rory very deliberately reached for his glass, raised it to his lips, and took a slow drink. He turned his head slightly to the right so he didn't look at her face-on. He set the glass down before speaking. "No. Not really."

Something akin to fear fisted in her belly, and she now regretted the half-downed beer. Somehow, some way, she needed to convince him otherwise. But why? Especially since she didn't believe in it herself.

Granted, she'd had patients under hypnosis who seemed to slide into a dream world where they claimed to be someone else, where their memories seemed as real and solid as their recollection of the here and now.

A song played softly in the background, and she noticed that Rory cocked his head to listen. She concentrated on the lyrics but only one phrase stuck— "But time keeps us apart." A sense of profound sadness settled over her.

"What is it, cailín?"

Startled, she stared at Rory. "What did you just call me?"

His eyes narrowed in a perplexed expression. "Delaney. That's your name, right?" He shrugged and looked away, his gaze roving across the room as nervous energy gathered around him. "What did you think I said?"

She shook her head. "I… Never mind. It doesn't matter. I thought you called me something else. A word I don't hear…often." *A word I've never heard before this one particular hunky figment of my imagination used it.*

"Yee think me to be a hunk then, cailín?"

Laughter burbled in her ear, and she jerked her head around looking for the source of that voice. No one. The music continued above the bass hum of conversation and the sharp clink of glasses at the bar. The song ended and she made a mental note to track it down. While listening to it, she'd almost felt a key turning in her mind, a key in a lock to a closed door and she longed to open that door.

She sipped her beer and watched Rory. He still checked the room, his eyes darting into all the corners only to focus on the front door each time it opened. The eyes were the same, she decided. Perhaps that bit of folklore was true—the eyes were the mirrors of the soul. There were subtle differences between Rory and the warrior of her dream, if it had been a dream. She needed to do more research on lucid dreaming. And reincarnation.

"That still doesn't explain things."

Delaney blinked several times in an attempt to focus her attention. "I'm sorry?"

"Your question about reincarnation. It doesn't explain why I found you sitting in the corner of the hall outside your office."

She avoided his gaze, following his move earlier and watching the other patrons in the pub. "No, I don't suppose it does. I need to do some research—"

"No." His brusque statement cut off her excuse. "You need to tell me what the hell was going on, Doc."

Could she tell him? Explain she thought she might be losing her mind? "Answer me this. What do you think about déjà vu?"

He tilted his head and watched her from eyes slightly askew. He didn't want to face her straight on. He didn't trust her. And that hurt far more than it should, both professionally and personally. Especially personally.

"What about it?"

"Does it happen to you? Do you feel like you've been some place before, done something before…" She swallowed hard. "Feel like you've known someone before?"

One corner of his mouth tugged upward. At least he didn't smirk at her. He tossed a one-shouldered shrug into the mix as she tried to read his expression. Delaney inhaled slowly and waited for his answer.

"Yeah. Sometimes. We talked about this, after the party."

She exhaled. "I know. But."

"But what?" He didn't quite blink as he asked but his eyelids lowered so that look he favored her with appeared almost feral.

"I'm a trained and licensed therapist, Rory. While the human mind is not built of hard scientific facts, the study of it is. I'm supposed to keep an open mind. I'm supposed to look for the best way to relate to my patients in order to help them relate to their environment." Now she got the smirk from him but she forged ahead. After all, she had no place to go but down, right? "When you found me…" She paused for another fortifying breath. "When you found me in the hall, I think I was having some sort of lucid dream. Or something."

"Or something."

She bit back a retort. Rory had no intention of making this easy for her. "That's why I need to do research. I'm not sure what I experienced."

"Why don't you tell me about it, Doc."

Delaney rolled her eyes. "Right. So you can make fun of me? I think not."

His hand descended on hers and enfolded her fingers in his strong ones. "It's called CISD, Doc. Remember? Whatever you experienced, it's left you shaken. It might not have been a critical incident like a hostage situation, but the stress is definitely showing. Let's debrief. Besides, if I can lucid dream, so can you."

He would throw her own words back at her. Critical Incident Stress Debriefing made sense for cops and firefighters, for EMTs and soldiers, even for people caught up in the middle of a traumatic event. The only trauma she'd suffered was wondering if she'd lost her mind. Heat from his hand warmed hers, and the warmth calmed her. Deep down, she knew he was right.

"I was… I experienced…" She sighed, searching for an explanation that would make sense. Then she realized that nothing she said would make sense. "I don't know what happened."

Her hand trembled in his, and Rory squeezed her slender fingers gently, surprised at how cold her hand felt. "Don't worry about making sense of it. Just describe what occurred." He watched her inhale, hold her breath and then exhale and did his best to focus on her face, not the luscious curves stretching the front of her sweater.

"Okay." A few more breaths and then she began, but she focused her gaze on their joined hands, not his face. "I was leaving the office for the day. I locked my door and then I heard…music. Then singing."

He wanted to interrupt her but remained silent. This was her story to tell.

"The voice… It was so sweet and…" She angled her head to the left as if she listened for some far off song. "Compelling. I felt compelled to find the man who was singing. So I went looking. Only no one was around. I even checked the stairwell. Nothing. When I turned around, I smacked into this guy and he grabbed me—"

"What!" He snarled and his hand tightened around her hand until she yelped. Now it was his turn to breathe deeply and calm down. He loosened his grip and soothed her by rubbing his thumb over the back of her hand. "Sorry. Did he—" Rory had to squelch the growl threatening to erupt from his chest.

"Hurt me?" she finished for him. "No. It wasn't… It was… I swear he was there. I felt his hands on my arms, but then things got a little fuzzy."

"Fuzzy?" Had the man drugged her? How long had she been alone with him in that corridor before he arrived? Rage churned inside him, but he managed to keep his voice even.

"Yes. Sort of swirly and dark and when I opened my eyes, I was…someplace else." She cleared her throat and continued before he could interrupt. "And this is the crazy part. It was some *time* else. I was in what looked like a medieval kitchen. Or something. Big hunks of meat roasted on spits in a massive fireplace and pots hung from chains cooking. And the people…" She glanced up to see if he believed her. He had his poker face on and didn't even blink. Evidently reassured, she continued. "The people wore historic clothes. Including me. And I wasn't…me. I was a young girl. But I felt like me. The *me* I am now. Nessa was there. And I knew she was my sister, and her name was Nessa. Or…no. It was Neasa. There's a slight difference in the nuance. And there was a woman there. I felt like I knew her." She swallowed and looked down again.

Rory squeezed her hand and tugged a little. When she looked up, he offered a smile he hoped would encourage her. "What are you not saying?"

"Everyone was there. Connor's parents. His sister. My brother. And…" She gulped in a breath. "And you."

"Me."

"You. Only not you. You looked different. Your hair was long and darker and you…you had a sword."

"A sword."

"Yes. You were…" She blinked. "You looked like a picture in one of the books I had as a kid. You looked like a Finian warrior. Do you know about them?"

His stomach twisted. The sharp clang of metal on metal and the stench of death surrounded him. He could taste the copper of fresh blood on his tongue. He felt fierce and…exhilarated. His right hand clenched and unclenched, as if searching for feel of something tangible and real…a sword. Rory pulled back from the brink and stared at Delaney. "I know enough."

She watched him as if she knew exactly what he was thinking, and then she nodded. "We'd been preparing a feast, waiting for the warriors to arrive. You saw me. But it's like I didn't exist."

"No, you saw Connor and I didn't exist." He clamped his jaw shut and prayed he hadn't said that out loud.

Delaney favored him with an odd look. "I ran from the great hall and the man from before—the one who I'd seen in the corridor outside my office—was there in the kitchen. Sitting on a bench against the wall and playing a harp. I asked him who he was, and he kept giving me riddles to answer. *Ayveen*, he finally told me, though I've never heard that word before."

"How do you spell it?"

"A-y-v-e-e-n. I think. That's the way he pronounced it."

Rory shook his head. "It's A-b-h-e-a-n. The Harper of the Tuatha de Danaan."

She leaned back against the seat and tugged at her hand but he didn't relinquish it. "How do you know that?"

"I'm not sure. Probably the same way I know about Fenian warriors. I read a lot as a kid." She shrugged at his explanation. She didn't believe his rationalization any more than he did, but he wasn't ready to talk about his conversation with Kieran MacDermot yet. "So what happened then?"

"Abhean talked. I listened. He told me that some king decreed I'd screwed up in all my previous lives, and I had to get it right this time."

"A king."

"Yeah. Manannan? Something like that. Of Tirenanoog."

"Tir Nan Óg."

Both of them jerked their heads around at the intrusion of the new voice. The little waitress smiled at them. "“'Tis the fae land of the ever young," she explained. "You'd be speakin' of Manannán mac Lir , the fae king who decides which souls can go there."

Her lilting accent danced toward them, and Rory smiled despite himself. "You sound like you should know…Alys." He glanced at her nameplate before calling her by name.

Dimples appeared on her cheeks. "Aye, I'm from Ireland, and the stories of the fae and of the feuds between Abhean and Manannán mac Lir are legendary. Me mum filled m'head with the tales when I was a wee cailín."

Delaney gasped. "Colleen? That word. What does it mean?"

"Cailín is a girl, miss, in the Gaelic."

Rory watched Delaney's reaction. She seemed almost relieved, but she said nothing until Alys set fresh glasses in front of them, cleared the empty ones, and retreated. With reluctance, he released Delaney's hand and sipped his beer for a few moments to regain his composure.

"So, you think you've been enchanted by the fae?"

She laughed, the sound high-pitched and a bit hysterical. "In my line of work, if a patient came to me and claimed all this stuff, I'd refer them to a psychiatrist for heavy duty drugs."

"But."

Delaney nodded. "But. It felt so real, Rory. And…"

He recognized the fear in her eyes and reached for her hand again. "And?"

"Tonight wasn't the first time."

Rory schooled his reaction and very carefully asked, "Oh?"

"At the restaurant. The day Connor and Nessa met? When I bumped into you?" She searched his face, her expression anxious. He nodded slowly and she continued. "I was coming from the ladies room. Abhean—or whatever his name is—he was there. And…" She shrugged and looked out toward the front windows for a long moment. "And I watched another scene. I was an on-looker, not a participant. There was a little girl and this humongous dog—"

"Hiding in the straw from raiders."

Delaney stared at him, her mouth slack-jawed and her eyes wide with disbelief. How did he know that? From her expression, he'd obviously guessed right. Only it wasn't a guess. It was the truth. And he knew with absolute certainty that he'd walked into that barn, found that child—found Delaney—and carried her to safety.

She shook her head, denying his words. “I have to go.”

The words whispered from between the dry lips she licked to moisten. His groin tightened as he watched her tongue. The need to kiss her almost overwhelmed him.

“No.”

She tugged her hand, but he refused to surrender it. “No. I’m not letting you go. Not this time.”

A shadow appeared across the table, and they both looked up, startled. The man blocking out the light was a stranger. Or was he? Rory narrowed his eyes, squinting to better see the man’s features.

“A lover’s spat? ’Tis no time for that, children.”

Rory blinked as the man’s voice washed over him. He’d heard that voice before, he’d swear an oath on it. It sounded like cotton candy tasted—so sweet it made your teeth hurt even as it melted away on your tongue. And he knew. “Abhean.”

“Aye, Riordan MacDermot.”

“What are you doing here?”

“Yee found me all those lives ago and begged me to save her, fool that you are.”

Shaking his head back and forth, Rory stared without blinking. “No.”

“You.” Delaney’s voice sighed out the word, breathless and shocked.

“Aye, cailín. Me. Time has run out. Mac Lir will wait no longer. Yee have precious little time left, Riordan. I will return then and escort you to Tir Nan Óg.”

He never took his eyes off the man even as he opened his mouth to protest. Darkness yawned, swirled, swallowed up the colors of the room and then winked out. The man disappeared, leaving them both blinking.

"What's he mean, Rory? What's going on?"

He lifted her hand to his mouth and kissed the back of it, his lips hungry for the touch of her skin. "I don't know, but I'll figure it out. Nothing is going to happen, Delaney. I'm not going anywhere."

Wide-eyed, her forehead furrowed with worry, she shook her head slowly. "No. This is all my fault. I know it is. And he called you the fool? I'm the foolish one." Tears gathered in her eyes. "I don't know what to do, Rory. I don't know how to fix it."

"Shhh, Doc. There's nothing to fix. I'm not a believer in all this New Age shit. But I do feel a connection to you, have since the first time I heard your voice, to be honest."

Delaney sniffled and dabbed at her eyes with a napkin. "When was that?"

"A couple of months ago. That hostage negotiation with the two gangbangers at the jewelry store."

"Music Man."

He wondered if she remembered that day as vividly as he did. Far from a poetic guy, he had to admit that meeting her added something to his existence—like color, love, life. He'd fallen in love with her voice and then with the woman herself. He'd continued his sessions with her simply to bask in her presence.

"Yes." He stumbled over the word and nothing followed, his tongue too twisted around his thoughts to add anything coherent.

Delaney looked guilty, and he realized she hadn't

shared his feelings. Then or now. Connor. Despite the fact the jerk abandoned Delaney for her sister, despite the night they'd spent making love, she was still in love with the asshole. Yeah, Abhean was right. He was a fool. Rory dug some bills from his front pocket and tossed them on the table.

"I have to go." He made it to the front door. Made it out onto the street. *Breathe.* He had to get home. He started walking, remembered his truck, found it, climbed in, and sat. *Breathe.* He could survive this. He'd get home. Think things through. *Breathe.*

****

Daylight brought no peace. The buzz of his cell phone only added to the sense of unreality—and the unease that had dogged him for hours. A call out? This was the last thing he needed, but he headed to the station, suited up, and responded with the team.

Working to find his focus, he climbed to the top of a building and set up. Ready, with his eye fixed on the scope, he acquired target. His heart stopped as if someone had sewn a block of dry ice into his chest and froze that fist-sized muscle solid. Rory couldn't breathe for a minute.

The captain's voice barked through his headset. "Where is she? She's been called and paged. Why isn't Dr. Burns on scene by now?"

Rory knew. Jaw clenched, teeth gritted, he choked over the words his brain hadn't wrapped around yet.

"Say again, Alpha One. You broke up." Dutch's voice, calm and collected, cut across the captain's.

Rory cleared his throat, but it felt like swallowing sandpaper down a throat raw with emotion. "The doc's already here."

“Where the hell is she? Why isn’t she at the command post?” Captain Davis, abrupt and demanding, overrode Dutch.

“Because she’s the hostage.”

Chapter 19

"Oh. Shit." Rory blinked and gazed around, stunned.

He no longer stared at Delaney's terrified face through his sniper scope. Turning a slow circle, Rory tried to figure out where the hell he was. And what the hell had happened.

A guy with long blond hair sat cross-legged on the ground playing a flute. The branches on the trees seemed to dip and sway in time to the music and his right foot started to tap along. Angry, Rory willed his feet still.

"Who the hell are you?"

The blond guy turned his head. Abhean. The man from the pub. Rory rubbed his eyes with the heels of his palms and looked again. Nope. Still the same guy.

"You know who I am, Riordan MacDermot. But perhaps you have forgotten that I am also the Harper to the Tuatha de Danaan."

"I'm dreaming. There's no such thing as fae harpers."

"So you'd like to believe. Welcome to Tír Nan Óg, Riordan. The time has come to keep your bargain."

"Bargain? What bargain? I don't know what you're talking about."

"Truly? Have you no memory of that day beside the river? The day you offered your life in exchange for the cailín's. I distinctly remember givin' yee the memory." The fae looked well pleased.

Rory relaxed his hands from the fists he'd made at his sides. This whole thing was nuts. Maybe he had finally gone around the bend. He closed his eyes. *Breathe.* Inhale. Exhale. Relax. *Breathe.* When he opened his eyes, he'd be across the alley from the restaurant, rifle in his hands, eye glued to the scope. Delaney was depending on him. He'd go crazy later, after she was safe, when it was convenient for him to occupy a padded cell. Not now. *Breathe.*

He opened his eyes. "Well, shit."

"'Tis no sense to fight the inevitable, Riordan."

"You keep calling me that. My name is Rory."

"Yee was born Riordan MacDermot, mortal, many lives ago, and no matter the moniker, yee'll always be Riordan."

"Put me back."

"No."

Rory's fists clenched in front of him, and he fought the urge to grab the other man and beat him to a pulp. Was it even possible to hit a figment of the imagination? "I have to go back. Delaney needs me."

Abhean returned the flute to his mouth and blew a few experimental notes, his fingers dancing along the instrument, coaxing and caressing. After a few measures, he looked up and stopped playing. "No."

"Yes."

"You made your bargain, Riordan. Do you now renege on your promise? Your life for hers, mortal, to be taken at my choosing."

"And you choose now, you damned freak? She's going to die."

"Perhaps."

"What the hell does that mean? I recognized the asshole holding a gun to her head. He'll kill her. If I'm not there to stop him, he'll kill her." His voice broke on those words, his heart knowing the truth of them.

"A bargain is a bargain."

The wind kicked up and leaves swirled around the fae. In moments, Rory couldn't see him in the center of the whirlwind. He closed his eyes against the sting of dirt and debris, and seconds later the wind died. Completely. He opened his eyes but he was alone.

"Damn you, Abhean!" He shouted the words to an empty sky and felt impotent. "If she dies because of you, I'll spend the rest of my life finding a way to kill you."

Laughter danced around him, followed by a merry melody played on that damn flute. If he ever got his hands on that thing, Rory promised to break it. A soft giggle wafted on the balmy breeze now rustling the grass at his feet. On alert, he searched for the source of the sound. Movement in the trees pulled him in that direction one reluctant step at a time.

"Well, this is definitely not Kansas." He hissed the admission even as he continued stalking the illusive laughter—laughter with a definite feminine lilt. A flash of color darting between tree trunks kept him moving deeper into the forest. Intrigued, he wasn't yet so enthralled that he ignored his surroundings. Getting lost in the woods was not on his to-do list, especially these woods. He heard the crack of a branch behind him at almost the exact moment a hand brushed across his back. Rory whirled but the—what the hell had he just seen? Sprite? Faerie? Wood nymph? Slender, graceful, the woman—girl—danced away. Diaphanous material draped from her shoulders but did little to hide her charms. Ageless, beautiful, the sort of woman a man fantasized over. But she wasn't Delaney.

Rory planted his feet and refused to follow her, despite the fact she peeked around a tree trunk and beckoned him with a crooked finger and come-hither smile. "What do you want?"

"Do yee not recognize me, Riordan. 'Tis Alys I am."

He stared at her. "Alys? The waitress from the Crossing?"

She pouted prettily and with bare feet skimming the mossy ground, she approached him boldly. Stopping an arm's width away, she smiled up at him. "Aye. From the Crossing and other places. I've never been far from you all your lives, Riordan MacDermot."

"My name is Rory."

She laughed, the sound gay and lilting like the calliope on the merry-go-round he'd loved as a child. He didn't move, waiting for her to continue.

"Yee think it matters what yee call yourself, Riordan MacDermot? I know your heart. I know the look in your eye when yee want a woman. More often than not, that's been me yee've reached for in the dark. After a battle, I warmed your bed, not that twit of a mortal. Delaney cannot see what's as plain as the nose on her face. Always pining for another, her soul seeking his, life after life."

Her eyes snapped and whirled, the once vibrant colors mixing and blurring into a muddy mishmash. She pressed the palm of her hand to his chest. "I've waited centuries for Abhean to take his vengeance. I've waited for you, Riordan. You are in Tír Nan Óg finally, and we can live a glorious life here, wanting for nothing but the touch of each other. Love me like yee've loved her, Rory. I won't refuse you my bed."

"Alys!"

She froze at the sound of her name. Rory could feel the tremble in her hand. He glanced over to the woman who approached. Memories stirred, shifted, and then clarified. Onagh. Queen of the Connaught Faeries. Alys dropped her hand, straightened her shoulders and turned to face the other's terrible beauty.

"Leave off, your majesty. 'Tis no affair of yours."

"There you are wrong, Alys. King Finvarra and I pledged our protection to those of Clann MacDermot. That extends to all in Ciaran's house. The man who is as much his brother as his cousin is chief among them."

Rory's hair lifted off his scalp as animosity crackled like electricity in the air between them. The women ignored him so he backed away, one slow step at a time. So intent on them, he had no clue another had joined his audience of one until he backed into the very solid body.

"Easy, boyo."

The voice, like hot caramel on ice cream, coated his skin and elicited a shiver. Hands gripped his biceps with bruising force and he couldn't turn around.

"Will yee not run if I let yee go?"

Why was he even thinking about it? He knew there was no place to run. He dipped his chin in a curt nod. Those iron hands loosened and dropped away. The man stepped up beside him.

"I am—"

"Finvarra."

The king chuckled. "Aye, I am. Your memories return then?"

"Some of them."

"More will come with time. Yee know where yee are now?"

"Tír Nan Óg."

"Aye. The Land of the Ever Young. Yee'll not age, Riordan—Rory." The king corrected his name without reminder. "This should be a place of peace for you, but I fear yee'll be no more content than Becca before yee."

Rory pivoted and glared at the man. The king was as beautiful in a strictly male way as Onagh was in female form. The expression in Finvarra's eyes appeared kindly, but he didn't trust the fae as far as he could throw him—which he doubted would be more than a few feet. "Abhean has condemned Delaney to die. Why the hell would I be content to sit here and twiddle my toes?"

Finvarra inclined his head toward the women, who still argued—Alys's voice raised in a shout, Onagh's husky and intent. "Yee'd be doin' a bit more than twiddling your toes, boyo. Little Alys has long had her sights set on yee, and yee've been content to diddle with her down through time. Why not simply enjoy her obvious charms? She'll help you forget the lives you've left behind."

"She's not Delaney."

The weight of his pronouncement stifled the forest. The women quelled their argument and whirled to face him. Birds and humming insects froze like hitting the pause button on a DVD player. Not even a leaf dared rustle in the silence. The three fae stared at him. Rory squared his shoulders and stared back, each one in turn.

"Delaney is mine. Has always been. Will always be. Despite Abhean and his games. I will not rest here while she is in danger. I will not relinquish her to another. And I will not love another. Ever." This last he directed toward Alys.

Color flared in Alys's cheeks as she stalked toward him. Her whole body fairly vibrated with anger. "And yet yee swore never to love anyone, once upon a time, Riordan MacDermot. I heard your vow. As did Abhean. Yee stood there in the seat of your clann, and yee vowed to the heavens that yee'd never love one woman as Ciaran loved Becca." She balled up her fist and hit him in the middle of the chest. Pain radiated from the spot.

"Even so, yee loved them all, Riordan, in your own way. Despite that yee were hidin' from your heart's desire." Onagh's voice felt like cool water on a bad burn, and the pain in his chest eased a bit. The queen exchanged a look with her husband.

"Yee were not tasked with the burden of the MacDermot Knot, Riordan. But that did not mean there wasn't a heart meant to companion your own." Finvarra patted him on the shoulder, the gesture oddly awkward for a man who seemed so in control and poised. "As yee've finally learned, Delaney is your other half, but consternation, man, yee've taken your own sweet time figuring it out."

"No." Alys all but screamed the denial. "Abhean promised me."

"Promised you what?"

The three fae shrank back from that question. Rory swiveled his head and stared. Manannán mac Lir in the flesh. He couldn't breathe—it was like the fae king had sucked all the air out of the forest.

"Alys." Icicles should have decorated Manannán's voice.

The little fae shivered as if she felt the frigidity. She refused to meet the king's gaze. "The harper promised me the mortal. Said he'd be mine for the next millennium."

"And what had you to do to earn this prize?"

She gulped, still studying the mossy ground around her toes. "Distract him."

"So you warmed his bed and bespelled his thoughts away from the cailín."

"Aye." With a sudden jerk of her head, she thrust her chin at mac Lir. "Aye, I did. And I'd do it again, Manannán mac Lir, t'get what I wanted." She pointed a shaking finger at Rory. "He was promised t'me and I want my due."

Rory opened his mouth to protest but no sound came out. Moments later, he couldn't move. Panicked, he struggled against unseen bonds.

"Cease, mortal." Manannán's words whispered from his mouth but swelled like the crescendo of a symphony with a clash of cymbals and roll of tympani drums as violins wept notes like falling leaves. Storm clouds gathered above and lightning flashed, strobing lights that left ghost images on the retina.

Rory stilled. He obviously couldn't fight whatever magic the fae commanded. Better to save his strength. He'd forgotten everything he'd learned on the streets. Intel. Without intel, an operation went to hell in a heartbeat. *Breathe.* He inhaled. Exhaled. Willed his heart to smooth out, to slow to a steady beat. *Breathe. Just...breathe.* The argument among the fae faded as he found his focus. Delaney. Delaney would die if he didn't get back to…? Where? Earth? Home? His real life? Yes. That was the answer. He had to find his way back to his life. The life where he was Rory MacDermot, Alpha Team sniper. With a job to do.

Breathe. Becca found a way, all that time ago. She'd returned to Ciaran on *Samhain*, after his cousin swore the binding oath. Crap. Rory had never sworn the oath to Delaney. They'd never been in the right place at the right time. She'd been eight, for god's sake, the first time he held her in his arms. His chest burned with need. Even then he'd known she was his, that he need only be patient to claim her for his own. But…

Breathe. He'd waited too long. He'd blown off everything, wanting only to ease himself between the legs of a willing cailín. Alys. Alys in all her guises. And others too numerous and vague for him to remember. "You were an ass," he muttered.

"Indeed you were."

He looked up to find Manannán's gaze boring into him. "How do I get back?"

The king's stare wavered, dropped away and a cloak of sadness descended on his magnificent shoulders. "How did you get here?"

What the hell did that mean? He'd been looking through his scope and then... He blinked and opened his mouth to speak then closed it with a snap. How did he get here? A bargain. He'd made a bargain with Abhean and learned too late that a bargain with the fae was tantamount to a bargain with the devil.

Manannán watched him for a long moment, expression unchanging, and he waited. Something in Rory's expression trigged a response. "Yes. You made a foolish bargain. And now you live to regret what was made in haste."

Rory whipped his head back and forth, a vehement motion meant to deny the fae's words. "No. I would do it again to save her life."

Did the fae actually sigh? He certainly looked saddened again. "Each life is finite, mortal. To be lived in the time allotted. The cailín's time had come. Had you let her go in that lifetime, the next would have come easier. And the next after."

"What are you saying?" Stunned, Rory swallowed against the bile rising in his throat. He felt like a raw recruit, called on the commander's carpet, and reamed out for being stupid.

"You feel in your heart my words, mortal. Know they are true." Manannán clapped his hands and in a kaleidoscope of colors swirled with darkness, all the fae disappeared.

Rory blinked his eyes. He'd been transported, not the others. He stood on wet sand, facing the sea as inexorable waves swelled to foaming whitecaps only to wilt as they neared the shore, lapping against the black-sand beach with nervous tongues. He turned a slow circle to get his bearings. The narrow strand gave way to craggy dunes and cliffs. Beyond, mountains made of blue stone reared their crowns to the sky. Which way was the forest? The standing stones? Instinctively, he knew the standing stones were the key.

His stomach growled and he licked his dry lips. Were the stories true? If he ate or drank anything here, would he be trapped forever? He laughed out loud, a biting, harsh bark of sound. "I am so screwed."

A dog bayed in the distance, the sound familiar and

almost comforting. He could see no path up those cliffs so he started walking in the direction of the barking. After quite a hike, he rounded a headland and found the dog—a huge Irish wolfhound. The animal bounded to him and leaped, placing front paws on Rory's shoulders with ease. With a lolling tongue, the dog looked to be grinning at him. Once more, memories flickered in his head, like old home movies, the film not quite threaded correctly.

"Broc?" He knew this dog. From before. Ciaran. Broc had been Ciaran's wolfhound.

The dog wagged his whole body and licked Rory's face before dropping to all fours. He rubbed the dog's ears and patted his shoulder. "Wish you could talk, big guy. I need to get back to the standing stones. Delaney needs me."

Broc woofed, turned and trotted up the beach. When Rory didn't immediately follow, the dog stopped and looked back. He barked again.

"Where're we goin', big guy?"

The dog's tail swept back and forth in a slow wag and he stepped forward again. This time, Rory followed. They walked along the beach for what seemed like several miles, but when Rory turned to check his back trail, he could still see the track of their footprints all the way back to the place they'd started. The dog trotted away from the waves, angling into a cut in the cliffs towering above them. Despite the prickle on the back of his neck, Rory paced beside the animal until he angled up a steep path. A bit more cautious, Rory followed, sometimes scrabbling with his hands to keep his balance.

For what seemed like an hour, though he wondered

about the passage of time in this place, he climbed the cliff trail. His watch remained on his wrist but the time registered different whenever he glanced at it. Sometimes, the hands raced ahead. Once they even retreated backward. The dog waited for him and the two of them climbed over the top together. Rory could only trust the dog, even though a part of his brain wondered if the animal really was a dog. Maybe the thing was a pooka.

Chapter 20

"No. *That* would be a pooka."

Every hair on Rory's body stood up and he shivered. The damn dog spoke those words, all the while staring at a big, black horse. "What the hell are you?"

Broc turned luminous brown eyes his direction and panted happily. "I'm a *cù sìth*."

"Cooshee?" He snorted. "And that would be what? A furry cover for a cold beer?"

The dog offered him a long-suffering look. "Somethin' you likely have no wish t'be knowin'. We have a long ways t'go, Riordan MacDermot. Arien has agreed t'take ya."

"My name is Rory."

"Nay. Yer name was and will be always Riordan. The sooner ya accept that, the sooner you'll be settled into life here."

He stood his ground, feet braced, hands on his hips. "Not gonna happen. I'm already crazy since I'm standing here talking to a dog. I'll damn sure hang onto my name and I am not getting on some creature straight from the Wild Hunt."

"Suit yerself then, mortal. The pooka and I have better things t'do with our time. But yee need to get yer sorry hide from here to there." Broc pointed his nose through a pass. The mountain fell away to a long valley and in the far distance, craggy hills smudged the horizon.

The horse—pooka—thing stretched his neck. Velvety lips nibbled at Rory's shoulder. "Do you talk, too?"

The horse whickered and shook his head. Then he nose-butted Rory as if to say, "Don't be so stubborn. Get on and let's ride."

Rory reached deep and hung onto his instincts and training. He'd ridden horses as a kid. Hopefully, it was like riding a bicycle—once you learned, you never forgot. Without a word, he fisted the horse's mane in his hand and leaped up, throwing his right leg over the animal's back. He got settled, griped with his thighs and knees, but still held on to the mane. Broc trotted off, Arien right behind him.

By the time their little party reached the valley, Rory had relaxed enough to trust the horse. Pooka. Thing. Though he paid attention to his surroundings, his mind also worked through the situation. OODA. He had to work on the OODA Loop. Observe. Orient. Decide. Act. The countryside was beautiful, the colors as clear as a photograph but objects looked hazy around the edges, smudged like a water color painting. Time still did a number on his watch so he gave up trying to determine its passage. Besides, there was no guarantee he could find a way home from that beach. Now he wished he'd spent more time pumping Kieran—no, Ciaran—for information. Better yet, Becca. Becca had been trapped here in Tír Nan Óg. And she'd tricked Abhean into revealing the secret to return. Or had she? What was Abhean up to, and more importantly, what was the deal between Abhean and Manannán mac Lir?

Rory suspected something dark and hateful existed between the two men. If he could discover what it was, what the root cause was, he could exploit it to his benefit. Divide and conquer, only they were already divided. He could use that. A sense of dread blanketed him and he couldn't breathe for a minute. Delaney.

"Damn you, Abhean!" Despite the futility, he tossed the curse into the cosmos.

"I already am, mortal."

Rory almost fell off the horse as he twisted his body to locate the man with that hated voice. Scrambling, he managed to stay on board. The horse didn't stop so he had to turn his head to keep the fae in sight. "Good."

Abhean threw back his head and laughed. "You amuse me, mortal. Perhaps I shall keep company with you on your journey."

The next thing Rory knew, Abhean rode knee-to-knee with him on a horse so white he had to squint to see the animal clearly. "Don't do me any favors."

"I don't intend to, Riordan MacDermot."

Refusing to engage Abhean, Rory clamped his mouth shut and stared resolutely forward, using only his eyes to scan the area. A bit of advice from Marine boot camp played on a loop in his head. After you know everything about yourself, learn everything about your enemy. In this situation, he had a lot to learn. About himself and the strange being riding alongside him.

"You have questions."

Rory gave no indication he heard Abhean. This was part of the learning experience. The fae held all the cards yet he was the one who broke the silence first. Interesting.

"Stubborn are you? I give you this one chance to indulge your curiosity. I won't offer again, mortal."

He wished he'd learned to play chess better but he had excelled at strategy planning. If he guessed right, Abhean would keep pestering him. The fae thrived on feeling superior, on having information someone else wanted. Rory took a chance. "Manannán mac Lir answered what questions I had." Abhean growled and the sound raised all the hair on Rory's head. Oh, yeah. First point to him.

"Bah. Then you didn't ask the right questions."

"Found out what I needed to know, though. I figure there isn't anything you can add to what he said."

"Did he tell you that I brought you here and that I'm the only one who can return you?"

The only reaction Rory allowed himself was the squeeze of his thighs against the horse's withers. "You have no intention of returning me, so the point is moot."

In a flash of light, Abhean and his mount disappeared. In the distance, thunder rumbled. "Frying pan, fire." He muttered the words, but the Irish wolfhound trotting beside him chuckled.

"Yee handled that well, human. Not many can put the harper into a snit."

"Bully for me."

The dog remained silent as he ran and the horse kept to a steady canter. Alone with his thoughts, Rory made plans. Escape. Evade. Survival. Get home to Delaney. His guts twisted. Delaney. The memory of staring through his sniper scope, seeing her face and the abject fear plastered on it, left him gasping for air. If she died because Abhean ripped him away, he'd spend the rest of his life searching for revenge. Magical being or not, there had to be a way. And by God, he'd find it.

His fingers twisted the horse's mane and yanked, the visible expression of his inner turmoil. Arien whickered and turned his head to stare at Rory with one baleful eye. With effort, he loosened his grip but the horse slowed to a trot and then a walk before stopping altogether. They'd reached the rocky hills he'd first glimpsed through the pass in the mountains. He turned, amazed that the mountains now appeared a hazy blue swathed in mist. A path led up the side of the hill amongst boulders and bracken. Music floated down—pipes, he thought, though something light and sprightly. He snorted. Sprightly? The air of this place seemed to soak into his bones, affecting him in ways he could only guess at. And therein lay the problem. The clarity of the air—in vision and with each breath pulled deeply into the lungs—proved as intoxicating as any alcoholic spirit.

Some part of his psyche remembered the old tales—of humans lured into the land of Faerie never to be seen again. Those who managed to escape told stories of lethargy, of amazing food and drink, of dancing and music—and no sense of the passage of time. He glanced at his watch. The second hand was spinning madly. Backward. Broc stared up at him.

"Why so grim, human?"

"My name is Rory."

The dog cocked his head and his panting bark almost sounded like laughter. "Me thinks, human, that the harper has bitten off more than he can chew this time." Turning his head, he pointed his nose up the path. "At the top yee'll find the standing stones, and there'll be someone to see you settled in."

"I don't want to settle in." Rory repeated his mantra in his head. *Escape. Evade. Survive.* And he added one more word. *Return.*

At the top of the path, a gentle meadow contained a circle of standing stones. Forest, looking impenetrable in places, surrounded the place on three sides. A lithe young woman, with long dark hair and laughing eyes, danced toward him, her movements languorous and seductive.

"Aye, an' it's about time yee be arrivin', Riordan." She threw her arms around him and peppered his face with kisses.

Rory stood stock still. He didn't even breathe for a long moment, and he made no move to touch the woman. She stopped kissing him and tilted her head back to stare at him.

"Don't yee know me, darlin'? 'Tis yer own sweet Alys."

Rory stared at her. "Why go to all the trouble to change your appearance, Alys? You might try to look like Delaney, but you aren't her. And never will be."

"Can't blame a cailín fer tryin' now can yee?" She tightened her arms around his neck and leaned in to whisper in his ear—erotic words of what she planned to do to him.

Rory didn't suppress the shudder running through him at her recitation. Once, he might have been that man. Once, he'd been a man who loved women freely and without reservation. And without commitment. Until Delaney. The moment he'd held her in his arms, her naked skin heating his, sliding together like silk and velvet—in that moment, he knew he'd never love another. Just her. His heart lurched at the memory of making love to her. He stepped back, tearing Alys's hands from around his neck. With space between them, he could think. *Observe. Orient. Decide. Act.*

"I don't care what Abhean promised you."

The fae woman blinked in surprise and took a step backward, putting more space between them. He watched her expression change from surprise to cunning. "I'll still be havin' yee, lovey. Abhean promised. We've been lovers, life after life, and I find myself cravin' yer kisses, hankerin' for the feel of yer boidín drivin' into me." With a seductive smile on her face, she stalked toward him.

Rory held his ground as his brain sorted through his options. Submission. Deception. Cooperation. Lead. Guide. Distract. Survive. He could use Alys. And he would. Whatever it took to get back to Delaney. Becca had returned to Ciaran, all those lives ago. He was determined to do the same.

Alys pressed against him, rubbing up and down like a contented cat. This time, he clamped down on his revulsion. He cupped the fae's cheek in his palm and kissed her forehead. He felt her elation shimmer through her body like an electrical charge. His lips curled into a smile despite his best efforts. She mistook the gesture and nuzzled his throat. "Come t'me bower, lovely man. Yee can show me how much yee've missed me."

Thunder rumbled and the sky darkened. Broc appeared, trotting out of the woods and ignoring the gathering storm. The dog sat next to Rory's knee and growled at the fae. Alys huffed and glared at the animal but backed away from Rory.

"Tell yer master he won't always have his way.

Riordan's been promised t'me." She pivoted on her toes and marched into the woods, which quickly swallowed her. One moment she was there, a blink and she'd disappeared.

Broc ducked his head and lazily scratched an ear with a back paw. The dog nosed a little lower.

Rory opened his mouth but snapped it shut. He had more important things to talk about than the dog's hygienic habits.

He waved his hand to encompass the standing stones. "Tell me, Broc. How do they work?"

The dog barked, and again it sounded like laughter. "Yee think it'll be that easy, human?"

"Rory. My name is Rory."

Broc cocked his head to the side, his tongue lolling from the side of his muzzle. "Stubborn. That'll bode well for yee here, hu—Rory."

He stared down at the animal. "I'd kiss the king's ass if it got me back to Delaney. Now tell me how to work these damn stones."

"'Tis all a dream, Rory MacDermot."

"What do you mean? If I pinch myself I'll wake up and things will be back to normal? I'll be in my own place, my own time?"

The big animal lumbered to his feet and padded over to the flat stone lying in the center of the circle. He put his front paws on the stone and stared out toward the misty-blue mountains in the distance. "Nay. This is your reality. There lies the dream."

Clouds continued to roil overhead, gathering and bunching like dark shadows. Forks of lightning flickered across the surface. Broc hopped down and turned his head, staring at Rory. "Each must find his own dream, human." He raised his muzzle, sniffed the rising wind, and barked. "Yee've a place in the forest, with food and drink. A bower t'lay yer head and stay dry." He paced back to the edge of the woods, stopped and stared back over his shoulder. "Yee can't follow Becca's path, Rory. Each human must find their own way."

Lightning lit the sky with fireworks to rival any Fourth of July celebration, and the thunder sounded like cannon fire. Rory squatted at the foot of the altar stone, squinted his eyes shut against the display, and didn't move even as the skies opened and rain drenched him. He didn't care. He'd been wet before. He'd be wet again. Sheltered partially by the stone, he pondered what the *cù sìth* had told him.

Dreams. Reality. Which was real, which wasn't. Manannán mac Lir snatched Becca on *Lughnasadh*. She didn't find her way home until *Samhain*. The whisper of a memory niggled in his subconscious. Sometimes, the veil between the worlds thinned and overlapped. Sometimes, unwary humans fell into the land of fae. And sometimes, smart humans found their way out. *Each human must find his own way*, Broc had said, and that Rory's way was not Becca's.

The storm passed, bringing sunshine and that clarity of vision that seemed so disconcerting to him. The craggy fingers of the mountains snared the tempest, trapping and holding the clouds as if to squeeze the last bit of thunder and lightning from them. As he watched, rainbows danced between the standing stones and the squall. And then Delaney's face swam in his vision. Surrounded by dancing colors, she was hard to focus on, but he narrowed his eyes and concentrated, willing her to substance from shadow.

Objects solidified behind her. Her office. The wall behind her chair, covered with certificates. Rory willed her to full form. Solid. Real. She was speaking. He watched her mouth move, form words, and he hungered to touch those lips with his own. Her image wavered.

"No!" He reached for her and her image faded. He leaned on the stone and focused once more. In his mind, he pictured tuning a TV. Picture. Volume. Brightness. Yes. There. Her image flickered a few times then found substance. Her voice whispered across his skin and he strained to make out the words.

"I know you don't want to be here. None of you ever do."

"I just want back on duty. Captain Davis said I couldn't roll out unless I finish these stupid sessions with you."

"Dean, I really can help you. You're having nightmares. Not sleeping. Let me help with that."

"The hell with that. I just need to get back on the job."

What? Dean Carter in her office? What was New Boy doing there? Why did he need counseling?

"You weren't there. It was a righteous shoot. When that banger walked out holding that woman, I took my shot. Blew him away, too."

"But he was surrendering."

"Ha. Shows what you know. You weren't there. Those two bangers had hostages, including a kid. I had the target. I had a green light. I fired. End of story. Not my fault the asshole moved. I got him with the second shot."

"But you killed the child with the first one."

Rory's gut clenched and he wanted to throw up. NO! He screamed his denial to the heavens. He'd been there. He'd relieved Carter. He'd never taken the shot.

"But you weren't there."

Chapter 21

He turned slowly, fists clenched at his sides. He wanted to hurt something. Beat flesh and bone until his rage drained away. The expression on Manannán's face drained his anger. Profound sadness surrounded the fae, dampening the very wind.

"What do you mean I wasn't there?" He stared at the king. "I. Was. There. I remember it."

"Do you wish the truth, mortal?"

Something in the king's voice made Rory hesitant, but he'd always been a man who insisted on the truth. "I do."

"Then walk with me."

The fae turned his back and walked away, leaving Rory no choice but to jog after him until he caught up. A path opened at the edge of the woods, wide enough for the two of them to walk side-by-side. The mulch beneath their feet rustled, the sound echoed by the leaves above their heads. Even here in the shade of the giant trees, the air's clarity persisted. A hush descended around them as they passed, then sound swelled after their passage as birds and little animals resumed their daily lives. More than once, Rory opened his mouth to push for answers only to clamp his jaw closed at the expression on Manannán's face.

"You made a bargain with the harper, many lives ago."

Rory held his tongue.

"You remember this bargain, your life for hers, thinking Abhean or I would take you then after restoring the child to her life. But your life and hers have been entwined always. When Ciaran found you, did he tell you of the binding?"

"No, but I remember."

Manannán chuckled, a dark, stormy sound that rumbled like thunder. "You MacDermots remember too much sometimes."

"I was there. In Tuam that *Lughnasadh* night when you took Becca from Ciaran. And I watched him wither and dry up, his will to live sucked out of him. He wouldn't take his own life but he was willing to die in battle to join her. Then she found her way back. She found a way to return. And Ciaran bound her to him, and she bound him, there at the *Samhain* fires."

"Ay, he did, with a bit of help from Onagh and Finvarra. To this day the *Taoiseach* of Clann MacDermot wears the MacDermot Knot. And do you remember the vow you made?"

Rory's brow furrowed. "I made no vow, especially not to a woman."

"Aye, you did, mortal. You vowed never to love as Ciaran did. Do you know the story of the binding?"

That stumped him. As if he rifled through a file drawer, he searched his memories but nothing came to mind. He finally shook his head, admitting defeat.

"As a very wise woman once told Ciaran, back in the very beginning of time, back before the misty blue mountains existed, each man had a woman. And each woman had a man. Two hearts. One soul. When they found each other, and pledged the vow, their lives joined throughout eternity. Life after life."

Manannán stopped and prevented Rory stepping past by throwing up his arm as a barrier. Luckily. They stood on a cliff. Down below, a wide river meandered through a narrow valley. As Rory watched, islands appeared or disappeared with no rhyme or reason he could discern. The big fae silently watched for much too long to suit Rory, but once again, he remained silent while questions burned the tip of his tongue.

"You vowed never to love like that, Riordan MacDermot, and Fate heard you. By your own action, you condemned not only yourself but that of your other heart to lifetimes of loneliness."

"Fate? Ha. I don't believe in fate. Life is what we make of it."

"Is it? Time is a river, mortal. And human lives are but islands in that stream."

Rory blinked several times, staring in shock at the scene below. "Wait. What? You mean those are people's lives?"

"Aye. They are."

Two islands, surrounded by mist, appeared. A man might almost jump between them they were so close. A figure appeared on one, insubstantial as if Rory watched through smoke and mirrors. A woman. A familiar ache lodged in his chest. "Delaney." Her name lingered on his lips and his hand reached for her of its own volition.

Manannán waved a negligent hand and the fog on the island danced and curled beckoning fingers around her before dissipating as if teased by a spring breeze. Rory could see her now. She looked the same but…not. A tightness around her mouth and eyes, furrows across her forehead, hunched shoulders—this was a woman tired and worn by the cares she carried. Behind her, like an antique kinescope, scenes from her life—lives—flickered. Mesmerized, Rory watched.

The ache in his chest expanded as Delaney loved Conor life after life, and lost him to Neasa each time. And in each life, a dim figure haunted her existence, always ready but never summoned. Sometimes she noticed that dark shade, but always her heart yearned for the man she was never meant to have. Anger warred with sadness within him as the mist once again enshrouded the figure and the island winked out of existence.

"What just happened?" He gritted out the question from between clenched teeth.

"You weren't there."

"What are you saying?"

"You were not there, Riordan MacDermot. You had no place in the life you remember but of which she has no recollection. You never existed. Everything changed once your vow to Abhean was fulfilled."

"What the hell do you mean I never existed?" His heart stopped beating, or so it felt from the pain radiating in his chest. "That island. Delaney's island. It disappeared. Why?"

Manannán stared down at the river, his silence wrapped like a shroud around them both.

"She dies?" Rory didn't breathe, terrified of the answer.

The fae laughed, a dark, brittle sound like nails on a blackboard. "All mortals die. Each in their own time. It was her time." He studied Rory for a time. "You made the bargain, Riordan. Abhean called your marker due."

Breathe. He had to remember to breathe. "Wait. If I wasn't there, what about Nelda Whitson? Does that mean she wasn't shot? That she survived?" He hated the hope coating his voice.

A fleeting ghost of emotion flitted across the fae's expression. Sadness. "Nay. Each comes and goes in their own time, mortal. 'Twas her time as well."

That caught Rory flatfooted, and he watched Manannán walk away. Realizing the fae was about to disappear, he jogged to catch up and the import of the fae's earlier words penetrated. "What do you mean I wasn't there?"

"You didn't exist. That life never happened." Manannán's steps slowed. "You were never born, Riordan. Not in that life. And because of that, you weren't there to keep Dean Carter from his mistakes. You weren't there when Delaney was taken hostage. And you weren't there when Carter pulled the trigger."

"NOOOOOOOOOO!" Rory dropped to his knees, the pain in his chest ripping him apart. Tears slicked his face as he rocked and moaned, unable to bear the knowledge. Rory stared at the remaining island, knew the shadow inhabiting it mirrored his actions, endured his grief. When he could breathe again, he had but one question. "Why?"

"That is the question, mortal. All of you ask it, but none of you seek the answer."

Rory pushed to his feet. He swiped his sleeve over his face to clear his vision then glanced at the magical being beside him. "Why? What have the MacDermots done to the fae? Why do you torment us?"

Manannán threw back his head and laughed, the

pealing tones ringing bitterly in the thickening air. "Torment you?" He waved his hand and islands appeared in the river, islands so thick they clogged the channel, bumping and clinging to their neighbors. "I have far too many lives to concern myself with one mortal bloodline. But Abhean forces my hand."

"Why?"

"Why indeed?" Abhean appeared in a shimmer of air, but only Rory startled at his appearance.

Deciding discretion was the better part of valor, he backed up a few steps, leaving the two powerful beings to face each other. OODA, he reminded himself. Observe. Orient. Decide. Act. As soon as he reminded himself to breathe. The hair on his arms prickled as static electricity crackled in the air. A human was pretty stupid to stand here and watch what could be an epic battle, yet he couldn't look away, couldn't run away even though his common sense screamed that's exactly what he needed to do.

Colors swirled around Manannán—blue, violet, red, purple—bruising the air. Abhean stood loose-limbed, seemingly unconcerned, but his long hair lifted, forming a nimbus of gold and silver around his head.

Dizzy, Rory closed his eyes, but then he opened them almost immediately when a whirlwind swirled around the two men, kicking up leaves and twigs. Rory backed up further, using his arm to protect his eyes.

"The mortal asked a question, Manannán. I would like the answer. Why?"

"I would ask you the same question, Abhean. Why? Why have you persisted in this mad feud?"

"Why? Is it not obvious?" Abhean's voice, once as sweet as spun sugar cracked. Brittle. Bitter, like rock salt, or unshed tears.

"Do you miss the mortal realm so much then?" Manannán's voice gentled, like distant thunder after a spring storm. "Do you regret so much that I removed you from there, that I brought you here?"

Abhean stared at the other fae, unmoving, not even to breathe. Rory held his breath, but whether in fearful anticipation or sympathy, he couldn't say. As if someone gave a signal, the two beings stepped to their right, circling, eyes unflinchingly on the other, Rory all but forgotten, much to his relief.

"Why?"

"You know why, Abhean. The answers lie within you."

"I want the words from your lips."

"Do you? Are you so sure of that, harper?"

"I am. I want to hear you say it. I want to know why."

"Because I loved her." Manannán waved a hand toward Rory. "Like he loves his Delaney. And like the two mortals, the love I had for your mother was like two shadows kissing without hope of substance. She was mortal, Abhean. And I am the King of Tir Nan Óg. He sighed and it seemed the whole land exhaled with him. "When she turned her back on you—on us and walked away, I brought you here."

Rory rocked back on his heels and considered slipping away, but he was too curious. He refused to consider how curiosity killed the cat. He wasn't a cat. He cut his gaze back and forth between the two fae. Was it possible?

"You've always loved the mortals, Abhean. Even as a child, your curious nature sent you to the standing stones to watch their lives. I wondered if you searched for her in the human realm, but you didn't. It wasn't her life that drew you, but those of the O'Connors and the MacDermots. You meddled even then, thinking you knew best." Manannán waved his hand and the islands in the river began their seductive dance once more. "You do not understand, even now. The mortals are but shadows. Their love gives them the substance to become real." He waved his hand again and everything around them disappeared.

Rory barely hung on to the contents of his stomach. His feet felt like they stood planted on solid ground, though nothing but fog swirled around him inducing a stomach-turning vertigo. He could no longer see the two fae, could no longer see the hand he held up to his face. Fear, stark and cold, knifed through him.

"Do you not understand, Abhean? We are the mist. Our essence is nothing but smoke. We don't exist beyond this place, except within the dreams of those who remember us. Love, Abhean. That is the stuff and substance of our existence." In the mist, a hand appeared—Manannán holding his out. "I loved your mother, Abhean, as I love the son she gifted me."

The wind whipped around Rory again, tugging his clothes with invisible fingers. He didn't move, watching as a vortex centered on where he'd last seen the harper. Abhean's face, contorted with anger, materialized briefly, and then was swallowed again. The next time the fae appeared, his body had more substance, and his anger melted into abject misery. Manannán solidified right in front of Abhean. He reached for the other fae and pulled Abhean's resisting body into his arms.

"I love the son, Abhean. Despite his rebellion. His rage. I steadfastly refused to bargain with you because I am selfish. I could not bear to lose you to the human realm."

Rory felt like his stomach was ripped out of him. This was far worse than any express elevator dropping straight into hell. Boiling blackness buffeted his body with a wicked wind. He couldn't hear. Couldn't see. Couldn't breathe. Was this death? Had he witnessed something so profound that his existence must now be snuffed out? The searing wind burned away his entire psyche, shredding skin and bone, thought, memories. Stripping him bare until only one thing remained.

Delaney.

Chapter 22

Delaney curled up on her couch with a cup of tea. She considered calling Bronwyn to visit but figured her best friend would be out on a date. Friday night. The whole world was out doing a mating dance. Except her. With a desultory stab of her thumb on the TV remote, she flicked through the channels. Four hundred channels later, she turned it off. Feeling sorry for herself didn't help but she wallowed in her depression anyway. Nessa always messed things up. This time Delaney had found the perfect man. Handsome. Intelligent. Wealthy. And yes, she admitted, she was shallow. She'd even tried the nerdy route, to no avail. Nessa always appeared. Beautiful, sexy Nessa with her big eyes and simpering manner. And the men in Delaney's life always fell for her sister. Every. Last. One. Of. Them.

She glanced at her cell phone and actually wished it would ring, especially if the call came from police dispatch. Her practice, so mundane and boring, offered no challenge, though why she thought she needed a challenge was beyond her. When she'd read the ad in the paper, something clicked and she'd applied. She was an expert on PTSD, doing work at the Veteran's Administration hospital with returning vets, and she'd done an interesting study of EMDR, too. Eye Movement Desensitization and Reprocessing had been around enough years now that it had credence within the medical community. Luckily, the police department realized the need for their first responders to be debriefed, psychologically speaking, after a bad incident. She'd been surprised by the number of those.

Her phone rang, but it was the landline, not her cell. Nobody important called that number. Delaney waited for the answering machine to pick up. After her short greeting, her mother's voice echoed from the speaker. She winced.

"Delaney Burns, I am so ashamed of you! Why aren't you here? The whole family is. Except you. Your father and I and poor Nessa are making excuses for you left and right. Good heavens, do you have any idea how embarrassing it is to explain to Connor's parents that his fiancée's own sister couldn't be bothered to attend their engagement party? They've come all the way from Ireland, Delaney. They are important people."

She rolled her eyes, hearing the capitalization of those last two words in her mother's voice. So typical. No one worried about her feelings. No one gave a second thought to the fact she and Connor had been dating exclusively, that he'd mentioned marriage. Until he'd met Nessa. One look at Nessa and Delaney ceased to exist. Logically speaking, she should be glad to find out what a jerk he was before things went any further, but it still hurt. Her entire family conveniently forgot that she had feelings, too.

"I've assured Mr. and Mrs. MacDermot that you aren't rude by nature. I've excused you, claiming health issues. Migraine, so you have the story straight since we're having lunch with them tomorrow. You will be there if I have to come and drag you there myself."

Dead air hummed. Her mother's hang-ups weren't nearly as dramatic if she called from a cell phone. When she had a handset, that woman could slam a phone into the cradle with a vengeance. Delaney sighed. Typical. A command performance but once again, her mother neglected to give her pertinent details, like where and when. She heaved off the couch and padded barefoot into the kitchen to deposit the cup now filled with tepid tea in the sink. She looked around her. All she needed was a cat and she'd be the stereotypical spinster spending her nights alone. Good grief, she even wore a threadbare flannel gown and fuzzy rabbit house shoes.

"I'm a putz. A total and complete failure." In the background, a song played on her radio—old but familiar. No one heard, so the singer said. "Boy, ain't that the truth, though." She fell asleep on the couch, trying not to think about the ordeal she faced the next day.

****

After a frustrating morning of unanswered phone calls and texts, Delaney finally received the location of her imminent embarrassment. Not that anyone would care how uncomfortable the situation was for her. She parked her car at the one bank branch with Saturday hours. She dashed inside with a few minutes to spare before closing time. She might be a little late to lunch but she wanted to deposit her fee check from the city and get some cash. Since her parents were hosting, she figured she could pay her own tab with the cash and escape when no one was looking.

The line moved slowly—several people deep and only two tellers on duty made for slow service. Not that she was in any hurry. Her phone dinged and she retrieved the text message from Nessa.

Feel free to bring a date.

She almost burst out laughing, but the lump in her throat refused to give way. Her sister now wore an engagement ring from the only man Delaney had dated in the last year. Bring a date? Really? She shuffled forward and debated whether to respond, upset with both the late *permission* and the sheer callousness. Her turn came at last, and she pushed her check, deposit slip, and ID across the cold marble counter. The teller barely looked up at her, instead remaining intent on stamping and shuffling paper before counting out five twenties. Taking the folded paper envelope, Delaney turned and buried her nose in a man's chest. A very tall man. With long blond hair. And a really nice chest—covered—barely. The shirt he wore, unbuttoned, revealed taut abs highlighted by the crisp white cotton and dark jacket framing all of it. She forced her eyes up to his face, but they fought her all the way.

"I'm…sorry…" Her apology sighed out as she got her first glimpse of his face. For a mad, crazy, insane moment, she thought about asking him to be her escort. She could get through anything with this guy beside her and what an absolute bust to Nessa's chops if she showed up with a man who could grace the runway of any fashion show in New York. Or Milan. Paris.

Ask him! Nothing ventured, nothing gained. He looks like he can deal with your crazy family. Her inner voice was all but jumping up and down to get her attention. The idea was completely insane. Invite a perfect stranger to a family function? But her fingers itched to get caught in the net of his gold nimbus of hair. His coffee brown eyes warmed her from the toes up as he watched her. And his lips? She remembered to breathe. And then, his mouth moved and all the air whooshed out of her lungs.

A lazy curl of his lips tugged at his cheeks, forming a smile. "Aye, 'twould be a lovely time, me thinks."

Delaney almost swooned at his accent, but she stepped back from him, her cheeks flaming. Had she uttered that invitation out loud? He offered his arm, and she slipped her arm through it without thinking, bemused but curious. He led her outside and with a gallant flourish, placed her in the driver's seat of her car. He leaned in, his eyes as warm and rich as Sumatran coffee. For a moment, she wondered if he was going to kiss her, and her tummy clenched in anticipation. Time with this man would alter everything. She knew that with a certainty she didn't pause for a moment to question.

"Seatbelt?"

"Uhm…" She blinked up at him.

"Safety first, Delaney Burns. Buckle yer seatbelt, cailín."

The tip of her tongue teased her lips and she tasted something sweet. Spun sugar. *Breathe.* She did, and fumbled to get her seatbelt fastened.

"Keys?"

She blinked several times, trying to focus. Keys? Oh, yes, for the car. To make it go. She dug in her purse and her fingers brushed across the hard metal edges. With a triumphant flourish, Delaney rescued her keychain from the bottom of her handbag and dangled them from her hand. "Keys," she announced, pleased that she'd accomplished her task as she awaited his praise.

"Well done, cailín. Now put them in the infernal machine and get yee over t'the restaurant. I've an errand t'run first but I'll join you there."

"Promise?" Oh God. Had she actually pleaded with him? She wanted to bang her forehead on the steering wheel. Mortified, she could barely meet his gaze, but his smile reassured her.

"Aye, cailín. 'Tis a promise. I'll be there, Delaney Burns, for all tha' 'tis t'come." He did kiss her then, but it was only a whisper of warm, dry lips across her forehead. "There, now. Our bargain 'tis sealed with a kiss."

Her skin tingled where his lips had touched her. She blinked as she looked at him, her eyes dazzled by rainbows and bright sun. She blinked again and he was…gone. Delaney twisted her head this way and that, looking for him, but he'd disappeared. As if he'd never existed.

Her knuckles turned white where she gripped the steering wheel, and she leaned her head on them. Had her worst fear finally come to fruition? Did she have a psychotic break in the bank? She inhaled to steady her nerves and her nostrils flared. Fresh bread baking in the oven. Brownies. Fall leaves wet with rain. She breathed again. The scents remained though less noticeable now. The man. That's what he'd smelled like. If she stood outside a bakery in an autumn rain, eating warm brownies, this is what he would smell—and taste like.

Delaney shivered. She'd had these flights of fancy since childhood. Her *moments*, as her mother called them, had been what prompted her interest in psychology. Self-diagnosis was foolish, but she'd always felt…different. Out of sync with her family and her world. She had one true friend in Bronwyn but her parents felt like strangers and her brother and sister seemed intent on tormenting her. Even now. The one man she'd fallen in love with was at that very moment planning a wedding with her sister.

Her phone dinged. Nessa. What now? She read the text. *You have to stop by Sweet Desires to pick up the cake. Mom forgot.* Before she could so much as sigh, the phone dinged again. *Take cash. They don't take credit cards.* Of course they didn't. And why would Nessa or her mother pay for it when they ordered the darn thing?

Delaney jammed the key in the ignition. In a series of fits and starts, she backed out of the parking space and headed to the bakery.

Forty-five minutes and four increasingly demanding texts later, Delaney arrived at the restaurant. She was over thirty minutes late, the only parking space left was in the very back of the lot, and the skies looked like they could open up and rain any minute. The summer had been hot and dry so any rain would be welcome, but couldn't it wait until she was safe inside?

She managed to get the cake out of the car without damage and was only a few feet from the front door when the first drops splattered the dusty pavement at her feet. She reached for the handle just as someone inside pushed the heavy wooden door open. Delaney squealed as she danced backward and juggled the massive cake box.

"Ah, and here yee are, cailín." The man from the bank caught the box and steadied her with a hand under her elbow all at the same time.

Delaney sighed. And then she chuckled, the sound as self-conscious as the flood of red staining her cheeks. But really, how could any warm-blooded woman *not* sigh around this man? "You came."

"Of course, I did, cailín. I wouldn't miss this for the world. Come along inside. Everyone is waiting for you." His eyes flicked over her shoulder and when she turned her head to follow his gaze, he tugged her forward. She caught sight of a shadowed figure, but she was inside and the door closed before she got more than a glimpse. A smidgeon of unease tickled the back of her neck, but then her escort beamed at her and she forgot everything but the radiance of his smile.

He led her to the private room at the back of the restaurant. Her mother and sister pounced the moment she walked through the door. She fielded their questions and tried to make sense of the hurried introductions that weren't really introductions at all. Her mother pointed to the members of Connor's family, said names, and then demanded to know why Delaney brought a stranger into their midst. A waiter retrieved the cake with a deft slide-and-glide move and was gone within moments. She stammered something about Nessa's text and tried to wrap her mouth around words that made sense. Her escort slid into the breach with amazing dexterity.

"I knew Delaney's mother must be a beauty," he purred taking her mother's hand and looking for all the world like he was going to kiss it. The harsh lines around her mother's eyes softened as the woman smiled at him. He didn't release her hand as he tugged her back toward the front table. "Delaney and I are old acquaintances, Mrs. Burns," he explained and sounded perfectly reasonable, despite the lie.

Nessa grabbed her arm and pinched. “I didn’t send you any text. What are you trying to do, Delaney?”

She fumbled for her phone, punched it, and held the text screen up. “You did to.”

“Well…it’s not like I expected you to actually bring someone. You’ll have to pay Mom and Dad back for his lunch. I can’t believe you sometimes, Laney. First you don’t show up last night and embarrass us all and now you show up with…” Her voice drifted off a bit dreamily as she waved a languid hand toward…

Delaney’s sigh sounded like, “Argh.” She *still* didn’t know his name. She really needed to discover what it was before her lie was totally exposed. She watched the man steer her mother toward a side table and wondered why he kept his back to the head table. Moments later, her mother returned with champagne glasses. She kept one and offered the other to Nessa. Delaney tried not to roll her eyes. So typical.

“Evan is a musician.” Her mother positively gushed. “He’s agreed to sing something after lunch. “Please tell me he’s not one of your patients or something, Delaney.”

She managed not to flush. “No, Mother. He’s not.” Evan. So his name was Evan. And now she saw the black leather case at his feet. Violin? How had she missed that earlier? “I do know people outside of my practice.”

“At least you didn’t drag one of those awful policemen here.”

Delaney bristled at that. Most of the police officers she worked with were interesting and polite and…real. Far more so than the crowds Nessa and Keegan hung around with. She bit her tongue. Her mother wanted to pick a fight and the only way to avoid one would be to walk away. She plastered what she hoped was a pleasant expression on her face. “Excuse me. I think I’d like a glass of champagne myself.” She walked away before her mom or Nessa could say anything.

Moments later, Nessa returned to Connor’s side. Delaney had to admit that her sister glowed as she basked in the sunshine that was Connor. With a tight pursing of her lips and a warning glare, her mother followed. Delaney exhaled. She’d escaped for now but figured she’d get an earful later when Very Important People weren’t around to overhear.

A deep chuckle ruffled her hair and she turned to look at Evan. “Thank you for charming my mother, Evan.”

The chuckle rolled into laughter. “Evan is it? Nay, cailín. M’name is Abhean.”

He spelled it for her, and she tasted his name on the tip of her tongue and her lips. Her ears heard ay-veen, and she could understand why her mother thought it otherwise, given his lilting accent. And his voice. Once more, his voice reminded her of spun sugar and marzipan. She realized she was swaying closer to him then saw a gleam in his eye that unsettled her. She inhaled deeply, steadying herself, and straightened.

He chuckled again. “Aye, cailín. ’Twas ever so. A cautious soul yee have.” He leaned closer. One hand brushed the hair back from her face, and his lips teased her temple with a feathery touch. “’Twill stand you in good stead, m’thinks, cailín, with what’s to come.”

His words sent shivers scurrying down her spine, and she did her best not to show how unsettled his nearness made her feel. Delaney gazed into his eyes and became immediately lost in a swirling miasma of colors. Her body leaned closer as if it was made of metal and he was a powerful magnet. Brief glimpses of scenes caught her attention, none lasting long enough for her to make sense of them. But there was someone. A man. One she didn't recognize, but she did.

Delaney blinked and found herself seated at the end of a table on the far side of the room—as far away from her family and the MacDermots as possible. She glanced around, confused and dazed. How had she gotten here? Where was Evan—no, Abhean. He was her date. He should be next to her, but he stood near the door, staring intently at the head table.

The hair on the back of her neck prickled, and a sense of unease raised goosebumps on her arms. She shivered. Something was very, very wrong here. She studied the people seated at the front of the room. Connor and Nessa reigned like a prince and princess over their court. His dark head and her fair one remained close as they leaned into each other, chatting in whispers and ignoring everyone else.

Her brother Keegan stared at the woman seated next to him, all but drooling over Connor's twin sister. Delaney couldn't fault him for his reaction. Ciara was absolutely stunning. She choked back a shuddering laugh as she realized Connor would have made a beautiful woman—a thought that unsettled her more than a little.

Rhea Burns talked to everyone within her sphere. The woman looked like an animated doll—perfectly coiffed and wearing a designer dress—her hands directing the conversation like a maestro. Connor's poor mother was forced to pay attention, and she might have looked bored but for the ways her eyes kept cutting to the man next to her.

Oh. My. Delaney's girly bits snapped to attention. Connor's dad was so handsome every woman in the room should forego dessert and just enjoy the sight of him. Just as filling and so many fewer calories. This was the first good look she'd gotten of him. He had to be tall, judging from what she could see of his torso. Broad-shouldered and still fit looking at his age. His blue-black hair showed no hint of silver, and Delaney would bet real money the man never looked at a box of hair dye, much less used the stuff.

As she watched, both Mr. and Mrs. MacDermot tensed, their gazes snapping in unison to the same spot in the room. Delaney glanced that way and gasped. Evan—no, Abhean. He held a violin and his nimbus of hair floated around his head almost sparking with static electricity. With effort, she dragged her gaze back to Kieran and Becca MacDermot. They *knew* him. And they were mad as hell he was there. She slunk lower in her seat and wished she could disappear. There'd be hell to pay now, from her mother and sister.

She glanced longingly at the door and wondered if she could slip away without notice. Adrenaline surged and she focused on the flight or fight sensation tingling in her body. But she couldn't move. As if mesmerized, no one in the room moved. No one but Kieran MacDermot. He rose to his feet, and a part of Delaney's brain realized he was *really* tall.

"Abhean."

"MacDermot."

The two men faced each other, both stiff, neither

yielding. A hush blanketed the room, and Delaney could feel the daggers thrown her way from Nessa and her mother. She refused to look at them, focusing on the two men instead.

"Why have you come then?"

"'Tis a time of joy for Clann MacDermot, *Taoiseach*. I come to play a blessing on the couple soon t'be wed." And with that, he lifted his violin and bow and began to play.

As the music swelled, Delaney could almost see the notes dancing like dust motes on the air. Her body swayed with the tune, her feet tapping out the rhythm. And then Abhean sang. She lost all track of time, all sense of reality, lost in the patterns of the unfamiliar words. Gaelic. Some small part of her brain still functioning managed to identify at least that much. And the words were a vow of some sort. A vow for lovers. A vow between lovers. A vow for eternity.

A vow she would never make. She snapped out of her trance with that realization. She stared at the man fiddling and singing, his long blond hair whipping about him as gold and silver sparks shot from the silken strands. He was at once the most beautiful and most terrible being she'd ever seen.

The music crashed into silence as the doors exploded. The scene segued into slow motion. A hulking man wearing dark clothing and a mask paused at the door, the nasty-looking automatic rifle in his hands covering the entire room with broad sweeps.

The spot where Abhean once stood now shimmered like heat waves flickering above hot pavement on an August day. The musician vanished as if he'd never been there. Kieran stood tall and angry, facing the intruder while sweeping his wife behind him—a warrior once and always. Delaney's father cowered, as did her mother and brother. Connor froze, half-standing, his hand on Nessa's shoulder to push her below the table. He looked scared but determined, standing there in his father's shadow. Connor's colleagues looked almost bemused, as if this was some sort of entertainment staged for their enjoyment. But she knew better.

Surreptitiously, she dug her phone out of her pocket where she'd dropped it after her confrontation with Nessa. Luckily, she hadn't put it back in the black void of her purse. Not daring to breathe, she turned down the volume and dialed 9-1-1. She slid it onto the table and surreptitiously flicked a cloth napkin over it, hoping it would go unnoticed.

"Man with a gun." She breathed the words, hoping the phone's microphone would be enough to pick up her voice. "Glen Ross Restaurant."

"Everybody shut up!"

One of the lawyers laughed. The gunman sprayed bullets his direction, barely missing the man.

Nobody laughed now. Everyone ducked behind the tables. Everyone but the MacDermots. And her.

She recognized that voice, and her insides first turned to ice and then blazed as if hell itself opened a portal there. She swallowed the bile rising in her throat.

Dean Carter waved his assault rifle again. "I want all the women to move over there." He jerked his chin toward the wall farthest from the door and the windows. "Now!"

She didn't move, but the other women, hesitant, some of them crying and shaking, did as he bid. Once they'd gathered behind her, all but Beeca MacDermot who stood by her side, Carter slipped sideways, closer to them and away from the door.

"You shouldav listened to me, Doc." His voice sounded flat, but Delaney recognized the suppressed rage hiding behind the words.

"You know this man?" Her mother, voice sharp and accusing sounded incredulous.

"Shut up! Nobody talks but me."

He spared a glance for the women before turning his attention to the men. "Get out. All of you. Cops'll be here before long. Tell them this won't last long." He pointed his gun at Kieran. "You first." Then the barrel shifted to point at her and Becca. "Move it or this lady goes first."

"Kieran." Becca said his name and Delaney shivered at the emotion in that one word.

Love. Hope. Faith. Trust.

Asking and giving.

Looking like he could rip Carter in two with his bare hands, Kieran dipped his chin once in answer to his wife's plea. He nudged Connor and helped John Burns to his feet. "Do as the man says." Though spoken softly, his words held the whiplash of an order.

All of the men rose from their hiding places and shuffled toward the door. Kieran herded them out and turned, planting his feet wide in a warrior's stance. "Know this. If a hair is out of place on her head, I'll hunt you through the shades of hell itself."

Delaney shivered at the deadly promise. She opened her mouth, but no words came out.

"Shut the door behind you."

Kieran and Becca exchanged a long look, and then

he reached for the edges of the double doors and pulled them closed as he stepped out.

Tears slicked the faces of some of the women, including Nessa's. Others stood in mute terror. All but Delaney and Becca. Strength and determination radiated from the other woman, and Delaney suspected Connor's mother was as much a warrior as his father.

"You screwed up, Doc."

Chapter 23

"Dean, think about what you are doing."

"Shut up, *Doctor* Burns. I'm in charge now."

Breathe. She had to get this situation under control—for everyone's sakes. "You've always been in charge, Dean." She furrowed her brow, the sense of déjà vu so strong she could almost taste it.

"Who is this man, Delaney?"

"This is all your fault!" The shrill voices of her mother and sister echoed each other.

"Shut up, you two."

One hissed out a breath, the other gasped. She didn't know who did what and didn't care. The situation demanded her complete attention.

Delaney felt Becca MacDermot shift beside her. She'd almost forgotten the woman was there. "Let me deal with this. Dean is here for me. Right, Dean?"

She wracked her memory for the lessons in hostage negotiation she'd so recently learned in hopes of expanding her consulting contract with the city. She eased her hands where they gripped the back of her chair, stretching her arms out in front of her just a hair, palms down, fingers splayed in a gesture asking for calm.

"Oh, I'm here for you, bitch. But all these others are my insurance."

Delaney repressed the shudder building in her

middle. "Okay, Dean. You're in charge."

Someone gasped, Nessa she guessed, and without thinking she whirled. "Sit down and shut up. Let me deal with this before you make it worse."

Her mother and sister looked stunned but they did as she ordered. All of them did, but Becca. The woman seemed frozen in place.

With her hands still making a placating motion, Delaney pivoted to face Carter again. No wonder Becca had stilled. Dean had the rifle pointed straight at Delaney.

"It's okay, Dean. You're in charge. I just wanted them to know that and to be quiet so you and I can talk. We can talk, right?"

"You talk too much. That's your problem, Doc. Talk, talk, talk. You should have cleared me back to duty. We wouldn't be here if you had."

Her lips felt as dry and cracked as a drought-parched field, but she fought the urge to wet them with her tongue. To do so would be a sign of weakness. She swallowed what little spit she could, but her throat still felt raw and scorched.

"I didn't think you were quite ready for duty, Dean. I didn't say you'd never go back to the team." She lied through her teeth, hoping he couldn't hear the pounding of her heart and know.

"Bullshit."

"No, Dean. Really. A few more sessions and I would have cleared you for duty. It's…" Her brain scrambled for an excuse. "It's mandatory. New rules that came down from the chief's office." She inhaled and sought a calm center within herself. "Look, we both know that you're fine."

Her mother gasped and Delaney wanted to stomp on her foot or something. “Mother, please? This is a conversation between Dean and me. Do not interfere.” She plastered a smile on her face. “Civilian, Dean. She doesn’t understand.”

“And you do?” Was there a plea in his voice?

“I’m trying to understand you, Dean. I do understand the system. How it’s stacked against you. You just want to do your duty, right?” Becca shifted again, but Delaney felt approval in that move. She remembered her impression of this woman as a warrior and the thought steadied her.

“Yeah. I’m a good cop. I belong on the SWAT team.”

She nodded and swallowed around the lie clogging her throat. “Yes.” There. Just the one word. Not so big a lie. “Look, Dean, you know they’ll be here any minute. You know the routine. They’ll want assurances. Why don’t you—”

“YOU! IN THE BUILDING!” A voice blared through a bullhorn cutting off her suggestion.

Delaney winced as Carter raised his rifle toward the windows. Made with patterned glass, except for a few panes, light filtered in, but there was no clear view of anything outside from where she stood. She pictured the restaurant in her mind, trying to find a frame of geographic reference.

Was this room on the back of the building? The front? Where would the SWAT sniper team set up? And how would they see inside? Camera! She had to distract Dean. He’d know. And then she remembered her cell phone. There on the table. Did the dispatcher still listen? Was their conversation being monitored by the police in the command post even now? She had to keep him talking.

"Dean? We need to answer them. You know how this works. We both know that if circumstances had been different, you'd be out there right now with your team." Was that enough information for them to figure out who they were dealing with?

"Shut up. I need to think."

Delaney glanced at Becca. The woman remained rock steady even as the others, now huddled on the floor against the wall, sniffled or sobbed quietly. Becca nodded almost imperceptively, a mute gesture of support.

"We want to set up a line of communication. One of our officers will bring a phone to the door."

"NO!"

"Dean…please?" She breathed, hoping her sudden panic didn't overwhelm her. "We need to listen to them. Listen to what they have to say, okay? I'll get the phone. You can trust me. I'll barely open the door—just enough to grab the phone, and I'll stay right here. Okay? Will that be okay?"

"C'mere, Doc." He wagged the rifle barrel at her. "Come here."

Delaney sidled over toward him. He reached out and grabbed her. She just managed to swallow her gasp. Doing her best not to shiver, she stood next to him.

"You!" He pointed the gun at Becca. "Go to the door." His gaze darted around the room as if he sought something in particular. He raised his voice, shouting again. "I know you have eyes, Captain Davis. Yeah, I recognize your gawddamned voice. I'm the one in charge, so you listen to me."

"I'm listening, Carter."

She almost wept in relief. They knew who they were dealing with.

"I have Doc Burns. She dies first if there's anything hinky. You got that?"

"What do you want, Carter?"

"I know you have a damn camera in here. Get rid of it. I want you blind."

"No camera, Carter. We haven't had time to get one set up."

"You!" He hissed at Becca. "Go stand at the door." He raised his voice. "You wanna talk to me? That phone better have a speaker. I'm sending a hostage to pick it up. I want it right at the door so all she has to do is reach out one hand to get it. If she disappears from that door, everybody is dead. We clear?"

"We're clear. The phone is in place. If she will open the right-hand door, all she has to do is grab it."

Carter dropped to one knee and surveyed the crack beneath the doors. Satisfied, he stood and nodded to Becca. She did as she was told. Once she retrieved the phone, she turned to face him.

"Answer it when it rings. Hit the speaker phone button. Put it on that table." Again, she did as he instructed then moved back to her former position, standing like a barrier between the shooter and the other women.

"Carter, can you hear me?" The captain's voice warbled from the phone's inferior speaker.

"Yeah. Nobody is going to win this. You know that, right? It's gone too far."

"No one's been hurt, Carter. We can still fix this."

"No. Nobody can. The doc screwed up, captain.

She shoulda cleared me for duty. This woulda never happened."

"The doctor just followed orders, Carter. Mandatory counseling and suspension after a shooting. She would have cleared you after you completed the sessions. She told me so in her report. She thought you could go right back, said your head was fine. But regulations... We all have to work within the regulations, Carter. Right?"

Delaney trembled. They had monitored her conversation. Thank goodness! She'd given them room to work. Maybe…just maybe, they'd all get out of this alive.

"Dean?" She modulated her voice, keeping it soft and encouraging. "The captain is right. We can talk this out. Work through it. But you need to let the others go. I'll stay. I'll talk to you. But there's no reason to keep them. Look at them—" With a careful wave of her hand, she drew his attention to seven women huddled together on the floor and the eighth who stood tall and brave. "I know my mother and sister. They're on the brink of hysterics. We don't want that, do we? There's nothing worse than a bunch of hysterical women." She didn't move, waiting for him to respond. When he didn't, she reached out her hand, with infinite care, and touched him on the shoulder. *Connect.* She had to connect with him. "Dean?" She whispered his name.

He shook himself like he was coming out of trance. Glaring at her, he stepped back, away from her touch. "Yeah. Fine. Get out, bitches."

Before Delaney could move, he snagged her biceps and squeezed brutally. "You're stayin' right here, Doc. This is all your fault. You're gonna pay for it, just like me."

No one moved at first, but then Becca galvanized the others, helping them to stand, shepherding them toward the door. Once she had them gathered, she cracked one of the doors open and yelled out. "There are eight of us. All women. We're coming out." Then she held the door a bit wider and pushed them through one-by-one. She turned to give Delaney a look and a nod before slipping through herself. The door whispered to a close, and Delaney was left alone with the man who held her life in his hands.

****

Rory's vision clouded and mimicked a kaleidoscope as dizzy images spun around him. He closed his eyes and breathed through the sensation. Voices. He kept hearing voices. Wait. Was that—? Ciaran? Or Kieran. Where was he? *When* was he? Becca. Another voice he recognized. Recognition was good. He concentrated. Focused on making sense of what they said.

"You know who he is?" The woman—no, Becca. That *was* Becca's voice.

"Yeah. Unfortunately, he is one of ours."

Captain Davis? Rory opened his eyes and wanted to throw up. He was still caught in the middle of the whirling dervish. He latched onto the voices in his head to anchor him.

"Delaney is handling him quite well, given the circumstances."

Delaney! Her name left him flash frozen with dread. She was in danger and there wasn't a damn thing he could do.

Focus. He had to focus. One of ours the captain

said. The dread flared, white-hot now. He could feel sweat trickling down his back. He could feel! *Breathe.* In. Out. *Breathe.*

"Where is the sniper?" Becca sounded matter-of-fact. That was good, right?

"On the building across the street. He has a view of the windows." Kieran sounded like he was in charge. That was good. Definitely. He trusted Kieran.

"It doesn't matter. He doesn't have a clear shot. That leaded glass is all wonky." Captain Davis. Wait? What was going on? Why were Kieran and Becca with the captain?

"There are some clear panes, intermixed with the pressed glass."

Rory heard Kieran chuckle as the man said, "Well done, darling. I knew there was a reason I still love you madly after all these years."

The wind whistled in his ears, and he could no longer hear. Sandpaper rode the storm, abrading his bare skin. Pain scraped across his psyche. Fireworks burst across his retinas and he blacked out.

Rory became aware of hot sun beating down on his prone body. Loose gravel on the tar roof poked his elbows. He opened his eyes and almost yelled in relief. He was on a rooftop across an alley facing a window. Captain Davis's words still echoed in his earpiece.

"The glass in the windows. One of the hostages says there are clear panes."

He shifted the angle of his scope searching the window. There. The captain was right. He scrambled to get a better firing angle. *There!* Yes. He had both of them in the scope. Delaney and Carter. His lungs labored while his heart skipped erratically. *Breathe.*

Sweat beaded on his forehead, and one drop trickled down the bridge of his nose. He ignored it. *Breathe.* Heart rate and respirations returned to normal despite the thoughts and sensations whirling in his brain. He swallowed bile. Couldn't decide if it was left from the tornadic ride or churned up by the sight of Delaney in danger. *Breathe.*

"I have target." Three words. Three words that would seal the fate of the man foolish enough to threaten Delaney with harm.

The air in front him shimmered. He could deal with heat waves—he already had target acquisition. Then his scope went black. What the hell? He raised his head. A man in dark jeans, a black shirt, and a dark leather jacket materialized. The apparition stepped to the side and leaned against the wall of the building next door, a negligent pose, all things considered. Abhean didn't smile as the two of them stared at each other. Rory tried to read the fae's expression but failed. He wondered what a brass jacketed steel slug would do to an immortal being. Then he ignored Abhean, returning his focus to the sniper scope on his rifle. Carter and Delaney hadn't moved.

"Your life for hers, mortal."

"Shut up, Abhean."

"She's going to die today, mortal, no matter what you do."

For just a moment, another face flashed in front of him—Nelda Whitson. Nausea roiled in his gut, and he swallowed bile. More sweat rolled off his forehead, dripping into his eyes. Rory ignored the discomfort like he ignored Abhean.

"One last chance, mortal. I will save her today, to

live out this life, unknowing she had another. And I will return you to Tir Nan Óg."

The heat waves intensified, a dancing curtain flickering between him and Delaney. Gray mist formed around the edges of his vision, spinning into a vortex centered inside his scope. *No. Not again. Breathe. Trust in yourself.*

"Rory!" Scott. Yelling in his ear. No. His earpiece. "Dammit, Rory, answer!"

The fog cleared. He gazed through the scope, vision sharp and focused through a pane of clear glass. Carter held Delaney in front of him, one arm wrapped around her upper arms and chest. The fool held a handgun to her head. Things had changed a little in this life, but not that much. Even if Delaney didn't remember him, he would still finish this. He would keep her safe this time.

"Fuck off, Abhean."

Laughter. And not from the damned fae. "Well done, Riordan."

Wrong fae then. Manannán. The king must have sent him back. And just in time. "My name isn't Riordan. It's Rory."

Chapter 24

Breathe. Inhale. Sight. Exhale. Squeeze. Carter's face disappeared from his scope. He shifted a half degree to his left and down. Delaney. Her body tangled up with Carter's. Blood matted in her hair. Eyes, wide and frightened like a doe, seeking out his position. She was alive. *Breathe.*

Rory didn't remember leaving his sniper's nest. Didn't remember clamoring down the stairs and bursting into the street. Scott had tried to grab him, but he broke free. Delaney. He had to get to her. Somebody…Jessie, maybe, loomed in front of him. He didn't pause, juking and ducking around every human barrier.

He barreled through the doors of the restaurant headed straight for the private room. A part of his brain recognized Connor and Nessa. Ciara and Keegan. The Burns. Becca. And Ciaran. No. Kieran. He slowed, realized he still clutched his rifle. That damnable gray mist fogged his vision again and his head swam.

"Riordan."

The bodiless voice raised the hair on the back of his neck. "Ciaran?" Or Kieran. Which man called to him across the mists of time? A figure appeared—not Ciaran at all. Manannán. The faerie king stared at him, unblinking, unemotional. Not laughing this time.

"Do you love this woman, mortal?"

He nodded mutely. His hands itched to take her into his arms, to touch her and make sure she was unharmed. He wanted—needed—to kiss her, to make love to her. He wanted to love her with all his heart for the rest of his life.

Manannán mac Lir seemed to grow, his hair a golden nimbus, his swirling robes infused with every color of the rainbow. "So be it. The vow, Riordan MacDermot. Bind her with the vow."

Rory staggered backward as thunder rang in his ears. Stars burst against his retinas, and for a long, frightening moment, he could neither see nor hear. Voices. Far away on the very edge of his hearing. He screwed his eyes shut until the skyrockets behind his lids stopped shooting into the darkness. When he opened them, the room appeared in sharp focus even though the people still wavered. He refused to let the vertigo swallow him, and in moments he recognized Kieran and Becca.

"Delaney?" Rory shook off the hands trying to hold him back.

"Rory!" He jerked his arm again, but Scotty held on tight. "Dammit, give me your rifle so I can secure it."

Hoss appeared and Captain Davis, both trying to block him, but it was the captain who issued a command. "Stand down, MacDermot. You can't go in there. You know the protocol, man, when there's an officer involved shooting."

He stripped out of his gear, passed it to the big man, while staring at his captain. "I don't care. Sir."

"Rory—"

He didn't stop to listen, pushing through them with

a singleness of purpose. Delaney. He had to see her, touch her, make sure she was okay. The doors at the end of the hall stood open and people milled around. Footsteps echoed his, and he spared a brief glance over his shoulder to see who was foolish enough to try to stop him. Kieran.

They stepped through the door side-by-side and Rory was struck by the sense of rightness in that action. They'd done this so many times throughout their lives. Paramedics and cops cluttered the area, and he couldn't see Delaney for a minute. When he located her, he grabbed the EMT closest to her and pulled the man away. He dropped to his knees next to her, reached for her hand until he realized his own was shaking. *Breathe.*

"Doc?"

She whimpered, her eyes closed. Her bangs straggled across her face, matted with something dark red and sticky. Blood. And other bits. But not hers. Dear God not hers.

Rory wiped his hand on his thigh before taking her hand. Kieran's voice, quiet but commanding, rumbled in the background, soothing the uniforms and paramedics. "Doc? Don't open your eyes yet, okay? Hold on just another minute."

Rory glared at a CSI holding a camera. "Get the damn pictures so I can get her out of here."

Galvanized by his voice, the CSI snapped photographs of the scene, focusing on Delaney first. At the investigator's nod, Rory leaned in. "Put your arm around my neck, baby. I'm getting you out of here." Her eyelids fluttered. "No, baby. Not yet. Don't look yet."

Her lashes teased her cheeks and then opened. Her eyes focused on him. “Rory?”

“It’s me, Doc. I’m here. You’re safe.”

She turned her head and he tried to stop her, but she shook her head. “No. I have to see. If I don’t, it will haunt me. What’s in my imagination. What I see when I close my eyes is much worse. I know it is.”

With reluctance, he helped her sit up straighter and turn. She stared at the man who’d been intent on taking her life. Thankfully, she couldn’t see the back of his head. One bullet hole blossomed in the middle of his forehead. The back would be a bloody pulp. Carter’s death had been instantaneous. His finger never had a chance to squeeze the trigger of the pistol he held to Delaney’s head.

Rory started shaking, hard shudders coursing through him. A warm hand clamped on his shoulder. Kieran. *Breathe.*

Steadier, he touched Delaney’s face. “C’mon, Doc. Let’s get out of here. Get you cleaned up. I want to take you home.”

Tears formed in her eyes but didn’t spill over. “Home.” Her voice remained steady despite the quiver in her lower lip. “I’d like that.”

He dipped his head and kissed her. “Me, too.”

****

They’d dealt with the paperwork, the hospital, and Internal Affairs. Kieran ran interference each step of the way. Now at Rory’s condo, Becca and Delaney had disappeared into the master bath while he and Kieran shared glasses of Guinness. Rory could breathe again, and his hand didn’t shake. Much.

“Thank you.”

“No need for that, Rory.” The other man watched him, a guarded look on his face.

“What?”

“Would ya mind tellin’ me what occurred? There in the hall.”

His hand shook again as he swallowed several large gulps of his beer. “Manannán mac Lir dropped by to visit.”

Kieran snorted. “I’m not surprised considering that bloody harper visited earlier. He arrived with Delaney. This whole affair stinks of fae.”

“Be nice, darling. I’m sure you’d hate a visit from the in-laws about now.” The two men stared at Becca. She snagged a beer from the fridge and popped the top, drinking straight from the bottle.

“Shush, darling. Don’t be sayin’ their names out loud.”

Rory raised a brow, his gaze tracking from one to the other. “I don’t want to know, do I?”

Becca laughed, the sound bright and joyful. “No, probably not.” She stared at her husband, and Rory realized something meaningful passed between them. “We can’t ignore the five-hundred pound gorilla, Kieran. We both saw Abhean before that man came in. And if that wasn’t Manannán mac Lir himself in that swirling mist in the hall, I’ll…well, it doesn’t matter. We know he was there.”

Kieran watched Rory, his expression inscrutable. “How much do you remember, Rory?”

“All of it.” He lifted one shoulder in a desultory shrug. “But I need the words to the vow. If I tried hard enough, I could probably remember the gist of what you said that *Samhain* night, but let’s just make it easy."

The sound of a pen scratching on paper drew his attention to Becca. She busily scribbled words on a paper towel she'd snagged from the stand next to the sink. The two men watched her in silence, and she pushed it toward Rory when she finished.

"Hope you can read my writing. Say the words to her, Rory. And she needs to say the words back, so be sure this is what you both want." She glanced at her husband and then down at the paper. "We think that's what happened before. You said the words and she didn't. You were destined to love her life after life, but because she didn't say the words back, she never loved you. Until now. Don't blow it." She straightened and opened her arms for a hug. Rory provided one. "Welcome home, Rory. We've missed you." She cleared her throat and wouldn't look at him as she stepped away.

Rory turned to Kieran and was enfolded in a massive bear hug. "Aye, Rory. We have. We won't let you be a stranger, yeah?"

"Yeah."

Once they were gone, he locked the door, turned out the lights, and headed to his bedroom. He didn't tell them that he was the one who'd screwed up before. Vows. Who knew simple words could be so powerful? He'd learned his lesson, though, and he would never take them for granted again. He heard Delaney in the bathroom and tapped on the door.

"Delaney? May I come in?" He heard the sound of splashing water and indecisive uhms.

"Okay." She sounded so unsure and timid.

Rory cracked the door open and peeked in. "I just

wanted to make sure you're okay."

She smiled and her expression relaxed. "Better now."

"When you're done, I'll help you get ready for bed, and you can get some sleep. I'll bunk on the couch." She looked crestfallen, eyes lowered, the corners of her mouth drooping. "Or…"

Delaney glanced up, hope brightening her expression. "Or?" Her skin flushed and the color climbed to stain her cheeks.

He pushed the door open and stepped in. "Or I can take you to bed and make sure that you are well and truly loved. Tonight." He swallowed around the lump in his throat. "And always."

Her eyes glistened and water dropped from her arms as she raised them. "Oh, yes, please. I like that idea very much."

Rory snagged a towel and offered his hand to steady her as she stood up. Then he wrapped her in the towel and picked her up. The covers of his bed had already been turned down, so he laid her on the cool white sheets. His voice hitched as he admired her. "You are so beautiful."

He knew the moment she had second thoughts. She shuttered the emotions in her eyes and opened her mouth to say something.

He stayed her with a gentle finger against her lips. "Shh. Yes, I know. I'm under suspension. Again. But the shooting was righteous. Yes, I'll have to undergo mandatory counseling. But not with you, Doc. No desks between us. No files. No official status. You aren't my doctor. You're the woman I love, and I have far more interesting plans for us."

He dipped his head to kiss her. He nibbled her lips then swirled his tongue along the seam of her mouth teasing and tasting until she opened to him. Their kiss deepened, and her arms circled his neck. He swallowed her sigh. And the words that followed.

"I love you, too."

He pulled away from her long enough to strip his clothes off. Stretched out beside her once again on the bed, he gathered her into his arms. His hands stroked along her side, savoring her curves, the silky feel of her skin beneath his rough calluses. She arched and sighed like a contented cat, and he enjoyed the sound. Rolling her to her back, he brushed his fingers across the tender skin of her tummy and teased up to cup one full breast.

"So beautiful." He smiled as her skin flushed again, and he dipped lower to nuzzle the nipple of her other breast. While his thumb teased one, his tongue laved the other. Her hips arched and she twisted them toward him. He slid his knee between hers, and she opened for him, her thighs clamping around his. She rubbed the center of her heat against his thigh, and his erection thickened as her thigh brushed against him. He groaned.

"I want you so much." He grit the words out, breathing in slow gasps in hopes of holding onto his control.

"I want you." Her hand circled his shaft and squeezed.

"God, baby. You touch me now—"

She squeezed again and slowly stroked her hand up toward the head of his erection, giggling softly. "I thought I was in control."

"You. Are. Killing. Me."

Delaney laughed. “Good. Now, come here.” She spread her legs and shifted her hips, inviting him inside.

His hand dipped low, barely brushing through her soft curls before seeking the wet warmth. His finger pushed inside and she gasped. Two could play this game, but he didn’t want to. He wanted to be buried deep inside her. He needed her wrapped around his heart in the same way she wrapped around his body. “Put me inside you.”

He felt her shiver, but she did as he asked. Raising her knees and widening them further, she guided his erection to her opening and pushed the head inside her. His balls tightened and he ground his teeth. He’d never felt a sensation more pleasurable. He curled his hips, and his shaft sank deeper, pushing slowly as her inner muscles caressed him with wet silk and fire.

Delaney wrapped her legs around his waist and cupped his face with her palms. “Make love to me, Rory. Tonight and always.”

“Always,” he murmured. “Marry me, Delaney. Right now. Right this instance. Marry me in the old way, and we’ll do it again in the church.” He held his breath, waiting for her answer.

She arched her hips against him, swiveled them, and smiled when he bit back another groan. Delaney raised her head and kissed him. “Say the words, Rory. I love you.”

He all but collapsed in relief, but his arms continued to brace his body above hers. His hips rocked, pushing into her and pulling out only to return. As he made love to her, the words tumbled from his heart.

“By the life that courses within my blood and the

love that resides within my heart, I take thee to my hand, my heart, and my spirit to be my chosen one. To desire thee and to be desired by thee. To possess thee and to be possessed by thee without sin or shame for naught can exist in the purity of my love for thee. I promise to love thee wholly in this life and beyond, where we shall meet, remember, and love again. There is no beginning, there is no end but in you. You are my chosen."

He quivered with the effort to keep from climaxing. If she didn't say the words back, he'd be in this damnable limbo for eternity. But he didn't care. Even loving her from afar was better than not loving her at all. He pushed deep inside her and dragged his shaft back out, almost leaving her warmth. She gasped and her grip, both inside and out, tightened around him.

"Say them again." She stammered a little. "Slow. So I can say them back."

He surged deep inside her. "By the life that courses within my blood and the love that resides within my heart, I take thee to my hand, my heart, and my spirit to be my chosen one." She repeated the words as he pulled back again. In. Out. Promise given. Promise received.

"You are my chosen." As she vowed the words, it felt like a key turned in his heart and everything just…fit. He felt her tighten around his shaft and she hunched against him.

Once. Twice. Three times he surged deep inside her before he exploded, his roar echoing her delighted cry. Spent and drained, he cuddled her, still buried deep.

He kissed the tears from her cheeks as she gazed at him.

"I love you..." Delaney's voice trailed off. "Anything I say or compare my feeling to will sound trite. It sounds so simple when I just say the words, but somehow it's not enough."

He kissed her. "It's enough, Delaney. More than enough. Always," Rory promised. "I will love you with my whole heart now and always."

Epilogue

Abhean stood in the circle of standing stones. His hands hung limply at his side. No breath of air stirred the grass or flowers. Even the leaves on the trees in the forest held silent. A golden red sun painted the misty blue mountains deep violet and the brilliant blue of the sky could blind a man if he stared too long. He ignored the trudging footsteps behind him, and said nothing for long minutes.

"You win." Like dry leaves tumbling before a winter wind, he admitted defeat.

"No, Abhean." Manannán appeared at his side. "This was not a contest between us, no matter how much you wished to make it so."

"The mortals made the binding?"

"They did, aye."

"Then you win."

"No, Abhean. Love wins."

"Ha! Love? What know yee of love, old man?"

"More than you, harper. You sing it into being with a heart closed and dark. You pervert it and twist it and use it to punish. But who do you penalize? The mortals? Nay. They find their way despite our interference. You wish to strike at me, but for all the millennium you have failed."

Abhean whirled, his eyes narrowed and gleaming with feral reds and yellows. "I will beat you." He ignored the look of profound sadness on Manannán's face.

"No, son. You will not. For I know your heart far better."

He opened and closed his mouth several times but no words came out. Before he could move, Manannán cupped his cheeks in his massive hands.

"I know that of which you seek. I know your hidden desires. I am the King of Tir Nan Óg, Abhean. I am the one who brought you here. Aye, perhaps for reasons far more selfish than I wished to admit at the time." He pulled Abhean closer and pressed his lips to the harper's forehead. "I could not bear to be apart from my son."

Abhean forced his knees to lock so he could remain standing stiff and aloof. He would not listen, would not be tricked by the king's lies.

"Love, my son, is a gift. I give it now to you."

Clouds bloomed against that dazzling blue sky and the wind whipped around the two men before chasing through the standing stones and making them sing. Abhean listened, for this was a song he'd not heard before. Caught in the web of music, his heart expanded until he thought it would burst, even as it felt like claws shredded it to pieces.

"Go yee, Abhean, Harper of the Tuatha de Danaan, son of Manannán mac Lir, King of Tir Nan Óg. Go yee to the mortal realm until yee find the other half of your heart."

Lightning struck the altar stone, sending up sparks, and Abhean, deafened by the crescendo of thunder that followed, stared at the man he'd hated all his life. Mist—swirling gray and black—enveloped him in a whirlwind. The hands cupping his face slipped away and he spun away into the vortex, his last word torn from his throat and lost in the void.

“Father!”

A word about the author...

With a rampant imagination aided and abetted by a Muse who runs with scissors, Silver James loves to share the stories created in that vast cosmic void pretending to be her mind.

Over the course of her lifetime, she's been a military officer's wife, mother, state appellate court marshal, airport rescue firefighter, and forensic fire photographer, crime analyst, technical crime scene investigator, and writer of magic and mystery.

Retired from the "real world" now, she lives in Oklahoma and spends her days at the computer with her two Newfoundland dogs, the cat who rules them all, and myriad characters all clamoring for attention.

To find out more about Silver, visit her at:
http://www.silverjames.com

www.ingramcontent.com/pod-product-compliance
Lightning Source LLC
Chambersburg PA
CBHW060543180626
46817CB00002B/705

9781612175591